Praise For *Christ Like*

"With *Christ Like*, Xavier demonstrates the literary splendor and heroic telling of Piri Thomas (*Down These Mean Streets*), and Junot Diaz (*Drown*) . . . Like the people that it represents, *Christ Like* is full of wit, charm, attitude, and resilience. This ain't no sad song. This is the story of how a rock can turn itself into a gem."

—Lambda Book Report

"Realistic and refreshing, Xavier's characters are flawed and feigning, and capable of making the reader both fear them and feel for them simultaneously."

—Book Marks

*Czerny,
Much love always!
Emanuel Xavier*

CHRIST LIKE

Emanuel Xavier

QUEER MOJO
A Rebel Satori Imprint
Bar Harbor, Maine

REBEL SATORI PRESS
P.O. Box 363
Hulls Cove, ME 04644
www.rebelsatori.com

Portions of this book originally appeared in *Men on Men 7*, *Besame Mucho: New Gay Latino Fiction* and *Best Gay Erotica 1997*, in somewhat different form.

Book design by Sven Davisson

Library of Congress Cataloging-in-Publication Data

Xavier, Emanuel.
 Christ like / Emanuel Xavier.
   p. cm.
  ISBN 978-0-9790838-5-3 (pbk.)
 1. Young gay men--Fiction. 2. Hispanic American gays--Fiction. 3. Gay culture--New York (State)--New York--Fiction. 4. Subculture--New York (State)--New York--Fiction. 5. City and town life--New York (State)--New York--Fiction. I. Title.
 PS3574.A85C47 2009
  813'.54--dc22

                                        2009005689

Dominic Brando
1967-2008

"If Christ were here now there is one thing he would not be — a Christian."

–Mark Twain

"If you bring forth what is within you, what you bring forth will save you. If you do not bring forth what is within you, what you do not bring forth will destroy you."

—Jesus Christ

INTRODUCTION

In 1999, the only feathers in my cap were a self-published poetry collection appropriately titled, *Pier Queen*, and some notoriety as an underground New York City based slam poet.

I had been working on a novel but despite featuring alongside notable literary figures, people were more interested in the slam aspect of my poetry.

One of the first few authors who believed in me and deserves mad props was gay Colombian writer, Jaime Manrique. He introduced me to Bill Sullivan, who was starting Painted Leaf Press, a small independent publishing company that offered me the opportunity to publish the novel.

Excitedly, I handed in the manuscript with no concept whatsoever of the editing process and relied heavily on Painted Leaf Press. The book was soon published and, only a few months later, the company filed for bankruptcy and went out of business. *Christ Like* has been out of print ever since. It is ironic that I would get an offer for a reprint during another terrible recession.

I continued to focus on my work as a poet and eventually published my first poetry collection and went on to put together and edit other poetry anthologies. I tried never to look back and forget my attempt at being an author.

Interestingly enough, some of those who read the initial publication liked something about it. They did not criticize me for being uneducated and inexperienced as a writer or mocked my humble beginnings as a slam poet. The original version was even a finalist in a small category for a Lambda Literary Award.

Throughout the past decade, I have come across fans who have told me the novel really meant something to them and they were not just trying to mack[1] on me. Perhaps because it was the typical story of a journey to self-acceptance but told through the eyes of that rare mythological creature which sometimes appears in literature—the urban gay Latino.

Enter Rebel Satori Press. The possible reprint of this book was in limbo thanks to the collapse of our economy. As soon as the publication rights were back on the table, they swooped in and made this happen.

Much like the main character of this novel, *Christ Like* got a second chance. With that, as the author, I had certain decisions to make besides coming up with this introduction.

The most important and necessary edits, besides the spelling and grammar corrections and breaking up the chapters, were the proper use of pronouns to refer to drag and transgender characters throughout the novel. I also admit the original ending was regrettably trite but I have been known to "flare disappointment like a challenge dance" and I grew up watching telenovelas.

The other bonus feature I wanted to add (as you may have noticed from the bottom of the page) is footnotes. With so much slang used throughout the novel, I thought these would be fun additions that would help the general reader get through the book. However, the Spanish dialogue does not get the pop-up-video treatment as much of it uses a Nuyorican[2] slang specific

---

1 The art of seduction or flirtation for the purpose of sex.
2 A blending of the New York City and Puerto Rican diaspora.

to that part of Latino culture (and I wanted to be a bit of a hard ass).

With the opportunity to tighten up the novel, I have made it a bit more of a memoir, though it remains a work of fiction. It was never a secret that I was the real Mikey X. Names have been changed and situations have been exaggerated but, without the unnecessary Hollywood ending, what is left is the story of my life before becoming a writer. I have watched many an author rise and fall for fabricating their lives and learned that, though I was not the best of writers, I actually had a genuine story to tell.

The main character of this novel is as melodramatic as people sometimes are in their teens and early twenties. Mikey was, by all means, naive and thwarted emotionally. He fell in love with a crack addict and eventually became a minor drug dealer and developed a bad habit himself.

Mikey was not interested in politics or the world around him. He came of age during Republican rule when Ronald Reagan was still President of the United States for eight years followed by George H. W. Bush. Around him—AIDS had already changed the way people engaged in sex; terrorists began hijacking planes; The Space Shuttle Challenger exploded within minutes of take off; savings and loan institutions went bankrupt; white police officers were recorded beating a black motorist leading to racially charged riots; and The USSR dissolved into individual autonomous countries.

Sometimes not caring is the only way to survive.

In a perfect world, no child would ever have to experience coming of age with so much pain and conflict. This does not justify Mikey's actions or absolve him from his crimes but it should at least grant him the permission to be angry and tragic.

Writing *Christ Like* was a soul-searching experience. Even while reading it over again for this reprint, I had to go back in time and realize how far I have come spiritually and emotionally.

Those of us who have survived sexual abuse understand our own difficult journey into acceptance. Without poverty, prejudice and struggle, there is already enough to overcome as individuals.

While I was out on the streets being 'Mikey', I did my best to find love and keep it alive in my heart. In writing this novel, it was my hope that others could learn to forgive and love themselves whatever challenges they may have had to face while coming of age. In reprinting Christ *Like,* it is my hope that we can also look back and laugh at ourselves. We often put ourselves through so much shit but, in the end, we all deserve to find peace and happiness.

—**Emanuel Xavier**
May 2009

LAMENTATION

Mikey felt the presence of undercover cops lurking inside The Sanctuary as he casually guarded his drug spot underneath the statue of St. Therese watching over him. Mikey had a wicked smile engraved on his youthful face, fully aware that they could never touch him. The paid-off security guards knew he was the life of the party and would never allow "Maggie"[3] to lay a hand on the club's designated dealer. Mikey and the House[4] of X were as much a part of The Sanctuary as the disco-ball hanging from the condemned church ceiling where New York City's most famous nightclub was located. Besides, unless you knew the secret password of the day, Mikey would deny knowledge of any drugs, curse you out, and send you off on your merry way. He was now an expert on determining who was undercover.

However, for forty bucks, Mikey would touch your hand, the cold vial of coke or K[5] contrasting against the feverish warmth of his Latin machismo. A wink from one of his pearl-black eyes, the one below his scarred eyebrow in particular, would be your signal to take the merchandise and disappear

3   A name used in conversation to refer discreetly to police officers.
4   Similar to the Houses prominent in the fashion sense, drag ball Houses serve as intentional families, social groups, and performance teams and are usually named after key members of the drag ball community. Throughout this novel, The House of X relates as a tribute to the House of Xavier which existed in NYC from 1998-2008.
5   K or ketamine is a drug used in human and veterinary medicine for the induction and maintenance of general anesthesia, usually in combination with a sedative. It is illicitly sold in powdered form, its appearance, and use similar to that of cocaine, producing hallucinatory effects similar to other dissociative anesthetics.

into the sweaty madness dancing around what would otherwise be early Sunday mass. The music pounded like his mother's fists when Mikey was too young to fight back but old enough to develop an insatiable dark side.

A hundred bucks and Mikey would still drop to his knees and feast on your supremacy with starving lips which, at the age of three, already knew hunger and submission, thanks to older cousin Chino. Two hundred and the gates of banjee[6] heaven could still spread wide open while you ripped through his soul like the needle on the record high above the altar from Dominick X's deejay booth.

They both still belonged to the House of X, a Godless gang of vicious gays whose wrists were only limp because of heavy knives used to slash their enemies. They were the kind to travel in packs, terrorizing the West Side Highway piers with loud exaggerated laughter, shady comments, and unapologetic homosexuality, the ones who would go to jail for mopping[7] clothes or cutting up ex-boyfriends and looked after by heartless criminals named "Bubba." When your own family puts you out on the streets of New York as a child for wanting the same sex, you create your own family or 'house' and deviance becomes a way of life, self-destruction giving you the only fleeting glimpses of survival.

The House of X and The Sanctuary had a lot in common—they were both christened in chaos; blessed in blasphemy. Neon lights, pin-lights, spotlights cast hues of red, blue and green over bitter souls and crumbling Catholic statues, glaring

---

6   *Banjee* is a term probably coined in the '80s that describes a certain type of young Latino, black or multiracial man who dresses in stereotypical masculine urban fashion for reasons that may include expressing masculinity, hiding his sexual orientation, and attracting male partners. The term is mostly associated with New York City and may be Nuyorican in origin.

7   Another gay slang term used to mean "shoplifting."

down with decadent beauty. Within these realms, the outside world meant very little, if nothing at all.

From the deejay booth, Dominick served as God himself over the dance floor blasting commands with every rhythm and beat, featuring an immaculate record collection of house and techno to entertain the children. Voguing[8] pier queens[9], possessed with the Holy Ghost, battled each other underneath Dominick's deejay booth for the glory of his flashlight to shine upon them. Walking, screaming, twirling, they threw shade[10] all over in preparation for the next ball[11] where Dominick would canonize them with trophies.

The highest of all angels was the legendary Damian X, the dark prince of voguing arm control and posing, who was battling Flaca from the House of Pendavis, not far from Mikey's spot. They created a fortress of spectators curiously involved with the intensity of the arrogance between the two of them. The battle was over who was the best but had more to do with a guy named Cesar, who Flaca was supposedly dating.

"Get huh! Get that skinny ass bitch!" Mikey cheered his sista[12] on. "Serve huh Damian!"

Damian danced more ferociously as Dominick spotlighted his every machine-like move. Dominick mixed in Damian's favorite house classic, "Love is the Message," as Damian served the floor with pops, dips and spins driving the crowd into

8   A highly stylized modern dance characterized by photographic model-like poses integrated with angular, linear, and rigid arm, leg, and body movements popular with inner-city urban subculture. It existed *way* before Madonna.
9   A slang term used in reference to gay urban youth of color who spent time hanging out at the West Side Highway piers of New York City.
10   Attitude
11   Not the Cinderella ballroom dancing type of ball. An event featuring voguing and runway categories where members of the House community get together and compete for prizes. Go out and rent *Paris is Burning* or *How Do I Look* for Christ's sake!
12   Gay slang used to refer to a best friend or BFF.

uproarious frenzy with his incredible energy.

"Work, Ms. Damian! Bring it bitch! Bring it to the ballroom!" Jorge X appeared from out of the darkness, taking over where Mikey left off.

"Walk for me! Feel the love break!" Jorge continued.

Damian, mean-spiritedly exaggerating Flaca Pendavis' trademark moves, mocked him in public. The crowd around them screamed support for Damian by chanting "Pendavis! Pendeja![13] Pendavis! Pendeja!" Flaca struggled desperately to keep up to the music to show any signs of success in the face of oppression but Damian had far too many skills. Damian moved to the music or was it the music that moved to him? He held his hands together and spun his sinewy arms around his back full circle; dislocating them and clicking them back into place. Damian flung his long muscular arms into the air and his silky wet black chest glistened naked under the blinding lights. His fierce eyes pierced through the smoky air, shooting Flaca down with a million daggers. The audience roared and Jorge jumped in, kissing him excitedly, while Damian's face succumbed to an undeniably enchanted smile. Dominick mixed in Junior Vasquez's "X," Flaca's ultimate humiliation. The battle was over and the category was closed. Damian X was once again a force to be reckoned with as Flaca and the angels from stained glass windows looked down at him with jealousy and contempt.

Mikey, now in his mid-twenties but still looking nineteen, was thirsty but unable to leave his spot because potential buyers would get confused about his designated location. Mikey simply caught Damian's attention with a penetrating

13 Spanish for stupid bitch.

stare, smirking in his sexy way before some shirtless muscle queen interrupted him with, "Yo, Mikey! Wassup kid? Got any vitamin C[14] for my cold symptoms?"

Mikey sized him up from balding head to construction boots, contemplating either a price or an excuse.

"Pookie says hello!" the wrinkling gym bunny insisted nervously while sweat raced down his bulging hairless pecs.

Arresting his pale blue eyes by raising an eyebrow, Mikey wondered if he recognized him from a previous encounter.

"Fifty bucks, papi!" Mikey half smiled, upping the price an extra ten bucks.

"Fifty?" the daddy freaked out, digging deep into his tight-assed daisy dukes for extra cash and working up enough nerve to ask, "Is it any good?"

Mikey's smile grew mysterious with anticipation. "About as good as those steroids you're on!" Mikey snapped, watching his face crumble to once holy ground.

"All right, I'll take it!" He hurried, handing Mikey the money quickly before Mikey changed his mind and called security.

Mikey, pulled out a yellow pen, marking the fifty-dollar bill to make sure it was not counterfeit before putting it away in the left front pocket of his baggy jeans. He pulled out a half gram of cocaine from his right pocket and reached over to surprise him with an unexpected hug while slipping the vial into his hand.

"By the way, I fucked your boyfriend the other night while you were in L.A.!" Mikey revealed into his ear, "Wouldn't you like to know if he was any good?"

With that, Mikey pulled away, giving him his signature wink. Wounded, the Chelsea Queen[15] turned from Mikey and

14 Slang term for cocaine.
15 A gym obsessed, lispy, disco dancing gay man (predominantly white) found but not limited to the Chelsea area of New York City.

walked away humiliated, losing himself somewhere on the dance-floor.

Mikey was approached with yet another opportunity for revenge.

"Hey, Mikey, can I get half a gram?" asked Hector, a tacky cha-cha queen[16] Mikey vividly remembered from his days living in the South Bronx.

"Shouldn't you be off smoking crack somewhere with my ex-boyfriend?"

"Mikey, that was years ago!" Hector begged. "Besides, Juan Carlos is dead!"

"Yeah, but you ain't! So, you betta get out of my face 'fore I beat you like the bitch you are and you could join him!"

Hector held himself back, gagging at Mikey's cold and heartless words.

"Pero Mikey, I've got money!"

"I don't need your welfare checks! Now fleece!" Mikey yelled loud enough for those around them to hear. Out of nowhere, Steve and two other security guards produced.

"Wha? Wha's da problem hea?" Steve asked with a rugged deep voice.

Mikey said something to Steve in his ear and, without a chance to defend himself; Hector was grabbed by six brawny arms and carried out of the club screaming.

"Me las vas a pagar! Maldita, me las vas a pagar!"

Mikey's face glowed like a crowned prom queen as he watched Hector being thrown out of the club. Revenge was sweet.

Meanwhile, up in the deejay booth, Dominick watched his

16 A gay man of Latino origin and ethnic proportions.

sistas prancing back and forth, longing to be out on the dance floor with the rest of them, dancing to his own mixes.

"Work, Mama, It's ovah[17] for you!" Jorge materialized from behind, racing toward Dominick with excitement. "The children, they live!"

"I didn't know you were here! Had I known you were coming, I would've baked a cake!" Dominick joked, mixing in the sample of a song he would not play for hours just to fuck with people's heads.

"That's too wicked!" Jorge shook his index finger back and forth, signaling a 'no.'

"Have you noticed all the pieces[18] out there on the dance floor tonight?" Dominick continued, his pale white skin lighting up.

"Um-hmmm!"

Using his flashlight, he pointed them out to Jorge. Shirtless bodies, flooded with his glory, threw their arms in the air and screamed for Dominick's attention. Dominick ignored them and searched for Damian, who was standing by the speaker closest to Mikey surrounded by an entourage of worshipping followers. Damian, stared back with two shining arrogant eyes fixed on his ex-boyfriend and best friend.

"Did you see him serve[19] Flaca Pendavis?" Jorge asked.

Dominick grinned, still staring at Damian.

"You still love him, don't you?" Jorge snatched the flashlight away from Dominick and searched for Mikey.

"Yeah and you still love Mikey!" Dominick came back

---

17 Gay slang which probably derives from the word 'over' and could mean either something or someone exceptional (as in this case) or, when used as part of a phrase, an end to something as in, "It's ovah for you, bitch!"
18 Potential sexual encounters.
19 Despite mainstream heterosexual appropriation years later, *getting served* was popular gay slang for winning a battle on the dance floor.

without missing a beat, exchanging a knowing stare with Jorge. "Or you hate him enough to date someone he once loved!"

"Whatever!" they both shouted. Rolling their eyes in unison, they fell into a fit of laughter.

"Excuse me, Miss Thing, but you're blocking my spot!" Mikey barked at some queeny little Puerto Rican from the House of Revlon, standing in front of him. "You're gonna have to move!"

"Eh-Q me?" he asked, no, demanded, turning to raise a perfectly plucked eyebrow to enhance what was meant to be a threatening stare.

"No, there is no excuse for you!" Mikey said unimpressed. The Revlon's eyes widened with disbelief.

"WHY can't I stand here?"

"Because I said so!"

"And WHO are you?"

"Someone you're not!" Mikey tucked it quickly into his sentence, "Now, would you PUHLEASE move!"

"Miss Thing, you are too fierce!"

"Thanks, I wish I could say the same for you! Now move!"

"Bitch, don't try it!"

"Security! Security!" Mikey yelled out nonchalantly, checking his nails.

From the deejay booth, Jorge and Dominick stopped laughing to watch the commotion along with everyone else looking into the spotlight. Steve and his henchmen emerged once again to haul the offending party out onto the streets. The Revlon crashed violently against the ground on the other side of the velvet rope, excommunicated forever.

"You know, I lose more customers that way!" Dominick sneered to Jorge while Mikey laughed sadistically up to them from down below.

"Do you s'pose that's why people don't like us?"

"You think?"

Laughter once again prevailed in the deejay booth.

Damian pushed and shoved his way toward Mikey's spot while Dominick conveniently mixed in a record, which repeated the words "Bitch Get Out." The crowd got louder and unsettled.

"Work, Ms. Dominick!" someone yelled out as Damian swam through the crowd like an eel, feeling up a few half naked bodies along the way.

"Damian! Damian, thank God you're here! Did you see that beast try it with me?" Mikey asked.

"Did you see me turn Flaca inside out?" Damian ignored his question and asked his own.

"Enough about you, let's talk about me! I'm parched! If I give you two drink tickets, would you get me a Corona?" Mikey begged.

"Bitch, I don't need your lousy drink tickets!"

"Oh, that's right, you slept with the bartender!" Mikey snapped his fingers in Damian's face.

"How'd you know that? Fine, have it your way but I expect a bump[20] of K for the pageant winner when I return!"

"Wait!" Mikey stopped him, changing his mind. "Better yet, why don't you stay here first? I've gotta spring a mad[21] leak before I'm stuck here for another hour!"

---

20 A small dosage of some illegal substance.
21 Used in slang as an adverb to mean extremely or as an adjective to mean many.

"Well, you would want to hurry it up or I'll just split and your customers will come together!" Damian said annoyed.

"I'll be just a second! When I get back, I'll let you go flirt with your favorite bartender, ah-ight?"

Damian returned Mikey's wink with an evil stare before nodding his head up and down half-heartedly.

"Ah-ight! I be out!"

Gliding as if he owned the club, Mikey made his way to the bathroom, where he discovered a notoriously long line waiting for the private stalls to do everything but pee.

There, the current love of Mikey's life, twenty-two-year-old banjee boy Eric Santiago stood in front of the line.

"Hey, where ya goin'?" someone yelled out to Mikey, who paid him dust, and walked straight up to Eric, smiling back at him with a glow on his smooth, ivory skin.

"Hey papi!" Mikey smiled, lowering his blushing face to disguise his unexpected shyness.

"Hey!" Eric returned with his rugged yet tender voice.

"How ya been?" Mikey continued coquettishly, zeroing in on Eric's recently shaved head.

"Ah-ight!" Eric blushed.

His dark puppy eyes fixed on Mikey, who was biting his lower lip. Both stood there smiling moronically, the cheerleader flirting with the quarterback, before one of the stool doors flung open and three drugged-up rave kids stumbled out onto the puddles of dirty water on the bathroom floor. Mikey casually stepped over them. Eric, right behind him, locked the door.

Without any forewarning, Mikey pulled his zipper down and whipped out his Latin pride, taking a mad piss in front of Eric. He was impressed by Mikey's brazen confidence. Eric noticing the color of Mikey's cock was darker than the rest of him.

Mikey sprinkled any remaining fluids before tucking it away inside his Marvin-the-Martian boxer shorts. Zippering up, he announced, "Well, what are you waiting for, a personal invitation?"

"I can't pee in front of other people!" Eric admitted nervously.

"That's ah-ight, I won't look!" Mikey lied. "I promise!"

"Yeah, right!" Eric giggled before shifting over to the toilet, blocking Mikey's view with his broad shoulders.

Mikey, however, reached over Eric's shoulder to catch a glimpse of his uncut beauty. He had waited for such a long time to enjoy this moment.

"Ooh! It's a masterpiece!"

"You little bitch, you lied to me!" Eric burst out with laughter, hurriedly zippering up.

"I couldn't help it! It's like going to Paris and not going to see the Eiffel Tower! Y'know? It's probably just as big!"

"I can't believe you spooked my trade[22]!"

"Ay, papi, you got nothing to be ashamed of! Trust!"

Confused about whether to kiss him or not, Mikey instead pulled out a half-empty vial of K.

"You like?" He raised his scarred eyebrow devilishly.

Eric's smile stretched across his rugged face, "Only if you feed it to me!"

"Papito, I'd feed you lots of things!" Mikey pulled out a Snuffly[23], scooping up a full bump from the vial before offering

22 Gay slang used to mean the offering of casual sex in exchange for cash, drugs, or other subtle means. In this case, he is referring to his cock.
23 Curiously sold at pipe and tobacco companies, a small pen like tool used to sniff powdered drugs without making a mess. The knob end is simply pushed down, twisted to lock, filled with the powdered drug, untwisted to close and the drug is sniffed through the knob end where there is a hole.

it to Eric ominously.

"How do you use this?" Eric asked.

"Ay, loca please! No te hagas! Just put it up your nose and take a deep breath!"

Following Mikey's instructions, Eric felt the powdery substance race through his nostrils, leaving behind an aspirin-like taste down his throat, a cottony feeling quickly taking over him as Mikey did the same.

Eric, in a K-hole[24], stood there staring at Mikey in bewilderment, traveling to distant waterfalls before Mikey broke the ice, asking that all-important question that every coke and K queen needs to ask after taking a bump, "Is my nose clean?"

To his own surprise, Eric reached over and passionately licked Mikey's freckled nose with his warm tongue. Hovering over Mikey with his breath caressing him, Eric tickled Mikey before grabbing him by the waist. Pulling up to meet lips, Mikey and Eric's tongues danced to their own sweet music. Mikey's heartbeat out of control, in spite of bitterness and multitudes of bad experiences, like the very first time. It did not matter that someone was banging on the door for them to get out or that they could be seen through the cracks on the door. At that moment, Mikey and Eric were the only ones in the whole wide world, removed to their own private island. Eric's mustache softly brushed Mikey's thick goatee, holding on to one another's dreams while the words 'Mikey X is a slut!' 'No he isn't!' 'Yes, I am!' bounced off the wall of the bathroom door.

Tired of waiting for Mikey and desperate to see Cesar

---

24 A slang term for a state of dissociation caused by sufficiently high doses of the drug Ketamine.

before Flaca got to him, Damian impatiently paved his way to the bar. Ignoring the customers vying for his attention, Damian slithered up toward the bartender who watched with lustful eyes.

"Can I get a Corona and a Sex on the Beach?" Damian flirtatiously leaned over the counter, practically sitting on Cesar's tongue.

Struggling for an intelligent response while his oiled skin glistened underneath the bar lights, Cesar fell short with, "We've had sex in more interesting places."

Within earshot, Flaca watched them ferociously, the hair in his nostrils quivering with anger.

"Too bad you had to get involved with that pendeja ... I mean Pendavis!" Damian snickered.

"That's it! It's curtains for you!" Flaca hollered above the music furiously before pulling out his pocketknife and lunging insanely through the crowds toward Damian. Club kids screamed out of the way as the glistening metal made its way into Damian's left arm, stabbing him underneath flashing strobe lights. Damian hollered as the blood quickly gushed out all over himself and Flaca. Flaca, pulled away by the crowd, dropped the knife to the ground as Cesar jumped over the counter and grabbed Damian who was still in shock from the attack. Through the madness, Damian's quickly infuriating eyes met with Flaca's frightened, tearful ones. Breaking loose from Cesar's tight grip, Damian jumped on top of Flaca and knocked him to the ground.

"Bitch! Bitch! Look what you've done! I'm gonna kill you!" Damian bashed Flaca's face in repeatedly with his right fist, a nameplate ring cutting deep into Flaca's skin. Flaca's eyes blurred as they bloating with blood.

Cesar pulled Damian off and the crowd engulfed Flaca like a flock of pigeons devouring bread. Underneath the disco lights, Flaca laid on the dance floor with his face quickly swelling. Choking in a pool of blood, Flaca was unable to let out more than a whimper. His legs spread and his arms stretched in a pose he would have never deemed possible.

ENTOMBMENT

"Dominick! Dominick! Damian just got stabbed! Maggie will be here any minute!" Steve yelled hysterically into his walkie-talkie as the doormen were already announcing the police's arrival at the front door into his headphones. Dominick and Jorge scrambled around each other with the flashlight, watching in awe as Cesar helped a bloodied Damian out onto the streets. Flaca was on the dance-floor, almost unrecognizable. Grabbing Jorge's hand, Dominick anxiously shifted the flashlight over to Mikey's spot, where he once held court.

"Shit! He's gone!" Jorge yelled, "He's gone!"

"Fuck!" Dominick lowered the music—Mikey's signal to leave the club immediately.

"Steve, find Mikey and get him out of the club NOW!" Dominick screamed into the walkie-talkie as the church doors burst open.

The dance floor flooded with God's wrathful light as an ocean of blue and cold air spilled into The Sanctuary.

"LIGHTS! LIGHTS!" Police officers infiltrated the club and Dominick's deejay booth, ordering him to turn on the lights and turn off the music. One of the officers, reaching for the microphone, made the dreadful announcement, "Attention everybody! This club is closed!" The words echoed, bouncing off sacred walls and raising loud angry curses from pissed-off club kids while others raced to the nearest exit.

Still making out, Mikey faintly heard the music lowered. He loosened his lip lock and pulled away from Eric.

"Wow, that shit was good! I think I've lost my hearing!" Mikey referred to both the kiss and the drugs.

Eric laughed his genuinely intoxicating laugh until the room stopped spinning and Mikey became dimly aware that the music had stopped altogether. Catching on to Mikey's inquisitive look, Eric opened the door to discover they were the only ones left in the whole bathroom.

"Did we take that long?" Confused, Mikey grabbed Eric's sweaty hand and led him out of their private paradise.

"Something must've happened!" Eric said, disoriented. Whatever K left in his system made him feel nauseous.

Suddenly, the entire bathroom washed with light. Mikey struggled to look beyond his blinded eyes, vaguely recognizing Steve's husky figure.

"Mikey! Mikey! Oh God! You have to get out of here! The club has been raided! Maggie's everywhere!"

"Mierda loco!" Mikey screamed, looking back at Eric with all the fear of the world in his eyes. Steve grabbed Mikey with a wrestler's grip and pulled him away, violently waking him from this dream.

"Nooo!" Mikey freed himself from Steve, racing back into Eric's arms. "Eric! Eric! I'm sorry but I've gotta run!"

"I'll come with you!"

"No!" Mikey insisted, "I mean you can't!"

"Mikey, we have no time for this! Save the romantic shit for later!" Steve yelled.

"Eric," Mikey pleaded, "if I get caught and you're with me, they'll take you too!"

"I don't care!" Eric begged.

"Yeah, but I do!" Mikey grabbed the back of Eric's head tightly with both hands, resting his forehead sweetly against Eric's, "I'm sorry, but I can't do this to you!"

"Mikey! Ya! Let's go! Let's go!" Steve said furiously annoyed.

They stared briefly into each other's eyes before Mikey kissed Eric with words he could never express and raced out the door forever.

Mikey was near tears as Steve directed him through a series of back doors and long tunnels until they were out on the streets, somewhere far from the main entrance. Mikey froze when he noticed the amount of police cars, sirens, and screaming queens going off by the church. The words of his cousin Chino, "If your Mami finds out, she'll leave you like your daddy did!" flashed across his face.

EMPTY TOMB

"Eh-Q me, offisah? Can you puhlease tell me wha is goin' on hea?"

The police officer looked down to notice a skinny black man wrapped in a white fur, addressing him behind huge Jackie O sunglasses surrounded by an entourage of faithful fans staring up at her. Officer Williams held back his smile.

"Ees these club goin' tah reopen?" Princess demanded to know, one hand on her leathered hips, the other pointing a long bony finger toward The Sanctuary.

"Not tonight, it won't!"

"But offisah, I pay twenty DAHLAHS to get in!"

"Princess! Princess, don't! You'll get yourself arrested-ed-ed!" one of the house children stuttered, the others giggled among themselves, fully aware that Princess was always on the guest-list.

"I'm sorry..." Officer Williams did not know whether to say ma'am or sir. "I don't know if it's ever going to reopen!"

Princess dropped her jaw, twisting her neck haughtily with exaggerated concern. Officer Williams walked away confused.

From the back seat of Steve's car, Mikey lit up a cigarette and watched the chaos outside with hopes of finding Eric or one of his sistas. As Steve drove by avoiding the congested traffic, the cross on top of the church reflected on the windshield. Mikey watched Princess chasing after some cop, who looked like an ex-boyfriend, Officer Williams, arguing about the closing of the club while others were escorted out in handcuffs. Further up, he noticed an ambulance swarming with a multitude of drugged up party people, revolving lights reminiscent of the red ones Dominick used on the dance floor.

"That's either Flaca or Damian in there!" Steve said, automatically locking the doors.

"What?" Mikey's eyes bulged out of his head, struggling with the door to jump out of the car.

"Cógelo con take it easy, okay! Flaca stabbed him in the arm! It's Flaca you should be worried about!"

"When the fuck did all this happen?" Mikey was unable to see who was inside.

"While you were in the bathroom with that kid!" Steve revealed a hint of bitterness. "Why do you think Maggie showed up?"

"Fuck, man!"

"Damian beat the shit out of her with whatever arm he had left! Flaca's lucky if he's still alive!"

"What's wrong with that bitch?"

"I don't know, but you guys are always fuckin' wit' somebody! How many times do I have to tell you? You had me throw out two guys today! I knew this would happen sooner or later!" Steve was yelling like the father Mikey never knew. Mikey rolled his eyes and pouted in the back seat, "Oh, daddy, just shut the fuck up and drive, will you?"

"I'm telling you, uno de estos días te van a matar!"

Mikey's beeper[25] suddenly went off with Dominick's home number and secret code—666.

---

25 Until cell phones became popular, beepers fulfilled the role of common personal and mobile communications.

"Ya cállate and give me your cell phone, it's Dominick!"

"Que tu te crees? Que yo soy AT&T? I don't have a cell phone wit' me!"

"Pues, pull ovah to the nearest phone!"

"At all! I'm taking you straight to my house in Long Island..." Steve mumbled on and on incomprehensibly.

"I don't think so!" Mikey snapped his fingers in the air, forming a semi-circle.

Steve continued, ignoring him.

"Ay c'mon Steve, it could be an emergency!"

"Mikey, I'm responsible for you! If anything happens to you, Ernesto would kill me!"

"Steve, the police don't know who the fuck I am! I could be standing right in their face and they'd ask me to get out of the way! Besides, I gotta find out if Damian's okay!"

Steve, still driving, tried to avoid Mikey's pleading eyes until Mikey put his arms around him, flirtatiously begging, "Please!"

A sucker for Mikey's come-on, Steve pulled the car over to a payphone, only a few blocks away from The Sanctuary, pressing the button and unlocking the doors.

Mikey kissed him on the cheek before jumping out of the car. Janet X raced toward him with bloodshot eyes, still tripping on a hit of acid.

"Me cago en Dios! Just don't take your sweet time like you did in the bathroom!" Steve groaned.

"Ay bendito, Mikey! Did chu hear 'bout Ms. Damian?" Janet was taking a deep drag from her Virginia Slim while her long curly hair waved in the wind to reveal her blemished face, tainted with acne and tons of makeup.

"I think he's okay but I gotta call Dominick back!" Mikey

studied Janet's tight Chicle jeans[26] and implants, which bulged out of her bright red bustier underneath a motorcycle jacket.

"I don't think he's gonna vogue f'awhile!" Janet's breath formed thick misty clouds in the cold late January air, "Es un escándalo! The locas ah screamin'! They got all pretty up to get thrown out onto the streets thanks to la Flaca pendeja, esa!"

Janet took another long drag before noticing Steve inside the car.

"Stevie? Stevie? Ay, Stevie! Papi chulo, I didn't know that was chu inside da cah! Espérate que tengo que contarte algo!"

Jumping inside the car, Janet harassed Steve while Mikey took the opportunity to slip the quarter in, dialing the number on his beeper.

"Hello!"

"Hello? Mikey?"

"Yeah! Dominick? What the hell is going on?"

"I'm at my house with Jorge."

"No, duh!"

"Where are you?"

"A few blocks from The Sanctuary, by some bodega[27]."

"Is Steve with you?"

"You mean daddy?"

"Yeah."

"He's in the car with Janet who's chewing his ear off as we speak."

"Janet?"

"Si! La Janet! I ran into huh on the way to call you back, but you still haven't answered my question!"

---

26 A popular urban brand of denim jeans that fit so tight-ass, it looked like someone was blowing a piece of bubblegum and it literally burst onto your legs. Chicle is a standard word for chewing gum in Spanish.

27 A Latino owned convenience store with a small selection of grocery supplies but most popular for beer, lottery tickets, newspapers, candy, cigarettes, and rolling paper.

"Flaca stabbed Damian in the arm and Damian fucked her up fierce!"

"Is he gonna be okay?"

"Who? Damian? Not if Maggie finds him! Listen, Finnegan, come over to my house!"

"Bitch! Are you for real?"

"Just bring your tired half Puerto Rican ass over, ah-ight? You've already left your dent on my couch!"

"Dominick?"

"What?"

"I think I'm in love! For real!"

"Good-bye!" Click, dial tone.

Mikey hung up the phone while Marsha approached him, a thin ratty shawl wrapped around her torn-up pink dress, still wearing the bonnet Sista Mama gave her last Easter.

"Hey Mikey! How ya doin' baby? Oooh chile, I is stahvin'! I do anythin' fah a dahlah! You got a dahlah? Baby, please tell me ya got a dahlah!" Marsha shivered violently to show how cold she was.

"Marsha, I ain't got no small bills but I'll give you a ten if I could find one!" Mikey went through his pockets until he pulled out a ten. Marsha smiled with joy to expose her rotting teeth while the lampposts cast a sickly glow on her coal black skin.

THE SHROUD OF TURIN

It was three weeks later and they were all together again, having coffee at Café Rafaela. Dim candles enhanced their hung over faces. Damian featured a bandaged arm while Dominick tried to conceal the bags underneath his frustrated eyes by hiding behind his trademark drooping sunglasses. He was miserably depressed about the closing of The Sanctuary. Jorge argued about waiting forever for a "damned tiramisu!" while Mikey stared out the window, hoping to catch a glimpse of Eric walking by.

They had already discussed everything there was to discuss about the other night. The subject was about as worn out as they were as they waited for the mother of the House of X, Sista Mama, to arrive so they could plan their inevitable attack on the House of Pendavis. Despite the fact she was annoyed with them for turning the House of X into a drug gang, she still held on to her title until finding a worthy successor. Damian suggested killing Flaca altogether while Jorge, the hopeless theater queen in the gang, preferred the old West Side Story-like battle at the piers.

"Are you goin' out tonight?" asked Mikey, changing the subject, the question directed to no one in particular.

"Where is there to go?" Jorge logged on.

"I dunno...maybe that new gay club, The Attic?" Mikey suggested, hoping to God maybe that was where Eric could be.

"The Attic? That place sucks!" Dominick interjected

bitterly.

"Well, if I go I'm going with Chris!" Jorge finally revealed, almost whispered.

"Chris? Chris Infiniti? Chris? My ex-boyfriend Chris?" Mikey silenced Jorge with an angry stare. The pain was obvious in his eyes.

"Oh, you'll get over it!" Damian jumped in defense of Jorge, the tiramisu finally making its way to their table.

"I thought Chris was going out with Jason Aviance?" Dominick wondered aloud, Jorge holding back his comment by stuffing his mouth with dessert as Mikey continued staring at him threateningly.

"Wait a minute! Back up! Didn't you go out with Jason Aviance too?" Damian asked, looking at Mikey as if the word 'whore' were stamped on his forehead.

"They weren't going out! They were just fucking!" Dominick clarified, Mikey nodding his head in agreement.

"Yeah, besides, Jason is cheating on Chris with Mark Magnifique!" Jorge took time out from his expedition to defend his curious date for the evening.

"That's because Jason found out Chris was cheating on him with someone who looks just like Mikey!" said Dominick, casually dropping the bomb to make Jorge choke. "But I ain't one to gossip so you didn't hear that from me! As a matter of fact, it was that guy Damian slept with last weekend!"

"Bitch! I only slept wit' him 'cause I got locked outta my apartment!" Damian yelled.

"That guy who looks just like me? Kenny? Did he ask you to pull his nipples while fucking him?" asked Mikey, happily turning the conversation over to Damian, mocking him by pinching his own nipples and comically feigning orgasm.

"I wouldn't talk if I were you 'Ms. Fifty dollars Grandpa, seventy-five the lover can watch!' Besides, weren't you the one who got fucked up the ass by Mark?"

"Mark? Mark Magnifique? Ha! Mark THINKS he fucked me but he was so high he can't remember it was actually Jorge he fucked!" Mikey belted out. Jorge pushed his dessert aside, defeated.

"That's right! He turned you out on his leather couch!" Damian said, excitedly turning on Jorge.

"How did you know he had a leather couch?" Dominick caught him, the whole table silently waiting while Damian gasped for a quick answer.

"Because...I fucked him...on that leather couch!" he let out a second too late.

"Yeah right! YOU fucked Mark Magnifique! With what Miss Thing? Your nail filer?" Dominick and the others burst out with hysterical laughter as Damian's face crumbled like ashes.

"Fuck you, all!"

The laughter eventually quieted, leaving them back to where they started, waiting humorlessly for Sista Mama X, late as usual.

Still dwelling on the previous revelations, Mikey turned back to Jorge, asking, "When did YOU start dating Chris?"

"When you was going out with that Chelsea queen, whatever his name was!"

"Cliff? The one I threw that drink on?" Mikey asked, raising his scarred eyebrow, contempt in his eye.

"Yeah! Cliff!"

"I'm surprised you never slept with Cliff considering how much you wanted him!" Mikey quickly blinked his eyes at

Jorge as if hoping to find a chicken in Jorge's place when he opened them.

"Who? Cliff? Bitch, please! It was cute for him but I don't do steroid-enhanced bodies!" Jorge said defensively.

"Ay loca, pleeease!" Dominick snapped, raising his hand up to Jorge's face like white trailer trash on the Jerry Springer show. "What the fuck was Troy, Fernando and all those other gym bunnies you slept with?"

"Yeah 'Ms. Big Cup'![28] I mean, 'Ms. Big Cunt'!" Mikey said, injecting imaginary steroids into his own ass, his face contorting in pretend pain.

Jorge, who wanted to jump Mikey over the table, could not resist laughing.

"I didn't know you slept with Troy too?" Jorge asked, aiming the question back at Mikey. He had finished with his tiramisu. "Didn't YOU sleep with Troy after we broke up?"

The conversation was once again on Mikey's lap, who quickly scanned the café with hopes of finding Sista Mama heading toward the ill-fated table.

"Yeah! I remember you were going out with Geo at the time! Oh! I'm sorry!" Damian gleamed. "You weren't going out with Geo! You were just getting fucked by him on a regular basis!"

Mikey returned on cue with, "Yeah, but haven't you heard the latest! Geo is now fucking your ex-lover Hector!"

Jorge and Dominick, joining forces, let out an astounded "Ooooooooooh!"

Speechless, Damian contemplated a comeback, the wrath of heaven and hell in his crunched eyes. "Yeah! Well, I heard Chris had messed around with your current little boy toy Eric!"

28 A popular coffee shop and gay hang out located in Chelsea, NY during the '90's.

Damian lied.

Mikey rolled his eyes, unimpressed. "Bullshit! Eric doesn't SEE[29] Chris! If anything, he feels threatened by him! Besides, Chris is Jorge's problem now. As for me, it's all about Eric!"

Managing to shut everyone at the table up for the last time with his bittersweet revelation, the entire café was invaded with tangible silence when the tall, black woman known as Sista Mama X finally arrived in all her wicked glory. Chanel sunglasses decorated her shaved head as Sista Mama sailed toward their table like an African goddess.

When they left, Marsha was outside begging for money with her Easter bonnet.

"Hey Sista Mama! Was goin' on girrrl?" She waved ashy hands at Sista Mama and the rest of them, her smile revealing a slew of missing teeth.

"Wassup Marsha girl? I dig your lubly ensemble!" Sista Mama reached her hand over to allow Marsha the honor of paying her homage.

Marsha dutifully kissed her calloused hands with dry lips.

"Ms. Damian ah heard 'bout what Flaca did to you at The Sanctuary! You okay, honey?"

"Yeah! I'm ah-ight!" said Damian, half-convincingly, shaking his bandaged arm.

"Back in da days, I got cut by Spiffy LaBeija at the Legends Ball right hea!" Marsha pulled up her dress to point a gray finger at a scar on her upper left thigh.

"The Legends Ball?" Jorge turned to ask Dominick.

"Prehistoric is more like it!" Dominick laughed.

---

29 Gay slang for not acknowledging or being interested in someone because they are not within your league.

"Anyways!" said Marsha, brushing him off, "Did I not set that bitch's hair on fiah da next day? Das right! I lit huh up!" Marsha accentuated the 'I lit huh up!' part with finger-snaps.

"I remember that baby! She jumped into the Hudson screamin'!" Mama laughed while reminiscing. "She wore wigs and hats 'til they found her floating dead in that same river years ago. Her hair never did grow back."

"She had it comin', attackin' po' lil' me!" said Marsha, hands on her bony hips.

"Are you taking notes? This is you in ten years!" Dominick said, teasing Damian.

"Oooh honey, chile! I is stahvin'! I'd do anythin' fo' a dahlah!" Marsha said, while Mikey mouthed off Marsha's trademark lines simultaneously with her.

"Really? Would you vogue for us, Mah...?" Dominick started to ask, Sista Mama silencing him with a stare, which was too late.

"Shuah, baby!" Marsha convulsed without a second to spare to some imaginary song in her head, arms flopping in the cold air, legs twitching to unheard rhythms. Her audience was appalled, desperately waiting for Marsha to stop. People were beginning to stare.

"Uhhh, okay baby!" Mama pulled out a few singles from her baggy slacks. "That will be all for today! The category is now closed! Here's your trophy. Now, walk for me!"

Marsha happily took the money, the others pulled out more.

"Go buy yourself sumethin' good to eat so you won't be stahvin'!" Dominick handed her a five before pulling to hand her another. "While you're at it, go buy yourself a new hat, 'cause that one is ready to pick up and walk its own category!"

Marsha was excited as they waved good-bye, heading toward the piers, leaving behind a homeless transsexual with a wad of money in her wrinkled hands and a lonesome tear racing down her charcoal face.

RESURRECTION

At the Christopher Street piers, Mikey rolled a blunt[30] to keep warm while Damian and Dominick fought over some leftover K. Staring out into the empty darkness of the Hudson River with "Master Blaster" playing from somebody's car in the distance, Mikey remembered the first time he ever stepped foot on to the piers. Choking on a mad puff, Dominick slapped Mikey on the back hard.

"Yo, chill out bitch!" Mikey managed to say between coughs, the air windy and cold.

Except for a few desperate hustlers, the piers were empty. New Jersey lit on the other side, Mikey imagined himself getting an apartment close to the Path train with Eric. Damian and Dominick were still arguing over the last few bumps of K. Mikey, in his own hole, recalled the days when the piers belonged to voguing faggots and house music blasted from parked cars. All that was left was but the carcass of a soul, the piers once so full of life now so full of death. Graffitied walls, once boasting "The House of Ninja Rules" now featured "Rest in Peace Supreme. We Love You!" The lampposts, which once served as spotlights for battling Houses, were lifeless. The nightfall still served the twelve-year-old who sucked some old man's dick behind the bushes— "Yeah! Suck it baby! Suck that dick!"

---

30 A cigar hollowed out and filled with marijuana. The term was originally a reference to Phillies Blunts, a popular brand of cigars.

In his drug-enhanced daze, Mikey turned to watch the cars drive by with locked doors. The West Side Highway haunted by the ghosts of men who once walked in the arms of other men, women who once kissed the lips of other women, men who dressed as women, women who dressed as men and children who dressed as adults. However, in spite of death and AIDS, the Houses still prevailed, lingering in the hearts of a new generation living out the legends of the past.

A speeding cab suddenly stopped not far from where they stood. Janet X dashed out of the passenger seat with one high heel stiletto on, struggling to run in a pair of ultra tight cut off shorts and a red lace bra, her bread and butter.

"Help! Help!" Janet screamed at the top of her lungs. Mikey and the others made out her bloodied face through the darkness.

"He's gonna kill me!"

A big black cabbie jumped out of the car, caught up to Janet, pulled her weave to yank her to the concrete floor, ripping open her shorts to expose Janet's tucked cock, punching her repeatedly in the face.

"You faggot! You faggot!" he screamed. Fresh blood warmed his clenched fist, before Janet used her long nails to scratch his face.

Before he could swing another near fatal blow, several arms, one of which went on to punch him in the face, snapping the bone in his nose, pulled the cabbie away. Someone else kicked him in the stomach, making him cringe to the ground before bashing him in the mouth. Unable to scream, belting out a groan, his mouth quickly filled with blood. Trying to cover his face with both hands, someone else kicked him between the legs followed by another kick to the ribs, cracking them as the blood in his mouth mixed with vomit. Through swollen eyes, he could only make out three shadows hovering above him before kicking him in his right ear, knocking his face into a pool of blood and vomit.

Janet watched in awe before they raced off, disappearing into the night, police sirens blaring somewhere in the distance. Holstering up against the floor, Janet stared through tearful eyes at the deformed figure before her, blood streaming through her hand, which held an ardent face. Slowly pushing off the cold cement, Janet limped toward him, eyes fixed on the disfigured face while holding her own hair back with one hand, the other reaching to touch a swollen cheek. The driver, still alive but closer to death, caught an angry glimmer in Janet's eyes.

"See wha happen when chu mess wit faggots! Now chu could tell all ya friends that chu got beat by faggots!" Janet screamed, gathering enough energy to give the sprawled out body one last kick.

That night, while sleeping on Dominick's couch, Mikey dreamt he was in a desert, the sun beaming down harshly, burning the skin right off him. Mikey, alone in the emptiness, sat underneath an ominous tree with the sand beneath hot as coal. Blinded by the brightness of the sun, Mikey could make out the shadow of a huge black bird sailing down toward the tree, thin legs clutching on a limb.

"Why are you still here?" the crow asked.

"I dunno!" Mikey said with sweat dripping down his tanned face.

"You've been here all your life!" the crow continued. "Hiding in the desert from your reality. Imagining yourself persecuted like me, wanting only to survive, to feed the hunger. Driven away. Driven away in flocks. However, you are not like me, always perched somewhere up in a tree, waiting, waiting for a chance to feed on the corn which gives life. The only one who persecutes you is yourself!"

Mikey forced a smile on his dried out face.

"Now tell me! Why are you still here?" the crow asked once again, his feathers ruffled.

Mikey contemplated the question for a moment before responding.

"Because this is all I know!" Mikey's smile became wry. "Suffering and pain."

With this, the crow turned, spread itself in benediction and flew away, vanishing over Mikey, leaving him behind still smiling wryly, alone in the desert.

IMMACULATE CONCEPTION

Maria Magdalena was born in Ecuador, the eldest of three brothers and one sister; she was remarkably beautiful. In 1969, at the age of fifteen, Magdalena's mother left her cheating father and moved to New York with her children. In pursuit of the American dream, they rented a one bedroom, rat-infested apartment in the Bushwick area of Brooklyn.

The three women took up working at a factory, packing cancer-causing sugar substitutes into small boxes, using rusty, old machines which sometimes stole their fingers for less than minimum wage—an industrialized step above cutting down sugar canes at the plantation but nonetheless slavery.

Magdalena was often victim to gossip throughout the factory, envied for her youth and natural beauty. A feisty rebellious soul, she often got herself into vicious fights outside the factory where she would beat the shit out of whichever bitch was giving her grief.

Her only friend was her younger sister Theresa, who after only six months of brutal weather and hateful subway stares, decided to return to the tropical trees and twilight's of South America.

Magdalena's father, a fledgling journalist, often wrote to her while her mother in the other room would sit alone and cry in the corner until she was too numb to feel the pain. Unable to discuss the separation, she would cry alone in a world she could not understand.

Magdalena's Titi Yoli and Tio Walter lived in the projects of Coney Island, across the legendary Astroland amusement park where all their seven children were somehow employed, legally or otherwise.

Already in the country for more than a year, they would throw the biggest parties, inviting other Latinos like Puerto Ricans, Dominicans, Mexicans, even blacks and fellow South Americans. These parties were a social structure where mailroom workers, house cleaners, janitors, cooks, delivery boys, factory workers and many other hard working immigrants came together to share their different cultures and dialects in deep fragmented conversations about their dreams and expectations from la isla de Nueva York.

At one of these parties, Magdalena, now a budding sixteen-year-old heartbreaker, met the tall, dark Puerto Rican that changed her life forever. Staring deeply into her pearl-black eyes, toying with the golden crucifix glistening above her already developed bosom, his first words to her were "Tu crees en Dios?" followed by a wicked, sexy smile.

Magdalena blushed flirtatiously and before she knew it, she was lying naked on his worn-out abused mattress with candles lit. The image of the Virgin Mary pounding against the wall with each thrust; knock knock knocking as he penetrated deeper, her virgin blood staining his white bed sheets.

A few bangs later and the Virgin Mary smashed on the plastic-tiled floor and Magdalena was pregnant.

The family law guaranteed that she would be disowned and thrown out onto the city streets she still could not even pronounce. She only had the baby's father to turn to but according to factory bochinche[31], he was solely responsible for

31 Spanish noun for gossip.

the next generation of factory workers at the sugar compound.

"Yo no quiero mas hijos!" he yelled before slapping her stunned face, waving his fists in the air as if he would beat the child right out of her.

Pushing her violently to the ground, he continued screaming, trashing his own apartment while she held tightly to her stomach, eyes swollen, silently praying for strength to an estranged God.

Asking her to leave was the last anybody ever heard of him. Rumor had him returning to Puerto Rico where he fathered a few more children and eventually settled down.

After a dreadful delivery, Magdalena gave birth to a premature baby boy in the month of May and in spite of many tearful fights, her mother never threw her out. The doctor, a plump Trinidadian woman, warned Magdalena that she could not have any more children and that her baby had been born with complications.

The first time she ever saw the baby, he was struggling to breathe inside an incubator, the size of a puppy, his dark brown skin wrinkled. The doctors gave him only a week to live but in spite of this, she named him Miguel, after her patron saint who she prayed to every night, San Miguel.

Miguelito survived—the joy of her entire family in spite of his dark Caribbean skin.

"Mija, te acostastes con un negro?" Titi Yoli would ask.

To keep her baby from being a bastard child, Magdalena listed her own father as the father of the child on the birth certificate, keeping the family name—Alvarez.

Magdalena quit her factory job in the midst of malicious rumors of her interracial affair with a moreno and took up welfare to raise Miguelito. Strolling him down Knickerbocker Avenue every day, she met other teenage mothers with babies from mixed backgrounds and they quickly formed an alliance of single women with children.

The baby hardly ever cried, saving all his tears for later in life. Magdalena, however, cried every night as she watched him in his crib, sucking on his bobo, staring back at her through Puerto Rican eyes, unaware of all the pain he caused her. Except for his round face and cholo smile, he was the spitting image of his father.

THE DIVINE INFANT

Two years later, at the age of nineteen, Magdalena took Miguelito, now with freckles, and moved in with her aunt, uncle, and cousins in Coney Island. Titi Yoli would watch over the baby while Magdalena returned to the factory, sick and tired of eating pan con welfare cheese.

Each of Magdalena's seven cousins doubled up in a bed and shared a room with the exception of eighteen-year-old Chino, whose brother Alberto had run away from home and left him with the room all to himself. Miguelito would have to share the room and sleep in the same bed with Chino. Late at night, when the entire world was sleeping, Miguelito awakened with the cold touch of Chino's hand fondling his soft baby butt. At times, wet sticky fingers would dig deep inside of him, searching virgin walls. Unable but to say a few words, Miguelito would scream when forced to go to bed.

"No seas malcriado!" his mother would reprimand, frustrated with her own miserable life. Unaware she was feeding him to this wolf; Magdalena would sacrifice Miguelito every night, planting a soft kiss on his terrified cheek. Chino would tease along, making sinister faces at him before Magdalena turned off the lights and left the room. Bottle in hand, Miguelito would cry himself to sleep only to be awakened a few hours later with, "Remember, if your mami finds out, she'll leave you like your daddy did!"

Blood gathering in the bottoms of his feet and his head,

everything in between became numb while Chino penetrated him, breaking down the only walls which ever made Miguelito Christ like. Chino, offered his thumb for Miguelito to bite on while forcing the resisting muscles to tear open.

Years later, he would remember how one of his cousins, Beto, had walked in on them by mistake. Unfortunately, Beto was only a few years older than Miguelito and mentally ill. Despite his best efforts to tell his mother what was going on, Beto's retardation did not do much to inform Titi Yoli that one of her sons was sexually molesting a little boy.

Miguelito became withdrawn during this time, playing quietly by himself, hardly eating anything at all. Titi, forced the food down his throat for hours before he would crawl underneath the table and fall asleep. He would spend his entire days with Titi in the kitchen, pointing his little brown finger up the stairs and screaming "El cuco! El cuco!" After long painful dumps, Titi would wipe his butt, the tissue paper smeared with traces of blood. However, without Medicaid, Magdalena did not have enough money to take him to the doctors, Miguelito staring at her with tearful, angelic eyes. Unable to understand what was happening to her child, Magdalena would have him sleep with her every night from then on, holding him tightly while they both cried themselves to sleep. She vowed someday to find the man of her dreams, the one who would save them from all this pain and suffering.

That day presumably came a few months later, when she met Emilio, a little on the weighty side and insecure enough to fall in love with a homeless mother on the rebound. Though he was also Ecuadorian, Emilio was white enough to pass for a gringo and he was ten years older to Magdalena's twenty years of age. Emilio had clear brown eyes hidden behind prescription goggles, which focused on Magdalena while she flirted shamelessly with him.

Emilio romanced her every day after work with chocolates, flowers, and dinners at McDonalds and trips to a Spanish movie theater in Jackson Heights in his olive green Buick. Sometimes he would drive her around Manhattan, introducing her to concerts at Radio City Music Hall, ice-skating at Rockefeller Center and picnics in Central Park. Though she had already been in the country for a few years, for Magdalena, a trip to the city was like discovering uncharted lands. Miguelito, mesmerized in the back seat, his pearl-black eyes lit up with Times Square.

Every Sunday, Emilio would take them to visit Magdalena's mother, who Miguelito had adoringly nicknamed Mamina in an unsuccessful attempt to call her either "mami" or "abuela." Even though he was now three years old, Miguelito still had trouble talking. Magdalena worried that he would grow up retarded after watching a show on Canal 41. He still seemed troubled, unable to communicate more than a few words at a time before gazing back at her helplessly.

Miguelito was beginning to acknowledge Emilio as some sort of father figure, dimly aware that he wasn't his real father and feeling lost in this strange family that devoured him at night and spoke of his differences in hushed tones.

After only a few months together, Emilio and Magdalena moved into a two-bedroom railroad apartment in Bushwick. Miguelito was subjected to their constant bickering about his real father coming to look for him someday. He spent his time drawing on the walls with crayons; keeping a lookout for the sounds of Mr. Softee, parading down the block; and watching the other kids harass their parents for ice cream.

Although still considered Bushwick, the apartment they lived in was located somewhere on the borderline between Brooklyn and Queens, the vast cemetery located just down the block, being the distinct division between the two boroughs. Frightened by the many tombstones and crucifixes, sometimes Miguelito would stay up late at night watching a strange gathering dressed in white, chanting foreign words, shadows cast on dark concealed faces from the candles held in their hands.

Emilio would take them to Coney Island to visit Titi Yoli at least once a month. Miguelito would cry in the back seat, plotting ways to jump out of the car. Chino was always waiting for him at the top of the stairs, calling him over to come up and play.

"Vete! Vete jugar con Chino!" Magdalena would insist. Emilio would pull her away to the living room before she had a chance to notice the terror on his face. Chino, smiling down at him, a bulge emerging from his shorts and the words "If your mami finds out..." written in his eyes.

During these visits, Chino would lock himself in the bathroom with Miguelito, squeezing his little mouth wide open before brushing his hard cock against Miguelito's lips. Shoving himself into his mouth, sometimes Chino would release a bitter tasting milky fluid inside Miguelito's mouth, rinsing it out before opening the door. Afterwards, he would put on cartoons for Miguelito to watch while he flipped through porn magazines.

At the age of four, Miguelito was enrolled in a Bushwick Day Care Center where everybody spoke English and called him

Mikey. The other kids would make fun of his strange behavior and Mikey often played alone. During naptime, he would sometimes wake up screaming, lunging himself off the mat to destroy the toys and artwork throughout the classroom.

Once, Mikey bashed another little boy dead in the face, busting his nose because Mikey woke up to find his leg over him. When the teacher reached out to grab him, Mikey kicked him in the crotch, running out into the hallway only to be stopped by security. He had developed a vicious temper and a terrible angry stare replaced the innocent, confused glow in his eyes. Magdalena no longer knew how to control him, as he became worse and worse, everyday getting into another fight.

It was not until the day he smashed up the brand new aquarium that Emilio had bought her that the cycle began. Mikey, curiously satisfied, gazed down at the quickly dying goldfish gasping desperately for life. Twenty gallons of water had slithered across the linoleum floor before Magdalena emerged from the kitchen, chanclas[32] dampened by the cold water, watching Mikey staring back at her with his father's wicked smile engraved on his face.

Grabbing him by the arm, she slapped him repeatedly until his cheeks were a soft, bright red. This new surge of control over Mikey escalated from one of his mischievous attempts at getting attention to a bad day at work to an argument with Emilio.

Magdalena's violence erupted unpredictably over anything at all and she dyed her hair blonde to coincide with this new attitude and new decade of life.

Emilio became more and more irritable, constantly

---

32 Spanish for slipper or any easily removable footwear that could be used as a weapon.

accusing Magdalena of having affairs while never proposing marriage and still having a relationship with the mother of his two sons. He went out every night, supposedly to visit them for a few hours a day while Magdalena stayed home, crying herself to sleep, looking much older than her twenty one years of age. They hardly ever had sex anymore unless he came home drunk and forced himself upon her, practically raping her in front of Mikey as she screamed to be left alone. Magdalena would later run to the shower in hopes of any hot water left. Nights spent touring Manhattan were a thing of the past.

Growing resentment toward his mother's boyfriend found Mikey placing nails inside Emilio's shoes and pulling many other stunts to express his hatred toward him, wishing for the day his real father would save them from this miserable life. Magdalena, just minutes after being beaten by Emilio, would chase Mikey with his leather belt, screaming "No grites!" before whipping him, the words echoing Chino's the many nights before he would cover his mouth and fuck him up the ass.

There were times one or both of them would end up at the emergency room after a vicious brawl. Mikey getting stitches in the back of his head after hiding underneath the bed from his mother and accidentally jamming a piece of sharp metal into his skull, trying to avoid her from pulling him out for a beating.

"What happened?" the Trinidadian nurse would ask her.

"Ay don know!" Magdalena cried, bruises throughout her own face and arms, asking herself the same question.

By the age of seven, every time his mother was beaten, Mikey did not know whether she deserved it or if he should kill Emilio with the box-cutter the landlord's daughter gave him. Everything flew in that house—vases, dishes, radios, his mother. Mikey learned to ignore the fights and pretend it was not happening just like with Chino, recently deported to Ecuador for drug dealing at Coney Island.

At school, he was not doing any better. On a school trip to watch Disney's "Swiss Family Robinson," Mikey sneaked out with a group of classmates, convincing them to watch "Saturday Night Fever" instead. The part where John Travolta walks into the club and passes a topless dancer was the first time Mikey had seen a pair of tits. After calling the police to report the missing children, the teacher finally found them and angrily pulled Mikey by the ears. Mikey proceeded to grab her by the tits, pulling them violently. That night, Magdalena smashed his fingers by slamming the door shut on them, leaving them a deep dark purple.

Mikey did not seem bothered except for the physical pain. The words cast between them, enough to put them all in prison for life.

"Eres un demonio!" she would yell.

"Y tu eres una puta sucia!" Mikey would repeat the words he often heard Emilio use toward her.

He was immune to watching Emilio grab Magdalena by the hair and shove her face into the plate, smashing it into pieces, slicing her eyebrow. Mikey would just chew his food silently while his mother's blood poured all over dinner.

Mikey became even more indifferent toward them with each passing year. His only comfort were the letters written to him by Magdalena's father who lived in Ecuador. He imagined running away to live with him in some foreign land. He secretly imagined his own father to be some sort of monster who would destroy Magdalena and Emilio and rescue him. He would look for him in the cemetery from the back seat of the car while Emilio punched his mother out in the front seat.

Screaming, Magdalena jumped out of the car while it was still in motion and ended up in the hospital recovering from broken bones for weeks. He learned never to even think about jumping out of a speeding car.

When he was violently getting a beating from Magdalena for purposely-staining Emilio's shirts with a magic marker, at ten years old, he finally decided he was sick and tired of his life. Mikey poured bleach into the soup his mother was cooking with hopes of killing her and Emilio, in order to run away in search for his father. He was caught and that day they both took turns beating him.

A few days later, Magdalena's father died of a heart attack. Mikey's grandfather had been the only man ever to attempt trying to be a father figure to him, even from a distant country. Something in them forever changed that day. With tears in her eyes, Magdalena gave Mikey the golden crucifix that her father had given to her on her quinceañera. Mikey would never know what it was to lose a father and Magdalena seemed to be aware of this. It was then that Mikey began to feel sorry for her. He allowed himself to feel the pain and cry every time he watched Emilio come home drunk to rape and beat her. For the first time in his life, Mikey understood her suffering and held on tightly to that cross every night before praying to his dead grandfather to save them.

"Tu eres maricón?" Emilio asked Mikey every time they were alone in the car while Magdalena shopped Knickerbocker

Avenue[33]. Mikey was twelve and traumatized enough by his own existence to respond. The beatings, his mother's and his own, had become sporadic. Mikey's hatred for Emilio became an obsession that overwhelmed him twenty-four-seven. Mikey, still waiting for the day his father would come save him from this hell. He had no friends, no girlfriends and if he were not out with his parents, Mikey would stay home alone pretending to be someone else. He wanted to be in somebody else's family—a happy family, a normal family, *The Brady Bunch* family, the *Little House on the Prairie* family. He would do anything to be Laura Ingalls and have Michael Landon as a father.

"No!" he would eventually answer in his low whispery voice, already the subject of much ridicule in elementary school. Whatever his motives, Emilio would persist, torturing him with the same question as Mikey waited angrily in the back seat for his mother's return.

Outside, some teenage Puerto Rican mother screaming up to a woman perched on a window.

"Yo Miriam ... Throw down the baby!

I don't wanna go up the stairs ... I'm too tired!

Just throw the baby out the window. I'll catch him!

I SWEAR!"

33 A popular shopping strip located in Bushwick, New York.

BAPTISM

It was the summer of 1984 and Madonna's "Borderline" ruled Coney Island Beach. Mikey was now thirteen and dangerous to know. He had finally made a friend, P.J. who lived only a block away from Mikey and like him, hated the prejudiced, evil, pretentious white fucks they went to school with.

"Spics! The spics are coming! The spics are coming!" they would yell at them when the yellow school bus that picked them up in Bushwick would pull into the Maspeth, Queens elementary school. Every weekend, they would go to Coney Island to smoke pot underneath the boardwalk before going to Astroland and riding the Cyclone, where many fell to their deaths.

On the way to the subway, Mikey would pass the projects where he once lived, where his mother had handed him unknowingly to the beast that lurked within.

"I don't remember much 'bout being a kid! 'Cept being really scared, frightened, that's all!" he would tell P.J. However, deep inside, Mikey remembered everything like it was yesterday.

P.J. ran away from home, leaving behind his abusive father and Mikey never saw him again, until years later when he would run into him stripping in some seedy gay nightclub. Inspired by P.J.'s audacity, Mikey tried running away himself twice but hey would always find him hiding out somewhere by Mamina's house. The beatings taught him never to try it again.

Therefore, he stayed and went on to some Junior High School in Ridgewood, Queens. Convinced that schools in Queens were better than those in Brooklyn, Magdalena lied about the zoning and forced Mikey to leave behind the few friends he had made to study in a completely new school. He argued everyday about wanting to go to school in Bushwick but when Emilio bought a gun, he learned to shut up quick.

The students placed in classes based on their abilities and previous performance. 01-03 were the honors classes for the smartest, most successful students. The numbers went as high up as 18, for the slower, difficult students. Mikey, now in seventh grade, placed in class 718. There, he got into fights almost every other day and quickly befriended the big black dykey girls which looked out for him. With them in his court, Mikey developed a big mouth and foul attitude.

One day, Mikey came home from school to find his mother on the living room floor, huddled with Mamina, crying. The image startled him. He slowly noticed Emilio's things were all gone. Emilio had gotten his ex-wife, the mother of his two children, pregnant and left to be by her side. For his mother's sake, he tried to hold back his excitement. He secretly wondered if he could have Emilio's closet now. Mikey could not understand why his mother was crying, she should have been happy. He walked over to his mother and she held him tightly while crying on her knees.

"Perdoname! Perdoname, mi'jo!" she cried.

Mikey flinched, half-expecting her to hit him as usual. Images of his mother swirled around him—in the hospital, her face shoved into a plate of food, jumping off a speeding car, slapped, punched, raped, and holding him tenderly as a baby.

Mikey reached down and held her tightly. Her eyes looking up at him—aged and swollen. They filled with tears and the love he had often forgotten she had for him.

By the end of the year, Emilio and Magdalena were back together. For the time being, the fighting and beatings stopped.

Mikey, disappointed by his mother's weakness, decided it was time for him to try his own twisted relationship. Mikey got involved with a voluptuous Puerto Rican mama, Raquel, obsessed with him because he looked "just like Ray from Menudo[34]." Raquel, domineering and manipulative, probably suspected Mikey's homosexuality but did not mind the challenge. He would take her to his parents apartment while Magdalena and Emilio were at work and fuck her on his parents bed, focusing on her large developing tits jiggling all over as she moaned loud enough for the neighbors to hear. When it came to eating her out, however, Mikey would get nauseous. It usually took her forever to get him hard if he did at all. He would have to browse porn magazines, noticing his excitement over the naked men and ignoring the nude women altogether, before their sessions.

"Why can't you just fuck me like the bitch that I am?" she would yell at him, irritated while Mikey lay there annoyed.

Magdalena hated Raquel and became so possessive of Mikey; sometimes it felt like he was her boyfriend instead of Emilio, who still went out every night to visit his newest son. She feared that Mikey would soon leave her too. Deep inside, Magdalena also questioned her son's sexual preferences and

---

34 Menudo was a Puerto Rican boy band popular in the '80's. Members would be replaced when they would turn 16, if their voice changed, if they grew facial hair, or if they got too tall.

was unclear as to who was using whom, Mikey or Raquel. Each day, she became more and more demanding and intolerable.

The memories of his childhood beatings still vivid in his mind, Mikey dealt with her by becoming more rebellious and difficult. He only stayed with Raquel because his mother hated her so much and did everything short of fucking her in front of Magdalena. He already knew he had no sexual interest in women.

One night, when he got home in the morning from partying all night with Raquel, Magdalena slapped him across the face the minute he walked through the door. Mikey responded by slapping her back. He felt a sudden thrill and bewilderment from giving her the same pain she had given him. Magdalena was shocked, aware by the look on his face that he felt absolutely no regret. Mikey was simply surprised he had not hit her back before. He was not taking shit from Magdalena anymore and she had the bright red cheek to prove it.

He remained with Raquel out of pure spite. It was only when Raquel asked Mikey what he would do if she were pregnant that he ended the relationship.

"I'd punch you in the stomach and throw you down a flight of stairs!" he said, half-seriously.

A new couple had moved into the apartment upstairs— Bobby, a twenty-one-year-old mechanic and Yvette, the seventeen-year-old mother of his daughter. The beatings and screaming now seemed to all take place upstairs—Yvette screaming louder than Magdalena ever did.

"Esos fuckin' boricuas!" Emilio would curse.

Mikey was dying for a chance to meet the family more dysfunctional than his.

"Where the fuck you going?" He would hear Bobby scream to Yvette.

"I'm going out with mai cousin. I need some air!"

"Well, then stick your head out the window and take a deep breath 'cause you ain't going nowhere!"

Soon, they would be outside in the hallway fighting viciously, Yvette holding her own by scratching Bobby and leaving him bloodied up.

One day, Mikey, cutting school, ran into Yvette and her gay cousin, a devoted Culture Club fan who would dress up like a Puerto Rican Boy George, smoking pot in the park. With the realization that Yvette was not only a tough bitch but also a fag hag, Mikey gladly went up and introduced himself as her neighbor.

From that day until the day they were evicted, Mikey would spend his afternoons upstairs hanging out with Yvette and her cousin. Together, they would watch bootleg copies of movies like *Purple Rain*, smoking weed and drinking Crazy Horse beer.

Mikey would bring his brown teddy bear hamster, Mr. T, which he stole from the school's pet club, upstairs to fuck Powder Puff, Yvette's white teddy bear hamster and together they would enjoy the wonders of mass reproduction. Mikey and her cousin would leave only when Bobby came home after a bad day at the garage with an evil glow in his eye. From downstairs, Mikey would listen to them beat each other up, Bobby leaving all black and blue while Yvette threw his clothes out the window. Mikey would watch in admiration, wondering why his mother could not be so tough.

In school, Mikey was surprisingly doing a lot better. Mikey

repressed the reality of his life by pouring over the lives of other people in the books he read. He would lose himself in these stories to ignore his pain. *The Great Gatsby* became one of his favorites, imagining himself as the lead female character. When he was not smoking pot with Yvette and her cousin, he was in the library studying and reading new books. Each semester he seemed to do better, becoming more ambitious, determined to be in an honors class. He became industrious and diligent—spending hours on his homework and extra-curricular projects. Yvette and Bobby were forced to move out from upstairs but, by that time, Mikey had become more fascinated with Greek tragedies than Puerto Rican drama.

Now in seventh grade, Mikey had jumped all the way to 703, befriending the smartest boy in school, an Italian named Gino Sabbatini from 701. They spent their lunch breaks together, dishing out the teachers, arguing over who was better—Madonna or Cyndi Lauper[35], Prince or Michael Jackson, making up stories, talking about everything and anything, except their own lives.

By the time he reached eighth grade, Mikey would make it into honors class 801. Gino, now the closest individual in Mikey's life, was rumored to be gay. They would watch *Dynasty* together over the phone, acting the scenes out the next day at school, and feign interest over Elena Stefano, the most popular girl in school. They simply wanted to be her. They formed a tight allegiance in junior high and were inseparable as the school's ambiguously gay duo.

Mikey would get hard-on's in the locker room while watching his classmates undress. He never discussed these feelings with Gino, simply assuming he experienced the same.

---

35 They were never rivals but the media tried to pit them against each other.

With words unspoken, they shared the same attractions and junior high school crushes. Everyone else thought they were lovers and rumors quickly spread about Mikey as well.

Gay was affixed to Mikey long before he had even figured it out for himself or learned how to define it. He did acknowledge that he had feelings for some boy named Mario Benito[36] who was also supposedly chasing after Elena. Everyone else in school hated Mario because they found him rude and obnoxious. Mikey, however, was drawn to his bad boy persona and went out of his way to get Mario's attention. Mikey became more involved in after-school activities and found himself joining all the clubs Mario joined. Although he was not Italian, he even joined the Italian Club. Though he hated everyone in the Junior Kiwanis Club, he joined because Mario was the secretary. It was not long before the rumors reached Magdalena that her son might be gay.

It was when openly homosexual Walter Vasquez slashed his wrists in English class and died before reaching the hospital that Mikey confronted his own reality. That was when the nightmares began.

He would be walking alone in a desert surrounded by an empty darkness. Wolves howling in the distance, Mikey would see himself wearing a white robe, which flowed without wind. Trance-like, walking towards nothing but more emptiness, he would wake up screaming, sweating, drenched in his own fluids.

Suppressed memories of his childhood now haunted him. He cried himself to sleep every night, becoming more and more detached from his friends and developing violent outbursts at school. The words of his cousin Chino reverberated in his

36 Apparently, there were many Italians in that school.

mind, engulfing him, until the one day Mikey threw his books on the floor and ran out of class. Heading toward the cemetery located somewhere between the school and his home, he ran as fast as he could as the wind sailed through his soul. Past tombstones and crucifixes, Mikey continued running from his God and his demons. Surrounded by death, he knew then he would have to confront his reality and a new life would begin.

Over the summer, Mikey started working at a department store in Queens, mixing paint in the hardware department. It was there he met Alex Diaz. Alex was a tall black Puerto Rican gay nineteen-year-old co-worker who wore green contacts. He seemed worldly, if only because he knew his way around New York City via the subway system. He would chew Mikey's ear off about a wonderful secret place in the city where gay men of color would congregate and make good money simply by returning sexual favors to rich white men. He spoke of fraternity-like groups of homosexuals that looked out for one another and demanded respect.

One day, Mikey decided to venture into the city with him and find out if this magical land really existed. He was officially introduced to the decadence of the West Side Highway piers. Alex was a part-time hustler and member of a group of vicious gays that called themselves the House of X.

They went around mopping designer clothes and terrorized the streets of The Village with their loud mouths and switchblades. They were a gang made up of fags, dykes, and transsexuals. However, the battles were staged at "balls"—events held where different Houses would compete in different categories for trophies and a Grand Prize. Alex took Mikey to watch a documentary called *Paris Is Burning*, and he recognized many of the film's stars at the piers and quickly became close to them. It was not long before he too was caught up in the ball scene.

However, Mikey nurtured stranger behaviors and soon befriended the street hustlers and drug dealers. He figured that if he was going to munch[37] or be munched[38], he might as well be paid for it. Mikey began hustling the piers. He would suck off old white men who spoke to him in idiomatic but rather flat Spanish as if he did not speak English. He gave blowjobs[39] everywhere from dark alleys, elegant offices and the bushes of Central Park. He did it simply to satisfy the darkness quivering in his heart. Mikey relived his sexual abuse by allowing these older men to take advantage of him, victimizing himself if only to feel he was making someone else happy.

The days of seeking success in junior high school seemed far behind, replaced by the memories of his childhood. Mikey felt that Magdalena would never love him in spite of any possible achievements or success. He was angry that he turned out to be gay and could not 'just fuck' Raquel. He was angry that he did not even know his real father. He was angry that Chino had molested him. He was angry that Emilio would beat his mother. He was angry that his own mother had beaten him in return. In short, he was really pissed off. An evil now surged from him, making him self-destructive, cold, and bitter. It was as if the devil had finally come to claim his soul. Mikey felt betrayed, abandoned by a God he never knew.

Now in Grover Cleveland High School and exposed to an exciting world just outside the boroughs of New York City,

37 Gay slang for giving a blowjob or eating someone out.
38 Gay slang for getting a blowjob or being eaten out.
39 Munched.

Mikey came on brazenly to Mario. He no longer cared what rumors spread about him and he was determined to bring Mario out of the closet. Mario soon started waiting for Mikey outside his classes and they would hang out after school—riding their bikes throughout Brooklyn, playing handball at the park.

"My parents aren't home. They're working, if you wanna hang out at my house for awhile," Mario finally suggested one day.

Mikey looked up at him, dumbstruck, with a faint 'sure' slipping past his lips. That day, Mikey made love to someone for the very first time. It was different from his previous sexual encounters because it was not forced upon, experimental or for money.

Rumors of their affair spread quickly throughout high school and Mikey confronted a furious Gino outside homeroom one day.

"Is it true?" Gino acted out the role of the spited lover.

"What are you talking about?" Mikey, nervously tried to walk away as a crowd gathered.

"You and Mario? Is it true?"

"What about me and Mario?"

"He's fucking you isn't he?"

"Gino!"

"He's fucking you! You faggot! You faggot!" Gino yelled before running into the crowd surrounding them.

That night, Magdalena received a call from Gino's mother and Mikey's world came crashing to an end. Mikey stared back at her, a fearful child again; speechless, afraid she would lunge at him.

"Quiero saber que esta pasando entre tu y el Mario ese!"

"Remember if your Mami finds out ... she'll leave you like your daddy did!"

"I love him, Mami!" Miguelito fell to his knees, defeated with tears.

He could not understand why he cared what she thought of him. Nevertheless, somehow it mattered.

The words she had feared all her life reached her, one emotion after another creeping into her pale face like a slowly developing Polaroid.

"No! No! Tu no eres maricón! No!" she yelled back at him.

Years later, Mikey would wonder why he did it—whether it was to reveal his secret to his mother or whether it was revenge.

"No! Mami, no! He raped me, Mami! He raped me! No! Mami, no!" Miguelito cried, his face salty with tears and mucus tingling his lips.

After all these years, he found himself stumbling to tell the truth, not about his sexuality or his love for Mario, but about the molestation.

"Quien? Quien? Mario? Mario raped you?" Magdalena picked Mikey up from the floor and shook him violently.

"No, Mami! No! Chino! Chino, Mami! Chino!" Miguelito freed himself from her tight grip and fell back onto the floor, convulsing with tears.

Magdalena was horrified, her face an ardent red.

"Nooo!" she pretended not to hear him, "No! Tu no eres maricón! Tu no eres maricón!"

Before Magdalena could say anything else, Mikey had run into the bathroom and locked himself in.

"Miguel! Miguel! Abreme la puerta! Abreme la puerta!"

she screamed, Mikey struggling to swallow an entire bottle of Extra-Strength Tylenol, searching the cabinets for more. He wanted a quick death before she could break down the door and kill him.

"Miguel! Miguel!" Magdalena screamed and flung herself against the door as Mikey furiously fought with a bottle of painkillers.

"Miguel! Que haces? Abreme la puerta! Abreme la puerta, por favor!"

When she finally broke through, Mikey was sprawled out on the floor repeating the words "... like your daddy did ... like daddy did!" before passing out, the sound of running water breaking the silence.

"Why are you here?" the crow asked Mikey, combing the desert, disoriented. The sun burnt him from up above, scorching his skin.

"I don't know!" Mikey mumbled before dropping to the sand with severe stomach pains.

The crow watched Mikey as he screamed, tilting its head, confused.

"But you haven't even seen the light!"

TEMPTATION

Mikey woke up in a hospital room, an elderly Russian man yelling for a nurse in the bed next to him. Tubes stuck up his nose, running down his throat. He started to pull them out, felt them crawling up inside his chest, through his throat before a black nurse rose from his side and tried stopping him. Mikey pulled them out his nose, coughing and gasping for air, as she screamed "No! No! You can't take those out!"

A short Asian man in a white uniform ran in and Mikey focused on the mole on his cheek before pushing up to vomit a pool of black charcoal all over him.

After two weeks of suicide surveillance and counseling, Mikey was released from Wyckoff Heights Hospital, returning home only to have Emilio confront him about his homosexuality.

"Tu eres maricón?" Emilio demanded.

Mikey smiled with slight disbelief, "Que tanto te importa?"

"Que esta pasando?" Magdalena interrupted.

"No te metas!" Emilio yelled, pushing her so violently she went flying to the other side of the room.

Staring at Mikey with all the hatred in the world, Emilio went to punch Mikey before Magdalena jumped in between the two of them. Mikey watched in horror as Magdalena grabbed Emilio's arm with all her strength before it settled somewhere in the middle of her face. The sound of his mother's nose breaking echoed throughout the room.

"Nooooooooo!" Mikey screamed, lunging at Emilio, both of them crashing against the linoleum floor. Mikey punched him repeatedly. "Don't you hit my mother! Don't you hit my mother!"

Pulling his stepfather off the floor by the collar, Mikey continued yelling insanely into his bloodied face.

"No Miguelito! No, por favor!" Magdalena cried out between her hands, which held back the gushing blood from her broken nose.

"DON'T YOU EVER HIT MY MOTHER!" Mikey yelled, remembering the many times he was too young to say those words.

His mother lay there crying as she had in the hospital bed, on the kitchen table, on the street by the cemetery. Memories of his abused mother raced through him like a sudden gush of wind before Mikey ran out as fast as he could. Aimless, Mikey ran down the streets toward the cemetery, past tombstones and crucifixes before falling defeated to the ground. He vowed never to return. If he did, he knew Emilio would either make his life miserable or try to shoot him with his gun. Besides, if Magdalena had not left Emilio by now, there was no way she would ever leave him.

Mikey went to see Mario but his parents had sent him upstate to be with his uncle. Mikey never saw him again but he did not have to. Though he felt something special for him, Mikey felt it best to leave Mario alone. Mario would always be alive, loving him through the eyes of many others.

With nowhere else to go, Mikey ended up back at the piers. Relying on the kindness of strangers for a place to stay or a couch to crash, sometimes the tricks would not even ask him to have sex with them.

Anji X, current "mother" of the House of X, even let Mikey stay for a whole week in her tiny East Village apartment before he felt the need to move on. He quickly became one with the night, lurking off from one trick to another, beating up old men he knew had more money than they claimed to.

Alex, now a homeless hustler himself after getting thrown out by his mother, introduced Mikey to cocaine, acid, and ecstasy to take away the pain and together they became the most notorious sex workers at the piers.

"When you accept your own homosexuality, it's like becoming a vampire. You learn to lurk in your own darkness. Hunt or be hunted," Alex would smile his corny smile.

The number of people Mikey slept with multiplied daily. He befriended a community of West Side Highway pier regulars—voguing queens, runaway twelve-year-olds, fifty-year-old sugar daddies, fellow hustlers, and drug addicts. They all seemed to have stories more horrifying than his, making him feel lucky just to be alive. His life paled in comparison to some of the things he heard but Mikey no longer cared about dwelling in his misery. He was in love once again, this time with a graffiti artist known to everyone as Supreme.

Supreme was a hard-core Puerto Rican banjee hustler with milky white skin. He cruised the piers with his wooden cane and rumor had it that he only liked transsexuals. Supreme often seen with Michelle Magnifique who paraded the West Side Highway in her tight tube tops, flaunting recently siliconed breasts. Mikey would catch Supreme gazing over at him with mystifying green eyes while holding Michelle's hand. Michelle would start cursing Supreme for not paying attention to her only to be bitch-slapped across the face or beaten in public with a cane for embarrassing him at the piers.

It was not until Mother's Day that Mikey and Supreme finally got together and exchanged hustling tips.

The fiercest, most notorious graffiti artist in New York City: a Puerto Rican banjee boy known to everyone as "Supreme."

A legend in the making with his "FUCK-YOU-ALL-while-sucking-on-a-lollipop" attitude: Mikey X.

They first lowered their sunglasses to clock one another while hustling at the West Side Highway piers.

Supreme: limping up and down Christopher Street with his wooden cane, spitting, crotch-grabbing, smoking big, phat blunts to impress potential clients, the whole time cruising[40] Mikey as he sat trying to sell away his bitter youth.

Mikey: feigning boredom with Supreme's played-out machismo and casting him shade, but lighting candles at night and praying to Oshún, Santeria goddess of love, for just one night with him—fantasizing the touch of Supreme's milky white skin against his own tanned, olive body; secretly worshipping Supreme while having sex with ugly, old fucks.

Mother's Day

After downing two Crazy Horse forties and smoking a joint, Mikey felt more than pretentious enough to step right up, staring deeply into Supreme's blood-shot green eyes, and make out with him right there at the piers. The lampposts hovering, cast carnal images over the Hudson River while sounds of lust were drowned out by inane laughter and blaring house music in the background. An overly excited

---

40 Gay slang which means to look for a sexual partner, usually in public places.

faggot beeps his horn as he drives by, hoping to experience a ménage à trois. "LUNCH BREAK! LUNCH BREAK!" Mikey sings out, making it perfectly clear that tonight, they belong only to one another.

Without as much as a gesture, they end up back at Supreme's West Side crib. The loft: small, dark, seedy, the smell of piss and Pine-Sol creeping in from the bum-infested hallway. Mikey: captivated by the graffitied walls revealed by the soft white candles Supreme lights.

"I'm gonna rape ya, kid!" Supreme gleams, ominously, his first spoken words, half-joking. "Yeah? ... well ya' can't rape da willin'!" Mikey smirks, bites his lower lip. Supreme lunges before Mikey says another word, thrusting his wet tongue deep inside Mikey's mouth, Mikey's sweet lollipop aftertaste lingering on his saliva, Supreme pushing his stiff cock into Mikey's growing erection.

Mikey: stunned, yet excited by the violent assault, sucking in his breath as Supreme attacks his neck.

Supreme: tossing him viciously onto a bed Mikey had not realized lay just behind him, crushing Mikey with unexpected thrilling strength, grinding on top of Mikey, pinning him to the worn, abused mattress, Mikey letting out angry screams as Supreme chews his neck, longing to produce hickeys Mikey will remember him by for days to come.

Mikey: fighting from underneath, desperately trying to push Supreme off, Supreme's teeth tearing through capillaries and sucking until he has left his tag, pulling away to admire it.

Supreme: watching the growing excitement in Mikey's pearl-black eyes.

"You bastard," Mikey curses through clenched teeth, the

irony in his fiendish smile making him concubine to the quickly reddening hickey.

Supreme: lifting himself off Mikey, reaches down to pull at his over-sized T-shirt, displaying a muscular chest with tight, pink nipples.

Mikey: quickly running soft hands down Supreme's definition before peeling off his own tank top, a golden crucifix glistening against his chest.

Supreme: marveling at Mikey's smoothly toned nineteen-year-old body and dark brown nipples, devouring them as if expecting to produce milk, arousing in Mikey a synthesis of pleasure and pain, swelling Mikey's dick.

At that moment, Mikey's beeper vibrates with urgent desperation, a trick paging to subdue an insatiable hunger. Supreme snatches it out of Mikey's pocket, tosses it across the room where it smashes against the spray-painted walls.

Supreme: seizing the moment to unzip Mikey's baggy jeans. Underneath, Looney Tunes boxer shorts wrap tightly around Mikey's smooth waist, a thin trail of pubic hair leading seductively from Mikey's belly button towards his bulging crotch, precum stains wet in the image of Marvin the Martian.

Mikey had just left Supreme's West Side Highway loft when Michelle and a group of Magnifique jumped him and tried slashing his face, managing to cut his cheek. Mikey fought them off with his switchblade and raced down Christopher Street in tears, his face and clothes bloodied. He ended up back at Anji's East Village apartment. In between all the phone calls and visits from her own children[41], Anji bandaged Mikey up and let

41 Members of a House are referred to as 'children' though there are no biological or legal rights involved.

him stay over until he was ready to face the world again.

With a face decorated by Band-Aids, Mikey went back to hustling, prepared to take on Michelle and any other Magnifique that would fuck with him.

It was during this time Mikey met Jerry, a heavy-set, full-fledged Dominican Santero who Mikey knew from Grover Cleveland High School. Behind a pair of goggle-like glasses, Jerry would watch Mikey hustling the piers with Alex. Mikey would never bother talking to him, bothered by the fact that Jerry knew him from high school. He remembered Jerry as one of the other boys routinely called 'faggot' because he always laughed too loud and talked too much. He had been the school clown, foolish in his zeal to be likable. Meeting him at the piers would be inevitable.

One night, while waiting for Alex outside some tacky gay Latin club in Queens, Jerry finally confronted Mikey. Like the Pillsbury doughboy begging for a squeeze, Jerry was gullible in his need to be accepted by him. Stuck somewhere on Queens Boulevard with no sight of Alex, Mikey had no choice but to talk with him.

"Aren't you Mikey? Mikey Alvarez? From Grover Cleveland High School?" Jerry asked.

"No!" Mikey denied, "My name is Angel ... Angel Gonzalez ... but they call me Junior! Pleased to meet ya!"

Mikey reached over to shake his hand, trying to hold back the smile developing from his own craftiness.

"You sure you nevah went to Cleveland?" Jerry laughed as if offended.

"Positively absolutely!" Mikey cracked, unable to hold back the laughter.

With nothing more than a chuckle, Jerry knew that Mikey was simply pulling his leg.

They would go on to form an impenetrable friendship that would last for several years. Mikey introduced Jerry to all the pier queens and Jerry introduced him to Santeria.

His apartment was a museum of altars worshipping statues of Catholic saints and American Indians, colorful beads and fabrics, cigars and rum, perfumes and fruits, candles flickering over photographs of cheating husbands.

A stone-sized rock with the outline of a human face surrounded by candy and toys was explained by Jerry to be Elegua.

"He was a young African prince. Elegua is a mischievous orisha[42]. One offers him candy, and toys, sometimes rum, and cigar smoke to ask for his help. He opens and closes all doors to the secrets of the religion, which is why you always keep him at the entrance but he's a crafty little motherfucker like you!"

"You know, I'm like jaded to everything. Very few things surprise me but this is wicked! Why are his hands missing?" Mikey referred to the statue of Jesus reaching out his stumps to him.

"Somebody stole them," Jerry said matter-of-factly.

"What does St. Therese have to do with Santeria?" Mikey pointed to the ceramic nun clothed in a brown and beige robe holding a crucifix and pink roses.

"In the religion, that represents Oyá, pendejo!"

Jerry went on to explain how when the Africans where brought into slavery throughout the Caribbean they were forced into Catholicism. However, they still practiced the

---

42 A spirit or deity that reflects one of the manifestations of God in the Yoruba religion.

Yoruba religion in secrecy by substituting the Catholic saints to represent the different orisha.

"Their religion lasted long before Christ even walked this earth and Oyá is one of the most feared of the orisha because she represents death. Rather, she represents the embrace of death. In nature, she is the wind. Oyá's main colors are burgundy and different shades of brown, which probably explains why St. Therese represents her. St. Therese is called 'the lily of the valley' and you'll find a statue of her in many funeral homes dressed in brown and beige."

Jerry continued his crash course on Santeria and all the other orisha until the phone rang. While he spoke, Mikey focused in on St. Therese with great awe. Mikey was drawn to her as if she held the key to his own duality. She stood out as the most beautiful and intriguing statue to Mikey. The mysteries and darkness with which Jerry spoke of Oyá somehow conjured up the childhood memories of finding his peace at the cemetery.

"Let me let you go cause I've got company and you know you can't keep them waiting. What? None of your business who! It's your husband, okay! I've got your husband here and I'm gonna suck his dick! Fuck you too, Miriam!" Jerry slammed the phone while a woman still talked on the other end.

Mikey's curiosity about the religion and Jerry's interest in becoming a pier queen brought them closer and closer each day. Mikey, however, would keep his hustling on the down low[43] and disappear for days without a trace until showing up at Jerry's apartment with flowers and gifts for Oyá.

Jerry would watch Mikey leave the piers with old men in black cars. Old men that would drive Mikey back to some cheap hotel room where they would pay him a hundred dollars

43 Slang for men who have sex with other men discreetly.

to sit on their faces and piss all over them.

"Why aren't you with your parents?" Jerry finally confronted him one day.

When Mikey told him the story about Emilio, Jerry suggested "Pon le los clavos!" —A Santeria ritual used to harm an enemy, which his own mother had often practiced. Mikey refused; afraid it would all come back to him in some way.

When Jerry's mother, Esperansa, returned several days later from her annual summer visit to Dominican Republic, Jerry convinced her to let Mikey stay with them. Unlike Mikey's parents, Esperansa was cool about her son being gay. Mikey agreed to pay utilities in exchange for a permanent couch to crash when he was not out all night with a trick. Unaware that she was housing a prostitute, Jerry and Mikey led her to believe Mikey worked coat-check at a New York City nightclub. Excited finally to have a place to stay, Mikey did not consume himself with the thought of selling himself for money.

When they were not watching telenovelas[44] together or sacrificing chickens, Jerry and Mikey would be found at the piers—dishing everybody out, cruising potential customers, learning new voguing techniques.

"Mama, don't forget to punch out!" they would scream when someone left the piers.

Everybody who hung out at the piers was family. The piers were a sanctuary for anyone thrown out by their parents, anyone whose father had tried to kill them, anyone harassed by fag bashers, anyone whose friend had just died of AIDS, and anyone who carried the package[45]. Every night, the West Side

---

44 A Latin American television soap opera with a limited run, much like a mini series. Lead characters are usually not representative of the racial fabric of the countries where they are produced with the main actors usually white and the more ethnic looking actors in supporting roles.

45 A derogatory slang term derived from prisons referring to AIDS.

Highway piers would be filled with gay and lesbian youth unable to afford the money to get into a club or not old enough to get in. With nowhere else to turn but the edge of the city, they were the forgotten children. They were the ones nobody else cared about or wanted to know. Condemned by the church, they lived out an inescapable hell where no God existed. Rebellion was in the air, taking many forms.

Mikey continued hustling at the piers until the day at Hatfield's, a gay Latin club out in Queens, when he met the short Puerto Rican papi chulo named Ricky.

"Are you in the House of X?" Ricky asked, referring to the black Malcolm X tee shirt with the letter "X" dripping in blood that Mikey was wearing.

Mikey found himself quickly drawn into Ricky's dark brooding Latin features and sexy smile, even though Ricky was terribly short.

The shirt quickly came off at Ricky's Ozone Park apartment but in spite of much kissing and foreplay, they did not have sex that night.

"I like you too much to have sex with you right away!" Ricky stared into Mikey's confused eyes. "I'd rather get to know you better!"

Mikey and Ricky became an instant item. Five years older, Ricky asked Mikey to move in with him after only a week. With no other options other than sleeping on Jerry's couch, he naively agreed, hoping lesbians were not the only ones successful at sudden shared living arrangements. Mikey did not mind that Ricky would not tell him where he worked at night. As long as they had food on the table and Ricky crawled into bed to be in his arms in the morning, Mikey had no complaints. Everything seemed like heaven until Ricky started disappearing for several days.

Mikey noticed things missing from the apartment. The television set had one day been "stolen during a break-in." Mikey's jewelry had somehow "been lost." In fact, Mikey "lost" more and more things in that apartment until the day Ricky dropped to his knees and finally admitted he was a crack addict.

Mikey was speechless. He had been through a lot in his short life but never had he fallen in love with a crack addict. Now it all made sense but Mikey felt stupid for not recognizing the obvious signs. He motioned Ricky to come into his arms with tears in his eyes. However, when Ricky reached over expecting a hug from Mikey, he was instead introduced to the back of Mikey's hand.

A few hours later, he was back at Jerry's apartment lighting candles to Oyá. Ricky began stalking him, following Mikey everywhere he went.

"Mikey, I LOVE YOU!" he would scream outside Jerry's window late at night unafraid to be shot down on the streets of Bushwick. Mikey, hiding behind the curtains, remembering the stories Magdalena would tell him about Emilio screaming out the window for her to come out.

Like his failed parents, Mikey got back together again with Ricky. However, he forced Ricky to tell his family and check into a detox center upstate for a month. Ricky agreed, writing letters to Mikey almost everyday and sneaking off to call him every night. When he completed his term, Ricky went into a rehab center while Mikey looked for legal work. Mikey landed a job at a record shop in the city where he mopped CD's everyday and sold them to his friends at half price for extra money. He would look out for Jerry while Jerry shoplifted the latest music and recording equipment. Mikey always came home with a new love song to play for Ricky.

Because they had apparently made it through the worst ordeal of their relationship and both swore to be HIV negative, Ricky convinced Mikey to foolishly experiment without condoms. Ricky wanted to feel Mikey while penetrating deep inside of him without anything to separate their love.

"I'm your lover not some trick you picked up at the piers for the night! Mikey, I love you! I want our love to feel special. I want to give myself to you completely without boundaries!"

Afraid of the AIDS crisis, Mikey fought Ricky off several nights but after a few drinks at a party, Mikey finally allowed Ricky to fuck him without protection. With nothing left to lose, they continued having unsafe sex until Mikey finally arranged to have them both checked for the disease at a free HIV clinic. It was then they found out that Ricky was HIV positive. By some miracle, Mikey tested negative.

Ricky had probably just become HIV positive and Mikey was in the clear. Despite the obvious fact that Ricky had been cheating on him, Mikey decided to stay with him.

Mikey fought to maintain a stable relationship with Ricky but the realization that he was dying made Ricky drop out of rehab and hit the streets again for crack.

"Do you think smoking crack is gonna save you from this disease?" Mikey confronted Ricky one morning when Ricky stumbled in drugged up with bloodshot eyes.

"No! But neither are you!" death clouding up in Ricky's eyes.

Fed up with the insanity, after almost a year, Mikey left Ricky for the last time and never looked back.

Sleeping on Jerry's couch, Mikey's nightmares now haunted him again with full force. The robe he wore in his dreams was now pitch black and continued to flow in a wind, which did not exist. Sometimes, Mikey would see a great wall emerge from the desert, painted with a fading portrait of him. He would watch his own eyes glaring back at him ominously with Medusa-like snakes covering his head. The image of him on the wall wore the white robe, which once adorned him, and his arms stretched out in a Christ like gesture. In one hand, the painting held a black crow. In the other, the image of him held a gold communion cup. Mikey would stand there, staring at this painting, confused.

When Mikey would wake up in the middle of the night, the statues staring back at him in the darkness would greet him. Candles cast an evil glow on their plaster faces, casting unholy shadows on virgins and saints. Jerry would be snoring away peacefully and his mother would be talking in her sleep. Mikey would cry himself to sleep if he slept at all.

Mikey abruptly quit his job at the record shop and became distant and withdrawn. With so much to deal with, Mikey could not care any less about selling records or dealing with customers. He was a walking corpse lingering in the death, which surrounded him.

Mikey contemplated surprising his mother who was now working as a secretary at the factory. However, what would he say?

"Mami, I've been a hustler and fallen in love with an HIV-positive crack addict!"

Mikey could not face his mother no matter how much he wanted to. Instead, he ended up back at the piers where one day he spotted someone else he knew from high school.

Lucky was a known crack dealer in Bushwick. Mikey and Jerry both had an incredible crush on Lucky but he was always with some gorgeous girl wrapped around him. Rumors throughout the neighborhood questioned his sexuality. Lucky's obsession with excess gold, however, offset his hard-core image, and rose more than a few eyebrows throughout the streets of Brooklyn.

Lucky pretended not to see him and held on tighter to the girl he was with. Mikey strolled over to another hustler he knew and asked if he knew the party in question.

"Who? 'Loca'? I mean Lucky! Of course, he's gay! He likes to get fucked by niggas!" Papo, a fellow hustler with long hair he kept in a ponytail, suggested. "You know Tyrone? Tyrone Pendavis? That's his favorite piece! Lucky pays him lovely to turn him out in bed! I heard he's a regular fixture at La Escuelita! Those cha-cha queens are the only ones that would buy crack! I hear he's looking for people to package drugs and sell for him."

That Saturday, Mikey and Jerry hopped on the L train from Bushwick and headed to Escuelita in midtown Manhattan for a planned encounter with Lucky. Escuelita was notorious for the seedy drag shows that would go on for hours to an audience of banjee hustlers, sugar daddies, and aspiring pre-op transsexuals. The place was run by Indian drug dealers and located in the basement of a Blimpies sandwich restaurant by Port Authority. It was a nightly haven for illegal immigrants and runaway gay and lesbian youth.

The minute Mikey and Jerry stepped foot inside the club they were attacked by a short older Dominican drag queen.

"Pero mira que lindo! Ay papi, tu tienes el 'look'!" she

screamed, pinching Mikey's cheeks. "They calleh mee 'Hollywood' because I'm a stah!"

Mikey forced a smile, biting his tongue so as not to offend anyone.

"Wai Hollywood, it's such a pleh-shah to meet chu!" Jerry carried on with her.

"Pero mira que muchacho tan chulo!" Hollywood continued pinching Mikey. "I must introduce chu to Angela!"

Before Mikey could say 'no', she was already screaming, "Angela! Angela! Ven pa ca!"

A tall anorexic-looking androgynous boy with a big nose emerged from the dance floor.

"Angela, mira te presento a unos amiguitos mios!" Hollywood gasped excitedly without even knowing their names, passing Mikey a wink.

"Wai heleaux Angela!" Jerry mocked Hollywood. "Mai name ees Jessica and these ees ..." Jerry looked at Mikey, searching for an appropriate drag name "Muriel!"

"MURIEL?" Mikey hollered.

"Yes, Muriel!" Jerry nodded back, insisting.

"Please to meet chu!" Angela extended a long thin arm to shake.

Uninterested in hanging out with drag queens and effeminate boys all night, Mikey left Jerry to make small talk with them while he combed the club for any signs of Lucky. They found a common bond in being Dominican and practicing Santeria as Mikey immersed himself in the salsa and merengue records, which his mother used to play around the house. He missed his mother so much and almost hoped to find her somewhere on the dance-floor.

"Muriel! Oh, Muriel!" Jerry called, "Look at Lucky right

ovah there!"

Pointing to a pole by the other side of the club, Jerry caught Lucky staring back at them like a deer in headlights. He donned his usual masses of gold and a black leather vest, exposing his mildly developed chest. His smile quickly became arrogant as he realized they were living for him.

"Oh! She's obnoxious!" Mikey snickered to Jerry as Lucky snaked past them, leaving behind a trail of social envy and cheap cologne. They casually followed their lead toward Lucky, trying to look aloof.

It did not help much that Mikey stood right next to him, pretending to be enthralled by the dancers on the dance floor. An old overplayed freestyle record by some one-hit-wonder vibrated from the speakers as Lucky stared at Mikey, waiting for him to say something. Mikey looked away and smiled, ignoring him. This went on for two sets while Jerry, Angela, and Hollywood cackled in the background until Lucky finally broke the ice.

"Ya know you certainly smile a lot!" Lucky said with an unexpected feminine voice, destroying the mysticism.

A few days later, Mikey and Jerry were working for him, cooking and packaging crack in Lucky's cluttered Bushwick apartment. In spite of all the money he made, Lucky would serve them watered down Kool Aid using half the packet like Mamina would make for Mikey. Not before long, Mikey moved in, sleeping on his couch while Lucky blew all the local bugarrones[46] in his bedroom.

Business was booming for Lucky with Mikey and Jerry

---

46 Latin slang for a heterosexual man that tops or receives oral sex from gay men for money while still engaging in relationships with women.

quickly becoming the most notorious queens in Bushwick. Feeling grand, Jerry would bring Angela down to meet all the homeboys and together with Mikey, they would carry on in the streets as if they owned the neighborhood. They would scour throughout the streets of Knickerbocker and Graham Avenue, buying the latest gear and Lucky more jewelry.

"Don't you think you have enough gold?" Mikey sneered at Lucky one day on Knickerbocker Avenue.

"You never have enough gold!"

"Spoken like a true queen!"

"I am not a queen!" Lucky yelled.

"Yeah, the only piece of jewelry missing is the crown!"

"Look, isn't that your mother?" Jerry interrupted.

Mikey's heart dropped as he spotted Magdalena looking at some sale footwear outside a department store. Even though her face revealed signs of age and depression, Magdalena still looked as beautiful as he had always remembered. His heart broke and he thought about running up to her and helping her find a nice pair of sensible shoes.

"Mami looks great. She loves shoes!" Mikey, starting to cry as Jerry held him back. "I should've never told her! I should've never told her! Maybe she'd still love me!"

"I'm sure she still loves you Mikey. She just needs time to deal with it. Pero, right now is not the time!" Jerry struggled with him while pointing to the police cars patrolling the block.

A car horn beeped and Mikey caught her face looking up, saddened and worn, watching her adoringly as she got into Emilio's car.

"Why can't she just leave him?" Mikey cried loud enough for everyone to hear, as Emilio's car pulled away.

Several days later, while making a drug deal on Knickerbocker Avenue, Angela started screaming, "Da police! Da police!"

"Calm down!" Mikey yelled at him, "You're gonna get us arrested!"

Angela pointed to a police officer on patrol who was scoping them out.

"Wow! He looks ovah!" Jerry drooled, unfazed by the fact that he might end up behind bars. "He can handcuff and rape me anytime!"

"I take that big black dick too!" Angela said enthusiastically, suddenly relaxed, and poised.

"Oh, God!" Mikey let out as the cop walked right up to them, "This is it! We're going to jail!"

"How ya doin' fellas?" the officer asked with a deep rugged voice.

"Fine!" they all said in unison, Angela trailing off coquettishly.

Silence followed as they sized each other up, the cop staring at Mikey hard as if he recognized him from a 'wanted' sign.

"What are you guys doin'?" the cop asked.

"Oh ... just hanging out!" Jerry began.

"Yeah, just hanging out!" Angela echoed.

The cop continued staring intensely at Mikey, nervously holding on tightly to the vials of crack in his pocket.

"He's a husband!" Jerry quickly whispered into Mikey's ear.

"What is your name?" he finally asked as Mikey looked away, searching for the quickest escape.

"Willie!" Mikey forced a smile, lifting the name off the officer's badge which read 'Williams', his right hand beginning to shake violently.

Officer Williams continued to stare at him as if he could see right past his fake smile and phony name.

"You know ... Willie? You have beautiful eyes!"

Everyone stood there in silence, wondering exactly what Officer Williams was trying to say. They all had this look on their faces as if wondering, "Did he just say 'eyes'? 'Beautiful eyes'?"

"Excuse me?" Mikey cringed.

"I said you have beautiful eyes!" Officer Williams repeated with a sharper tone to his voice.

Mikey, Jerry, and Angela stared at him in disbelief.

Officer Williams pulled out a pad and started writing something down.

"Oh, great! We're getting a ticket!" Mikey started fidgeting.

"What are we getting a ticket for?" Jerry started screaming. "I thought you said he has 'beautiful eyes'? Mikey! Show him your eyes!"

"Bitch! Don't give him my real name!" Mikey yelled.

They started yelling at each other, going off in Spanish, the words 'puta', 'sucia', 'asquerosa' flying out of their mouths like daggers.

"They alwais git like dis!" Angela batted his eyelashes, flirting with Officer Williams as Mikey and Jerry continued their verbal assault.

"Excuse me! Excuse me!" Officer Williams demanded silence.

They stopped, looking at each other the way angry children do.

"This is for you!" he said, folding the ticket and handing it over to Mikey.

Mikey opened up the piece of paper to discover a phone number scribbled on it, raising his eyebrow to express uncertainty.

"My name is Officer Williams but YOU can call me Tony!" he reached out to shake Mikey's hand.

Mikey shook his hand, still confused as to what was going on.

"Are you ... gay?" Jerry asked for Mikey.

Officer Williams answered by smiling to reveal perfect white teeth against his coal black skin.

"Oh!" Mikey said.

"Ooooooooooh!" they all sang out together.

"See! I told you he was gay, Ms. Thing!" Jerry continued arguing with Mikey.

"You did not, bitch!"

"You thought we was gonna get arrested!"

"At all! Who? Me? Arrested? Loca, please!"

"So!" Officer Williams silenced them, "Willie?"

He stood there mockingly; waiting for a correction but Mikey just watched him curiously. "I will hear from you tomorrow?"

For the next couple of months, Mikey and Officer Tony Williams shared a passionate illegal affair while Mikey continued dealing crack for a living. At first, Mikey lied and told him that Lucky was the drug dealer and they had known him for years, unwilling to turn their backs on their friend.

"Sometimes we help out with the packaging" he smiled innocently.

Slowly but surely, Tony figured it out on his own but only after falling deeply in love with Mikey. Mikey was the light that shined on his dark side, spinning his morals out of control. It made no sense for a police officer to pursue a relationship with a drug dealer but at the same time, it felt so good. Tony tried desperately to father Mikey and lead him on the right path, aware of his dysfunctional background and the insanity of his life. Mikey, however, was in too deep in deviance and showed no signs of wanting to leave Lucky's influence. Experience had developed a thick skin on Mikey, manifesting through his cold heartless determination to fuck the world over. He delighted and indulged in the notoriety he acclaimed while selling crack on the streets of Bushwick.

Tony finally disappeared one day, transferring to another precinct without a trace. Mikey only tried once or twice to hunt him down, showing up at other precincts with pockets full of drugs, before brushing him off as missing in action. He walked away from the abrupt end to their relationship unaffected and unbothered.

Mikey, now creeping twenty, was still a little boy inside and quite impressionable. He admired Lucky and looked up to him. Lucky, however, was becoming rather envious of all the attention Mikey was getting, especially from his suitors. They would walk out of his bedroom and stare at Mikey with lustful eyes as he lay pretending to be fast asleep in nothing more than his boxer shorts on Lucky's couch.

It was not until Lucky walked in on Mikey getting head from one of his pieces that Lucky finally gave him his walking papers.

Back to hustling at the piers, Mikey would end up sleeping on Jerry's couch when he was not in bed with a trick or two or three at the same time.

One night, sneaking into The Monster[47] with Jerry, he was surprised to hear a vaguely familiar voice calling out his name.

"Miguelito? Miguelito?" Mikey turned around, startled that someone would call him by that name.

"Alberto? Oh my God!" he rushed excitedly into the arms of a man Jerry waited impatiently to be introduced to, clearing his throat loudly for attention while noticing a vague resemblance.

"Jerry, this is my mom's cousin Alberto!" Mikey yelled as if he had just won Lotto. He had not seen Alberto for a long time and only remembered him as a strange distant relative he would see at holiday gatherings throughout the years. He would be the one to come out briefly and say 'hello' before retreating to hide out in his bedroom. They were never close but the fact that he was a relative and at a gay bar instantly made them sistas.

"I was hoping I'd run into you sooner or later!" Alberto turned to Mikey, ignoring Jerry's extended hand.

"What do ya mean?"

"Your mother ..." Alberto began, Mikey's smile quickly fading, "She's been sick! She's been looking all over for you, worried!"

Mikey formed tears, which he fought hard to hold back.

"How do you know?" Mikey was suddenly defensive.

"Well, she talks to my mother every day and insists that she'll do anything to have you back!"

Mikey just looked at Alberto as if making sure he heard correctly.

---

47 A popular gay bar and dance club located near Sheridan Square in the West Village with a piano bar upstairs, a dance floor downstairs and skanky bathrooms.

"Miguelito, Magdalena loves you!"

That is all he had to say. Before the end of the night, Mikey had brought Alberto to the piers and debriefed him on all the events of the past several years since he came out. Alberto just sat there with his mouth wide open, disbelief in his eyes.

"My brother Chino molested you?"

Mikey stared at him through watery eyes, having forgotten that Chino was his brother, the answer in the tear, which trickled down his face.

Alberto went on to reveal that he had run away from home when he was in his teens but returned a few years later and his own mother knew he was gay and accepted him.

"Titi Yoli knows you're gay?" Mikey asked, Alberto nodding his head up and down. "And she's cool with it?"

"She has no choice!" Alberto smiled grimly, "I'm HIV-positive."

Mikey finally allowed himself the permission to cry fully as they sat there, two men hugging on a pier at the edge of New York City.

"Jerry! Jerry!" someone screamed outside the window later that night. Mikey got up off the couch, wrapped in some old blanket while Jerry and his mother snored away in their bedrooms.

"Jerry! Jerry!"

Half asleep, Mikey almost tripped over the wires, which lit the small excuse for a Christmas tree, perched on one of the altars. Opening the window, he discovered Margie, the neighborhood butch-dyke who all her life had tried to pass as a boy.

"What's da mattah?" Mikey yelled down, annoyed.

"Mikey? I didn't know you lived here too. You've got to wake up Jerry!" she screamed from below, waving her hands like all the other bodega boys in the neighborhood. "They just smoked Lucky!"

Jerry and Mikey rushed over to Lucky's apartment where his mother, holding her three-month-old baby tightly, fought off questions from police officers and reporters. Lucky and two other dealers he worked for were found dead by the Belt Parkway, shot in the head. A deal with some Dominican drug dealers had gone wrong and Bushwick was hot with police cars and news vans crawling all over.

"What the fuck are you doin' here?" Officer Williams grabbed Mikey and threw him up against a brick wall.

"Don't you know they'll haul your ass in if they find out you used to work for him?" Officer Williams lowered his voice to an angry whisper. "You better get the fuck out of here, Mikey! Now would be a good time for you to get out!"

Mikey Alvarez, hustler turned crack dealer, nodded his head defeated.

Things did not get much better. A week later, while hanging out at the piers, Mikey and Jerry were approached by Papo.

"Hey, Mikey! Yo wassup kid? Heard ya ain't in the business no more! That's cool! Sooner or later, you gotta pull out!" Papo smiled, looking rather sickly like he was carrying around the package.

"Do you remember Supreme?" Papo asked, Mikey's face lighting up.

"Yeah! Where is he?" Mikey asked, the look on Papo's face sinking him back into his initial depression.

"He's dead! Got shot by da police tagging up a wall!"

Mikey remained motionless.

"And that little twelve-year-old hustler, you know the chubby one?" Papo tried narrowing it down.

Mikey and Jerry nodded, stupidly looking at each other in search of an answer because there had been so many chubby twelve-year-old hustlers at the West Side Highway piers.

"Well, he was found crucified in a hotel room with his balls cut off!"

Almost a year had passed and Mikey had taken up a job at another record shop before meeting the next fuck-up in his life, Juan Carlos, a few days after Valentine's Day at Hatfield's. Juan Carlos was an attractive stocky older Puerto Rican, openly HIV—positive. He had only been in the country for a few months and was living on welfare with his Santeria godfather, only known to everyone as Padrino, in the South Bronx. He seemed sweet and honest, romancing Mikey by cooking him fancy dinners and taking him out to the movies. Juan Carlos caught Mikey's heart by driving him around Manhattan late at night like Emilio used to with Magdalena. Mikey did not mind that he had HIV.

"At least, this time I won't find out later like I did with Ricky!" he would tell Jerry.

Mikey would spend most of his spare time with Juan Carlos, listening to Latin CDs he would steal from the record shop by Luis Miguel, Jerry Rivera, and Ana Gabriel. The neighborhood Juan Carlos was living in was far worse than the streets Mikey grew up in but Mikey needed to get as far away from Bushwick as possible.

After only two weeks together, Mikey packed whatever he had in Jerry's apartment and moved into Padrino's roach-infested South Bronx apartment with Juan Carlos. They slept on Padrino's living room floor and had a nice view of Yankee Stadium from their window.

Still, living in Bushwick brought with it the idea of his mother not being too far behind. Mikey cried himself to sleep every night wondering why his life was so fucked up. He wondered how he could ever face his mother after everything he had done. He wondered why he cared so much anyway.

Now almost twenty-one, Mikey had been through enough to put anyone else into retirement. Mikey would stay up all night with Juan Carlos snoring next to him. Mikey hardly knew anything about this man, was not sure he even loved him, was not sure he even loved himself. Mikey blamed himself for the fact that his father had abandoned him and his mother. Mikey blamed himself for the fact that his cousin Chino had molested him as a child. Mikey blamed himself for the fact that his stepfather beat his mother. Mikey blamed himself for the fact that his mother had in turn beaten him as a child. This was exactly what he deserved—to be unable to sleep on a cold floor in the South Bronx next to a perfect stranger. How could anyone love him? Mikey felt himself growing weak, tired of survival.

Mikey's insomnia was enhanced by the voices he heard all night and the images in his head. *When you accept your own homosexuality, it's like becoming a vampire. You learn to lurk in your own darkness. Hunt or be hunted. He was found crucified in a hotel room with his balls cut off. Mikey Alvarez found crucified in a hotel room. Now would be a good time for you to get out. Quiero saber que esta pasando entre tu y el Mario ese. Mikey Alvarez found crucified in a hotel room.*

Tu eres maricón? Remember, if your Mami finds out ... with his balls cut off. They just smoked Lucky. She'll leave you like your daddy did. Mikey Alvarez was found crucified with his balls cut off.

When Mikey would finally fall asleep, wolves howled in the distance and the chanting became louder. There was no moon in the darkness and sweat flowed down his flesh. There was only a bright light, which became brighter as he walked toward it. The small wooden crucifix that he carried had now become a huge, unbearable cross. He struggled with it toward the light, which he now made out to be a church. He wanted to run to the church as if it was his only salvation from the weight of the cross, the darkness, the evil.

Once he reached the church, the chanting and the howling stopped. There was only silence, only the church. He dropped the cross, the weight lifting off his shoulders. The doors opened slightly, a streak of light spilling out into the desert.

He pushed the door open further, bathing in the light as the chanting started up once again, louder than before. It echoed in his ears as he stepped into the church, into the light. Once inside, he was dazzled with overwhelming beauty.

There was gold and diamonds sparkling everywhere, adorning the most stunning statues of Catholic saints. They welcomed him, following him with moving eyes as he passed them by. St. Anthony held baby Jesus in his arms. St. Barbara stood warrior-like with her sword. St. Martha crushed the dragon with her feet. St. Michael held his sword up high, prepared to slay the demon beneath him. They seemed painted to perfection, almost human, as he walked toward the altar. He stopped in front of the statue of St. Therese and watched her smile. She had never looked more beautiful and heavenly.

As he walked to the altar, he found his mother kneeling by a wooden bench on the front row. Magdalena was praying, dressed like the Virgin Mary in a white and blue robe. She did not acknowledge his presence even when he called out to her. Strange enchanting voices, however, called him by name to the altar. He did not recognize them but left his mother behind to reach the altar in a trance.

He noticed he was now naked and felt a sudden breeze surround him. It almost carried him as the voices continued calling out his name. He closed his eyes and lay down with his arms stretched out, the voices soothing him. He became aroused and felt the blood quickly race to his erecting penis.

Then the hammer pounded and his eyes jerked open as the pain surged from his right hand. He screamed as the hammer pounded again, nailing down his left hand. The voices were coming from figures in black hoods which surrounded him as he screamed louder. He could almost make out the faces of all the men he had slept with.

"Nooooooooo!" his voice bounced off every corner as the blood poured through his fingers. He looked over and reached for his mother but, unlike the Virgin Mary, Magdalena did not try to stop the crucifixion. The hammer pounded down again and the pain now raced up his legs, reaching his groin as he raised his head to look down. A huge metal nail emerged from his quickly reddening feet.

"Nooooooooo! Nooooooooo!" he continued screeching as the chanting became even louder, drowning him out completely. His body became immobile until he lost sensation in his head, his eyes, his mouth, his tongue. He was crucified, nailed to the cross he had carried through the desert.

MINISTRY

Things never quite worked out with Juan Carlos in the South Bronx with all kinds of shit going on up there. Every day, someone else was shot, stabbed, or killed in his neighborhood. Mikey was afraid to befriend any of the local drug dealers— here today, gone tomorrow. One female doctor, trying to stop a brother from stealing her car, was shot three times outside the crack house next to Mikey's building—once in the leg, once in the arm, once in the chest. Mikey was coming home from the bodega when he saw her getting slaughtered in front of him; he dropped his 40-ounce bottle of Crazy Horse. As quickly as the stolen car speeding away, the piss-yellow liquid raced toward the pool of blood surrounding the young black woman sprawled on the ground. Her dead mouth was open, the scream frozen in silence. Her eyes were staring at Mikey's bloodstained brand-new sneakers.

The next day, in an effort to look really tough, Mikey went down to Paul's Boutique to shave off his hair, revealing the scars on the back of his head from many childhood brawls and his mother's abusive fits of anger. With a thicker, fuller twenty-one-year-old mustache, goatee, and an already decadent glow in his eyes, Mikey blended in nicely with the rest of the neighborhood. He walked hard, spittin', crotch grabbin', with a slight limp for allure, down the overcrowded streets where the salsa boomed over Rottweiler fights and gangsta bitches argued over imprisoned boyfriends.

Picking up welfare checks and cupones[48] to do the compras, he played the numbers every day in hopes of hitting the lottery. Mikey, in order to survive, had become everything he had promised himself he would never be. He would fight every day with Juan Carlos about going back to hustling at the piers and making enough money so that they would not have to eat pan con welfare cheese again. He spent his days learning Santeria rituals from Padrino, a wise thirty-something gay santero, who would eventually become his godfather in a religion which fascinated Mikey more than anything in the world did. He dreamt of the day that he could make a living by casting brujos[49] on cheating boyfriends and estranged lovers while listening to the sounds of growing winds outside South Bronx windows.

Padrino was also trying to teach Mikey how to cook for Juan Carlos, who would leave home every day supposedly looking for a job and coming back with marks on his neck and the smell of someone else's cheap cologne. Mikey failed to impress him with half-cooked arroz con pollo and the worst pernil since Titi Yoli poisoned the entire family on Mami's birthday with her bacalaito cakes.

"Mira, nene, you gotta start learning how to take care of your husband, because he won't always be this healthy, you know," Padrino would lecture.

Frustrated with Juan Carlos's up-front attitude about his affairs, Mikey would spend his midnights stoned with Padrino in the park across the street from Yankee Stadium. Padrino filled his head with stories about rich old men coming up from the city to pick up poor little Latino boys for sex. The park was legendary for street trade and it was usual for Padrino to

48 Spanish slang for Food Stamps.
49 Translated literally, a *brujo* is a Spanish word for a male witch but used in this context, it means witchcraft spells.

disappear behind the bleachers, leaving Mikey alone from time to time while being sucked off by strangers, coming back with enough money for a six-pack and a dime bag.

Mikey, never a step behind, frequented the parks until he had enough money to buy a new pair of sneakers, sucking on his Blow Pops while waiting in the bleachers late at night for rich, horny old men desperate for a taste of banjee heaven. He wanted to make enough money to leave Juan Carlos's tired ass and move to the big city where he would not have to worry about whether or not he would wake up alive the next day.

"Well, well, well! If it isn't the Grand Pier Queen of the South Bronx herself tryin' to work the park!"

Mikey turned around from the bleachers where he sat to come face to face with Hector, a tacky cha-cha queen who lived on the second floor of their building.

"What's the matter, Mikey? Need more money to buy food at the cuchifrito[50] so Juan Carlos won't find out you can't cook for yourself?"

"Yeah, well at least I don't be giving my ass away for some crack like you, you nasty ho!"

Hector walked away with his tight Daisy Duke shorts and flip-flops, pretending not to hear him.

"I HATE MY LIFE!" Mikey broke down later that day when he opened the fridge and the milk carton spilled onto the floor.

"Here, I'll clean it," Juan Carlos offered.

"No, forget about it! Just go away!"

"Hey! Hey!" Juan Carlos grabbed Mikey by the hands as

---

50 A Puerto Rican soul food restaurant popular in Latino neighborhoods with colorful external lighting and flashy signs. The word derives from *cuchi*, which is short for *cochino* or pig, and *frito*, which means fried.

he tried to soak up the milk with a sponge. "Calmate, okay! I thought I was your life!"

Mikey pulled his eyes away from Juan Carlos.

"I love you, Mikey! I motherfuckin' love you, ah-ight, kid!"

Juan Carlos was giving his best performance since Mikey's cousin Alberto busted him in the bathroom at La Escuelita one night getting a blowjob from some queen.

"It's all about you, papi!"

Mikey freed himself from his grip and headed toward the door.

"Why you frontin'? Stop fuckin' wit' my head, Juan Carlos! If you love me so much, then how come you have to fuck around wit' other guys? Huh? Tell me, Juan Carlos!"

"Look! If I fucked around wit' other guys it's because I'm sick, all right! You know I'm sick, Mikey!"

"No, YOU look! Don't make me go off! You don't wanna see me go off!"

"I'm dying, all right! I just want to have a little fun before I'm good and buried!"

"Ay! Not for nothing but just because you got AIDS don't mean I'm gonna let you fuck every Jose, Luis, and Victor you can get your dick into! That's shady, Juan Carlos! Too shady!"

"I'm scared ah-ight! I'm scared of getting too close to you so you can up and leave whenever the next fly papi cruises you in a club!"

"Oh! Just because other guys they look at me, that gives you the right to make a cabron[51] out of me! I don't think so!" Mikey picked up his baseball cap and unchained the door.

---

51 Translated literally, it means a male goat but it is used throughout Latin America as some sort of insult with different meanings depending on whom you ask. However, here it means a person who is being cheated on by their lover.

"You know, maybe if you didn't think about yourself all the time, Juan Carlos, I wouldn't be going out to the clubs running into all those putas you be calling 'baby' thinking everyone else doesn't know your bochinche!"

Juan Carlos grabbed him before he had a chance to storm out, turning him to stare into his face. "I never meant to hurt you, Mikey! I said I was sorry, all right, but what do you want me to do? Can't you just let it go?

Mikey forced back the tears, "Whatevah, okay! I'm tired of you playing me for a fool!" He pushed him off and stormed out of the apartment, running down the dark stairs as fast as he could, past all the bodega boys and drug dealers, heading toward the park.

That was the night Mikey was approached by the fiercest, most expensive car he had ever seen. An older man in the driver's seat stared him down. Mikey's mind raced with a million and one reasons to steal his car. Mikey had never seen anything like it except on television and in magazines. The lamppost lights bounced off the white shield of the car, glistening in Mikey's eyes. The driver watched from beneath the shadow of his baseball cap that concealed his wrinkling forty-year-old face, wearing an expensive jacket Mikey had seen on Fordham Road for like thirty dollars.

As a car alarm rang somewhere in the distance, the sugar papi parked his car in front of the bleachers where Mikey sat. He stared at Mikey in the way every young boy wants to be looked at by a potential trick. Mikey stared back at him, feigning an innocent smile, and giving him his best puppy dog eyes ever.

Juan Carlos had run out after Mikey, lurking underneath the bleachers. He watched the stranger in the car, thinking the same thoughts as Mikey: about what he could do with a car like that. He remained motionless in the shadows.

"Would you like to get in?" the man yelled out to Mikey, drowned out by the hip-hop record blaring from his speakers.

"NO!" he yelled back defiantly, like when he was a little boy and his mother asked him if he had smashed the aquarium while the goldfish struggled desperately for air.

The man bit his lip and pulled out a wad of money, flagging it at Mikey as if he was about to land a plane.

"Oh, come on! I won't hurt you!" he taunted him, as if Mikey really felt threatened by his corny old white ass.

Down below, Juan Carlos lit a joint, the smoke rising up to get Mikey's attention. Mikey searched underneath, through the holes, only to find Juan Carlos's cheating heart smiling up at him devilishly. Even through the darkness, with the help of the remaining lampposts, which had not been broken, Mikey could see his eyebrow raised and a knowing smile on his face.

"I promise I won't!" the old man begged, thinking Mikey was looking away in contemplation.

Mikey and Juan Carlos silently voiced the plan laid out before them with their eyes.

"Ah-ight! But you have to promise not to hurt me!" Mikey yelled to the driver, glancing back down to lock eyes with Juan Carlos. Juan Carlos mouthed the words back up to him "I won't!" before he rose off the bleachers and headed toward the car, the old man's face crumbling into one big smile.

Mikey opened the passenger door, making himself comfortable inside, nervously glancing over at the man, trying to avoid eye contact, the smell of alcohol reeking from his slightly built, older body.

"What's your name?" the man asked.

Mikey was quiet, searching for any signs of a weapon while contemplating an answer. "Ricky!" he said, using his ex-lover's name, a thrill on his rebellious face.

"Ricky!" the old man repeated in disbelief. "That's the perfect name for you!"

"Well, what's your name? John?" Mikey asked with a fuck-you-viejo-maricón tone of voice.

The man cracked smiles, which for a moment made Mikey reconsider his plot with Juan Carlos.

"How'd you ever guess?"

Sitting in silence for a moment, Mikey anxiously awaited for Juan Carlos to give him a signal.

"Tell me, Ricky? How much does a boy like you ask for these days?"

Mikey glared at him with attitude "Oh! You mean besides the car!" he sneered sarcastically.

Mikey played it off by laughing along with him, before "John" reached over, crushing Mikey with unexpected strength, feeling around for Mikey's rising erection, lost somewhere in his oversized baggy jeans.

Finding it, he pulled back and happily smiled down at Mikey's overwhelmed stare.

"You can have more than just the car if you play your cards right, pretty boy!"

With his other hand, he moved Mikey closer to him, forcing his tongue deep into Mikey's throat, almost choking him while unzipping his jeans.

"Wait a minute! Cógelo con take it easy, ah-ight!" Mikey struggled to push him off, the old man chewing his neck before being taken by surprise and pulled out of the car.

There was a ferocious rustling sound and loud screaming

outside the door as Mikey zipped up his jeans and raised himself enough to see Juan Carlos pounding the old man in the face, yelling like a bitch as Juan Carlos kicked him in the stomach.

"The wallet! The wallet! Don't forget the wallet!" Mikey shouted as Juan Carlos kicked the old man in the face again.

"Scream again and I'll kill ya!" Juan Carlos reached into his back pocket to pull out the wallet, kicking him one last time before jumping into the driver's seat.

"Hurry up! Hurry up! Let's go! Let's go!" Mikey cried.

Juan Carlos fumbled with the cars keys still in the ignition.

"Ahhhhhhhhh!" the man screamed.

"Come on! Let's get the fuck out of here!" Mikey screeched.

Juan Carlos finally started the car, pulling away, leaving the old man behind, his baseball cap on the ground exposing his bald head, crying for help as blood poured out from his mouth.

They made enough money from that car to pay the rent, buy some phat new gear, reconnect their beepers, get Santeria beads from Padrino, and pay off the hospital bills, which Medicaid did not cover for Juan Carlos. Juan Carlos's health worsened daily until finally he developed respiratory problems and his cell count dropped to only sixty-three.

"You know, Mikey, not for nothin', but he don't look too good!" Padrino would tell Mikey, "He ain't even gotta try to hide from da police 'cause they wouldn't recognize him if he was standing in their face. He may be whatever but he is still your man!"

On his twenty-seventh birthday, Mikey gave Juan Carlos

a surprise party. However, after smoking plenty of pot, and a very revealing game of truth-or-dare, the only surprise was for Mikey.

"Truth or dare, Juan Carlos." Padrino asked facetiously.

"Truth!"

Padrino contemplated whether to ask the question, until an evil glow in his eyes caught everyone's attention.

"Did you ever sleep with anyone else in this building other than Mikey?"

Juan Carlos's face turned pale and his mouth dropped in disbelief.

"Come on, Juan Carlos, you know you can't lie to los muertos[52]!" Padrino insisted.

No matter what he said, he was cornered, so Juan Carlos looked over at Mikey, who shook his head back and forth begging for a no.

"Hector from 257!"

"Hector from 257? You slept with Hector from 257? D-E-S-G-R-A-C-I-A-D-O!" was all Mikey said before lunging from his seat and landing on Juan Carlos.

Padrino raced to pull Mikey away, hands gripped tightly around Juan Carlos's neck, while the locas screamed in horror.

"Get off me! Get off me! I'm gonna kill him! I'm gonna kill him! You son of a bitch!"

"Olvidalo, papi please! He's not worth it! Just let him be! He's not worth it!" Padrino urged. Mikey fell into a fit of tears.

"I believed in you, Juan Carlos! I believed in you! How the

52 In Santeria, *los muertos* are usually dead family members or friends, but often random spirits, who live with and guide a practitioner throughout life. Creepy shit!

fuck could you do this to me?"

The entire room fell silent. Padrino reached out to comfort him before Mikey ran into the kitchen, emerging with the birthday cake in his right hand and a crazed look on his face.

"No! No! No, Mikey! Not the Valencia[53] cake! Por favor, not the Valencia cake!" Padrino begged as Mikey screamed maniacally, making a hundred-mile dash toward Juan Carlos's face.

"Bitch! You're crazy!" Juan Carlos yelled as the sticky gooey frosting from the cake glued to his gagging face.

"Happy motherfuckin' birthday, you hijo de la gran puta!" Mikey ran out of the apartment.

That was the last time Mikey ever saw Juan Carlos. He returned to the piers and hustled for a place to crash every night, until his cousin Alberto caught him out there one night.

"Miguelito, what the fuck is wrong with you? How come Padrino's the one who has to call to tell me you are back on the streets working the piers?"

Mikey was too choked up to argue with him. That whole night, they sat at the piers. Mikey told him all about his miserable life since they last ran into each other. Alberto insisted that Mikey move in with him and his lover up in Riverdale.

"I'm not taking no for an answer! I told you que ese hombre era no good for you from the get-go! He made a pendeja out of you! Ooh, if he was here I would cut him! Ay, dios mio, if your mother only knew!"

The following day, Mikey returned to the South Bronx while Juan Carlos was out and packed his bags with the help of

53 Valencia is a city in Spain from which the name of this popular New York City Latino bakery chain derives. The logo is a *torero*, or Spanish bullfighter, and the yellow sponge cakes with butter cream frosting are reasonably priced and big.

a mortified Alberto and his lover, Johnny.

"You were living here?" Alberto's eyes bulged with terror.

"No, I was just vacationing!" Mikey snapped, tossing his suitcases into the trunk, breaking into a smile.

"Mikey! Mikey!" Mikey recognized Padrino's voice before turning around to stop him dead in his tracks with a wicked stare. Padrino's face was flushed to a sickly color, his urgent eyes foretelling the bad news he was about to unleash. "It's Juan Carlos! He's in da hospital!"

Mikey shrugged his shoulders and turned away to slam down the car trunk—his excessive force a dead giveaway.

"Mikey, he's got tuberculosis!" Padrino ranted on. "The ambulance came to pick him up this morning! He thought he was gonna die! They won't let anyone near him because they say its cun ... cun ... What's the word I'm looking for?"

"Contagious!" Alberto jumped in.

"Yeah, that's it! Cunt-agious!" Padrino said, acknowledging Alberto's presence by raising an eyebrow.

Mikey turned to look at Padrino; all dressed in white with his collares[54], dropping his stare to the ground and focus on all the bubble-gum wrappers glistening like jewels under the sun. Padrino reaching his arms out for him like the Christ at the church, only Christ had stumps, not hands, since they always stole them. He felt bad about Juan Carlos, but at the same time, he felt it was just another trap to keep him by his side. It would not be the first time Juan Carlos used his illness to get what he wanted out of Mikey.

"Now, I'm not telling you this so you go running back to him like you always do! I'm telling you 'cause you would WANT to

54 Spanish word meaning necklace. In Santeria, initiated members receive several beaded ones representing different orisha by colors to protect them from evil.

go check yourself, chulo! You're the one who was with him the most!"

Mikey looked away so Padrino would not see the tears in his eyes, only to catch Hector watching them from behind the curtains in his window.

Mikey, falling into Padrino's arms, embraced him, planting a tender kiss on his cheek in full public view before running away towards the brightly lit bodega.

"Mikey! This is no time for you to go to the park! Mira, nene...Where you goin'?" Padrino screamed out to him. Mikey returned with a 40-ounce bottle of Crazy Horse.

"This is not the time to be gettin' drunk!" Alberto insisted.

Mikey tapped the bottle from underneath three times, like Padrino had taught him, opening it, closing his eyes and whispering a Yoruba chant while spilling the piss-yellow beer onto the concrete ground below. When he opened his eyes, he caught his cousin and Johnny's bewildered stares and Padrino's motherly smile.

"It wasn't for me! It was for the muertos! So that they could look after Juan Carlos while I'm gone!"

"Ay, Mikey! He'll be ah-ight!" Padrino cried. "Pero, you need to get your ass out of here before you get sucked into this life! Fuck Juan Carlos, he's a big girl! You need to follow your dreams, baby!"

Mikey pulled out a wad of money and handed it to a startled Padrino.

"Que'eso?"

"Some money left over from the viejo's car! Go buy yourself something pretty!" Mikey said, trying not to sound like the sentimental pier queen that he actually was.

"Mikey! I can't!"

"Loca ... please!"

Padrino quickly put the money away before Mikey changed his mind.

"Don't be a stranger!"

"Jamas!" Mikey smiled, fully aware that he would never return to the South Bronx and that this part of his life was, for better or for worse, behind him.

"Are you ready?" Alberto asked.

"Yes! Yes, I am!"

With that, Mikey kissed Padrino one last time, giving Hector the finger before getting into the back seat of the car and being driven away, never looking back at the streets of the South Bronx.

Though only a bus ride away, Riverdale seemed worlds apart from the South Bronx. Only when Mikey went out for walks, finding himself struggling up steep mountains of streets and climbing down marathon stairs, did he remember he was still in the Bronx.

"No wonder all those Boogie Down homeboys walk all slouched and shit! People think they're trying to look all tough and what not but they've got all these fuckin' hills and mountains to climb every day!" Mikey would complain to Alberto, missing the flat plateaus of Bushwick.

Alberto's studio apartment was what the queens at the pier would call "white woman cunt." It was decorated immaculately with black furniture, large exotic plants and a beautiful black green-eyed Cheshire cat named Sheba. The walls featured framed photographs of beautiful muscular men and fine crystal sculptures perfectly scattered throughout. Mikey had slept in many wealthy apartments and studied many expensive art pieces while getting dressed after cumming on some old man but he had never actually gotten to stay or asked to make himself at home.

Though small, the studio was comfortable enough for the two of them since Alberto was always working as a waiter and Mikey was always exploring Van Cortlandt Park. The couch where he now slept when Alberto wasn't staying over at his lover's was drowned with assorted pillows to which Mikey added stuffed animals Juan Carlos had won for him one night at Coney Island. Otherwise, he would sleep on Alberto's bed, an elegantly placed mattress in a large walk-in-closet-turned-love-shack.

Alberto reluctantly allowed Mikey to build a small altar dedicated to Oyá on the corner by the kitchen. Mikey took it the extra mile by placing his Elegua[55] by the entrance door. Mikey decorated his Elegua with McDonald's Happy Meal toys, rum, cigars, lots of candy and even a chicken he killed to feed his Elegua and initiate him into his new home.

However, after plucking and deep-frying, the chicken became his dinner and a drunk Mikey ate all the candy for dessert. It was not long before the apartment cluttered with small candles glowing beneath Santeria statues, which Mikey would find on sale on Fordham Road. Alberto would come home to find Mikey puffing thick cigars while plowing through every book he could find on the occult religion.

Mikey learned how to read coconut shells and was soon making spare money by giving people consultas[56]. Prophecy

55 Anytime there is a sacrifice or ceremony in Santeria, Elegua has to be given something first. Because Elegua is such a complicated deity, there is no specific answer as to why he is represented as a small clay head with cowrie shells.

56 Santeria readings or private sessions using any number of methods such as playing cards, cowrie shells, coconut shells, a glass of water and a candle, etc. This practice sometimes engenders the possibility of extortion or fraud (as in Mikey's case) but most Santeros are devoted to their beliefs and fear retaliation from their spiritual guides.

was about predicting the future but Mikey entertained himself with the idea that he could somehow help other people even when he could not help himself. He was clueless about the course of his own life but he could speak on the history and culture of Santeria at the drop of a quarter.

Alberto eventually gave Mikey the space by the bathroom to build yet another small altar to feature Mikey's new obsession—St. Martha. The martyr saint dressed in bright red, green and white colors, crushing a dragon at her feet, represented dominance over evil. Alberto's art deco apartment quickly became a mausoleum. It was as if Better Homes & Gardens had run a feature article on Walter Mercado[57].

Alberto allowed for all the changes but kept insisting that Mikey pick up the phone and call his mother to let her know he was alive. After several exhausting walks and sleepless nights, Mikey finally gathered enough strength and courage to call Magdalena.

When she heard his voice, her throat, full of aching, grieving beauty, told only of her unexpected joy. Mikey fell apart over the phone as Magdalena herself fell silent to shed painful tears.

"I'm not gonna run away from you anymore Mami, okay! You could hate me all you want but I'm not running away anymore!" was all Mikey was able to let out in between the crying.

The next day, Mikey was back in Bushwick visiting his mother but the tears from the night before had given way to an unexpected mix of emotions.

___

57 A flamboyant Puerto Rican astrologer famous in the Latin culture and known for his suits, capes, and acrylic nails. He is featured regularly on Spanish television and radio shows and appears in print in books and syndicated newspaper columns. He was a huge fan of Quentin Crisp (personal inside information from the author—Hey Walter!).

When Mikey finally arrived at Magdalena's door, they both stood there curiously staring at each other. Neither of them showed any signs of affection or extended open arms. They both seemed to be holding back their emotions; Magdalena still angry at Mikey for the way he disappeared and Mikey still annoyed that his mother could not accept his homosexuality.

Mikey felt that in Magdalena's eyes, he had ruined his life by being a faggot and Mikey could not do shit about it. The angry words they failed to verbalize gave the happy reunion an air of uncomfortable hypocrisy. Magdalena tried really hard to fight off the images of her son being molested by Chino and having sex with numerous men.

Though they loved each other very much, their relationship would only heal with time.

Later that night, Mikey ventured out to Hatfield's in search of love and romance once again. What he found instead was a gathering of depressing and desperate queens standing around pretentiously staring each other down. They wore the same clothes, danced to the same records, and used the same lines Mikey had used back when he had first set foot inside the club. It was on his way out, however, that he ran into one of Lucky's many ex-boyfriends, Victor. Mikey had spotted him inside the club earlier but, trying to forget the entire Lucky incident, had chosen to ignore him altogether.

"Aren't you at least gonna say goodbye?" Victor asked in a robust voice, grabbing Mikey by the arm.

Staring viciously where Victor's hand wrapped around his arm, Mikey shot back with "I wasn't planning to but now that you've stopped me ... GOODBYE!" before pulling his arm free from Victor's grip. Mikey stormed away, annoyed.

"Wait! Wait!" Victor chased him down the street.

"What? What?" Mikey yelled back.

"I just wanna talk to you!"

Mikey searched Victor's eyes for a purpose.

"C'mon! Why ya gotta be shady? I just wanna talk to you!" Victor begged.

"Talk? Talk about what?"

Victor's gaze dropped to the floor, humiliated.

"What is there to talk about?" Mikey continued, cocking an eyebrow in demand.

"I just wanna know why you pay me dust every time you see me!" Victor raised his clear brown eyes to see Mikey's reaction.

Mikey's eyes narrowed, debating whether this was all Victor really wanted. By the time Hatfield's had closed and all the faggots had spilled out onto the streets, Mikey had given up all sorts of information to Victor. Victor had not known that Lucky had been a drug dealer and played him out left and right. He only knew Lucky had been shot and killed. Victor sat there in his brand new car, speechless and stunned. Mikey, sitting in the passenger seat, bopped erratically to a house tape Victor was playing in the background, unbothered.

"Do you like this?" Victor asked.

"Wha? Talking 'bout Lucky? No! Not me! Uh-uh!" Mikey held himself back.

"No, stupid!" Victor laughed. "The music! Do you like the music?"

"Oh! Oh, yeah! Who mixed it?" Mikey's thick eyebrows formed a frown.

"D.J. Dominick X from the House of X taped it for me!" Victor name dropped and stared, waiting for the usual reaction of excitement from Mikey.

"Who the fuck is Dominick X?" Mikey asked instead.

"You never heard of Dominick X? I can't believe you never heard of Dominick X!" Victor snickered.

"The name sounds familiar. I've slept with many people but I don't think I've ever slept with a Dominick X!" Mikey looked out into the streets, trying to remember.

"Have you ever been to The Sanctuary?" Victor continued.

"The Sanctuary? Isn't that like for priests or something?"

"No stupid! Not a sanctuary, The Sanctuary!"

"What sanctuary?"

"THE SANCTUARY!"

"The Sanctuary?"

"YES, THE SANCTUARY!"

"Is that the name of the club? That's a stupid name for a club!"

They fell into a fit of laughter, the kind of laughter that, curiously, they could not control.

"So? Do you wanna go?"

"To The Sanctuary?" they both asked simultaneously, still laughing.

APOSTLES & DISCIPLES

The first time Mikey ever went up to the velvet ropes of The Sanctuary, he entered with no problem. The Sanctuary was notorious for exclusivity and only celebrated the in crowd. With a few unusual exceptions thrown in for good measure, only the beautiful and famous were allowed into the club while others clamored to be noticed by the watchful doormen.

Once inside, Mikey stood wide-eyed at the edge of the world-famous dance floor enthralled by the hedonistic orgy of flesh grinding before him below the watchful glare of Catholic statues. Mikey had been to his share of clubs before but, reincarnated from a deconsecrated church complete with stained glass windows, The Sanctuary was a magical kingdom of marvelous lighting and surreal music with a cardinal pattern of starting off slow then gradually building to an intensive peak. It was at this peak, usually late into the night, that the club would become overcrowded and all hell would break loose under one roof.

Only the finest personalities from the entertainment industry and the most fascinating club kids attended The Sanctuary every weekend like a mass ritual. They were admired from a distance while mingling on the dance floor with a feast of muscle boys, expensive models and a never-ending parade of voguing divas.

All the infamous Houses emerged from the darkness to serve as choirboys for the evening, chanting their ensuing battles of "Bring it! Work it! Learn it!" They only served the prime in shade and attitude.

The Sanctuary received Mikey with mixed emotions. Recognized by many faces from the pier scene, pretending not to notice him, they whispered comments to one another. Mikey glided past the knifing stares, which wanted him dead for his youth and beauty. They stared at him with eyes he had seen millions of times before, never bothering to acknowledge him. They were people he knew nothing yet everything about from rumors. Faces he remembered waking up with, men without names, hidden underneath the distinct dimension of lights and sounds. They were strangers, united, experiencing the joys of drugs, the thrill of life and death together—all under a once holy roof.

Mikey became a regular to the dependable excitement of The Sanctuary, exchanging his spiritual awakenings for disco naps, lighting up the queens instead of candles at night. He was now studying modern voguing instead of ancient Yoruba ritual dances and inhaling drugs again instead of exhaling cigars.

His goal to become a Santeria priest was replaced by pulling notorious stunts[58] in order to be noticed by the houses. He only cared talking to anybody who would get him on the guest-list. Santeria had kept Mikey focused on his soul but the drugs that flowed over his tongue and up his nose had no competition from religion.

"So when do I get to meet this Dominick X?" Mikey demanded one night.

Dominick would half-heartedly wave to Victor from the deejay booth; sometimes shine a flashlight on his face. Otherwise, Victor knew about as much about Dominick X

58 Slang for showing off.

as anyone who read the local fag rags[59]. Mikey would stare up at Dominick, a white street-hood type, with a gleam of premature bitterness in his eyes. Mikey, like legions of others, sexually attracted to Dominick who only seemed consumed by his music. Mikey became obsessed with getting Dominick's attention. Mikey thought that by sheer force of will, he could make Dominick his boyfriend, if not his friend. Determined to have Dominick's flashlight shine on him, Mikey would dance ferociously to his music.

In spite of all his efforts, Dominick refused to acknowledge Mikey. Mikey was completely unaware that someone he had once flirted with named Frankie had been Dominick's lover at the time. In spite of the fact that Frankie and him were no longer together, Dominick was very possessive of his HIV-positive ex. Frankie and Mikey had cruised each other fervently during the time Mikey was hanging out at Hatfield's. Mikey had just broken up with Ricky and Frankie was still involved with Dominick. They became good friends, flirting constantly with the knowledge that in another place and time they would have had an intense relationship. For this, Dominick despised Mikey, tearing him apart in his mind every time he saw him walk into The Sanctuary.

Every weekend, Mikey closely studied the moves of the most skilled voguers and quickly became an amazing dancer himself, full of energy and emotion. It had helped that during the brief time he had stayed with Anji X, she had taught him some basic voguing techniques. When Mikey felt the crowd, felt the energy, there was no stopping him. He would become one with the rhythm, one with the music, until the day he met Damian X.

59 Publications focusing on gay issues.

Damian X was the type of character who would walk into a room full of people and seek out his competition. Once established, his mission would be to conquer and destroy. Light skinned black, muscular body, flawless face, street boy image; the greatest dancer in New York City—Damian X was practically unapproachable.

His stare demanded attention. With just a mere glance, in less than three minutes, he could have anyone he wanted. He was young and beautiful, a treasure in the gay world. In four words, Damian X was 'the shadiest queen alive.'

The day Damian spotted Mikey tearing up a storm on the dance floor was the day the earth moved.

"Who the fuck is that queen?" Damian commanded while his friend Jorge watched Mikey in awe.

"I don't know! But he better work!" Jorge drooled.

Noticing the glimmer of lust in Jorge's eyes, Damian decided it was battling time. Parting the crowd surrounding Mikey, Damian walked right up to where he was standing. Looking up to the deejay booth to make eye contact with his ex-lover and best friend Dominick, the battle plans laid out before them. Damian stared at Mikey with joyful anticipation as Dominick began mixing in Damian's favorite house classic, "In the Dark We Live (Thee Lite)" by a group called Aphrohead.

The lights went out dramatically and a spotlight featured Damian, thrusting each arm to exact precision with every beat. The crowd drowned in a sea of smoke and Mikey stopped dead at his feet.

Damian lunged himself at him, hiding his face with each arm movement and gesture, cutting Mikey with his imaginary switchblade. Damian flung his legs to kick Mikey, trying to knock him to the ground as a siren blasted from the deejay booth. Bright lights exploded into the darkness like lightning as Dominick reached his orgasmic peak and the crowd roared in unison.

Damian was turning Mikey out as Mikey smiled, with both envy and admiration. He watched, hoping Damian would miss a beat or break a leg as Damian called him out to battle, singling Mikey out as the enemy. He ended by dipping into a floor spin, sprawled out on the floor. The battle was over. Mikey was defeated. Damian was the crown contender. Dominick was the legend.

Though Mikey had lost, he knew by the fact that Damian had even bothered to battle him that he had made an impression. Mikey also indulged in the knowledge that he had gotten the attention of the House of X. His world was about to change again.

"So who's ya friend?" Jorge X asked Victor.

"Who? Mikey? Why? Do you like him?"

"Let's just say I wouldn't mind getting to know him better." Jorge smiled to spread his perfect cheekbones.

By the time Mikey had pushed and shoved his way back from the dance floor, Victor had revealed everything he knew about Mikey to Jorge. Mikey, returning Jorge's intense stare while Victor sucked lavishly from his Newport Light, a tickled look on his stocky face.

"Mikey, I'd like you to meet Jorge X!" Victor making sure Mikey picked up the vital importance of whom he was meeting. Victor's voice bubbled with excitement.

"Yo!" Mikey forced out, unimpressed, breaking into an unconvincing smile.

Jorge returned this warm salutation by simply biting his

lower lip, eyeing Mikey from shaved head to Timberland boots without much else to say.

This unbridled passion which he had experienced plenty of times at the piers by his tricks, made Mikey feel extremely defensive and he stared back at Jorge like he had a bug on his face.

"Victor! VICTOR!" Mikey yelled as Victor cruised a potential date for the evening, "Would you come get some water with me?" Before Victor could complain, "I'm parched!" Mikey commanded by raising his eyebrow.

"We'll be right back!" Victor told a doubtful Jorge, leaving him behind to be swallowed by the crowd.

"Well? Whaddaya think?" Victor asked as they paved their way through the clubs half-naked bodies and smoky air. Mikey gave him a disgusted look, as if he had just asked the dumbest question in the world.

"What's wrong with his mustache?" Mikey complained.

"Whaddaya mean? What's wrong with his mustache?"

"It looks like he drew it on with a pencil liner!" Mikey continued, "I mean it's so fuckin' thin! I've never seen anything like it! It looks like he sneezed a caterpillar!"

Victor stopped for air, gasping with exaggeration. "Oh, you're just being too damn picky! Jorge X is motherfuckin' flawless!"

Mikey turned to smile at him facetiously, secretly thrilled by the fact that Jorge was interested in him.

"Whatevah!" was his only reply to Victor before walking away, losing himself on the dance floor.

"What about the water? I THOUGHT YOU WERE PARCHED!"

In spite of the irritating mustache, Mikey went on to pursue a relationship with Jorge, fully aware that this would be his ticket into the House of X—a street gang of vicious, Godless faggots who, like himself, were legendary for attitude. To be in the House of X meant respect, worship, and admiration within the club world. At least, that is what Mikey really believed.

Mikey introduced Jorge, like every other lovesick puppy before him, to his cousin Alberto for approval. Alberto was already familiar with the predestined fate of Mikey's pieces. Soon enough, Mikey would ask him not to take his calls, lie to him when Mikey was out with someone else, or entertain him while Mikey ran home from another date. Mikey had already warned Alberto that Jorge was much different than he had originally appeared and had turned out to be "too nice, too sweet, and too boring"

"Maybe one day you'll stop being such a diva cunt and realize someone like Jorge is exactly what you need!" Alberto would lecture.

Mikey would roll his eyes, putting his fingers together to form a 'W', the international sign for "Whatever!"

Jorge was attractive, sweet, and sincere. Mikey tried desperately to uncover his dark side, simply entertaining himself, if not just passing time, while Jorge attached himself everyday.

Mikey was still burnt by his last relationship to Juan Carlos, who was probably pimping off some other young boy for money to pay his hospital bills. Mikey knew he was being a total asshole by using Jorge in order to join the House of X but figured it was his turn to take advantage of someone else.

On Mikey's twenty-second birthday, Jorge showed up with a box of Godiva chocolates, two dozen pink roses ("One for each twenty two years of your life, one for good luck and one for love" Jorge would later say) and the biggest white teddy bear Mikey had ever seen. It was then Alberto realized the shit had hit the fan.

"You have to tell him sumethin' Mikey! He be hanging around here twenty-four-seven like he just moved in here or sumethin'!"

"Mind your business! I like him, ah-ight! Besides, I don't see you complaining when he picks up your tired ass from the supermarket or drives you into the city!"

"Sangana! I saved you from Juan Carlos and the South Bronx and this is how you talk to me!"

"Look! I was just fine living at the piers selling myself to rich old gringos! I didn't ask you to bring me here and mother me, ah-ight!"

"Oh! So now you just gonna keep being the little puta you are and hustle your way into the House of X so you could be 'the legendary Mikey X', right?"

"Why I gotta tell him anything? Huh? Why I gotta fuck everything up for myself 'cause I don't know how I feel about him?"

"Oh, but you do, Blanche! You do know how you feel about him!"

Mikey simply ignored the sound advice of his cousin Alberto and continued on his selfish quest to conquer the world—or at least The Sanctuary—maybe just The House of X.

"Mikey, I'd like you to meet my friend Damian!" Jorge smiled, "Damian, this is Mikey!"

Weak hellos ensued. It was brutally obvious that Damian did not like Mikey or at least he was making his best effort to make it appear that way. Damian was waiting for Hector X, father of the House of X, outside the Angelika Film Center[60] before going in to see the new Pedro Almodovar film. Attitudes were about to collide and Jorge was just picking up on the tension, dimly aware that this moment was somehow predestined in Mikey's mind. With daggers in his eyes, Damian had been dying to meet Mikey. Mikey was in awe of Damian. Neither of them, however, budged any gestures of friendship. It was the classic movie scene where the most popular girl in school meets the newbie in town.

"Hey, you guys!" Hector said as he arrived. Hector was older, in his early thirties, and wealthy. With a charming smile, highlighted by thick eyebrows and mustache, Hector had conquered the fashion scene. Former model turned fashion designer, he was Damian's greatest trophy. Damian gleamed with Hector by his side and Mikey realized he was not the only one using someone for status. He was also aware Damian was the resident slut of The House of X, having also dated Dominick X.

"What's up? You must be Mikey!" Hector extended his hand out, "I've heard a lot about you!"

Mikey shook his hand, impressed by his friendliness while Damian gave him a knowing smile.

Jorge would foolishly go on to introduce Mikey to just about everybody in the New York City gay club scene. Alberto would joke about Mikey going "From pier queen to club scene!"

As Father of the House of X, Hector's approval was enough to make Mikey the newest addition to the gang. Aware that

60 A movie theater chain featuring independent and foreign films located in New York City and Texas.

the reason for his dislike of him was that they had so much in common, Damian began to warm up to Mikey. They were both hustlers in one way or another struggling to survive. They would viciously read each other to filth only to end up laughing their heads off at their contempt.

"So, I heard you used to be a hustler at the piers!" Damian asked Mikey one day outside a bodega while Jorge bought a pack of cigarettes.

"You should know a thing or two about hustling!" Mikey replied.

"Excuse me? Are you trying to call me a slut?"

"Well, you're not exactly Christ Like, Ms. Thing!"

"Ugh! You've got a lot of nerve, you filthy bitch!"

"I've got a lot of everything!"

"You think you're fierce now, don't you? Just because you slept your way into the House of X!"

"Why? Isn't that the way you did it Damian? Because I know that voguing positions were not your only qualifications!"

"What's going on?" Jorge asked when he came out of the store in time to watch Damian's jaw drop.

"Nothing, baby! Damian and I were just discussing politics!" Mikey smiled to Damian who raised his eyebrow knowingly.

The other X-men adored Mikey. They surrounded him at whatever club they ran into him, feeding him drugs, dancing with him, dishing out anyone he did not like. He quickly became popular with all the members of the House of X except for one main constituent.

"So, you're the reason Frankie could never love me?" Mikey asked Dominick when they finally met up on the terrace of Hector's West Village penthouse apartment.

Dominick smiled off-guard, not expecting Mikey to approach him so brazenly. Damian had tipped Mikey off about Dominick's reasons for disliking him in exchange for a Santeria spell.

Dominick caught Mikey's determined gaze. His own eyes were sleek like a tinted limousine where one could look out but nobody could look in. Dominick suspected that Mikey had no idea the man in question was very ill.

"What do you mean?" Dominick asked curiously.

"Well ..." Mikey, avoided his stare, "He was still in love with you!"

Dominick held back a smile.

"As a matter of fact," Mikey continued, "I bet he's still in love with you."

At this point, Dominick allowed himself to laugh.

"What the fuck do you know about anything? You're just some little pier queen Jorge's fucking! You're nobody!" the words thrust out of his mouth like stones, watching the pain he caused in Mikey's eyes.

"Fuck you, asshole" Mikey shouted before starting his way out of the penthouse.

Dominick stared out at the traffic lights below, trying to look unbothered.

"You know ..." Mikey threw the stone back at Dominick before leaving, "Maybe if you weren't such an arrogant piece of shit, Frankie wouldn't have left you!"

Despite his facade of composure, Mikey knew he had left Dominick with the same ache he had felt before storming out. Jorge ran out after him as everyone else stood staring at Dominick. Dominick just raised his eyebrows and shrugged his shoulders, brushing Mikey off as a mental case.

The following night, when Dominick saw Mikey walk into The Sanctuary with Jorge, he ordered Steve, one of the security guards, to grab him and bring him up to the deejay booth. Steve returned with a frightened little boy who thought his brief flirtation with the New York City club scene was, by all means, over.

"You know, very few queens ever get to read me like that!" Dominick told him with an enviable tone of confidence in his voice while mixing in the next record.

"Very few queens ain't me!" Mikey growled, pretending to be unfazed, aware Steve was waiting right outside the door and there was no way out without one of them dying.

Dominick turned to look at him searching for the right words to say without offending him. His white tank top drenched with sweat, outlining Dominick's muscular build, which Mikey tried hard to avoid staring. He could not help but notice, however, the multiple tattoos, which adorned Dominick's milky white skin. Dominick, speechless, was unable to apologize for his raucous brutality the night before. Mikey stood there staring, waiting, and ready to fling a stack of records at him if Dominick decided to move towards him.

A certain glow in Mikey's eyes reminded Dominick of himself when he was a few years younger, making him aware of his repressed fascination with Mikey. He realized then what Frankie must have seen in Mikey. Mikey, frustrated, turned to leave the deejay booth.

"Wait up, bitch!" Dominick demanded.

Mikey stopped. Dominick noticed for the first time Mikey's freckled face.

"You ain't goin' anywhere! Steve! Steve!" Dominick yelled, snapping his fingers with command.

"Oh, great! Listen, don't bother doin' me any favors! I know my own way out!" Mikey said as Steve emerged out of nowhere.

"Get this child some drink tickets, will ya?" Dominick raised a mischievous brow.

Mikey and Steve looked every bit confused before Dominick turned back to his turntables.

"Oh! While you're at it," Dominick continued, Steve reaching over to hear Dominick's request. "Put him on the permanent guest list!"

"Are you sure about that?" Steve began.

"Just do as I say!" Dominick yelled before breaking into a grin.

Mikey looked back at him, glowing, and smiled a 'thank you' before Steve escorted him like celebrity back down to the dance floor. The speakers boomed, *"Music is the basis of all life/without music we have no meaning/ no joy/and no soul/ It comes from the innermost thoughts and emotions/Music is a celebration of life ..."*

Dominick stared down at Mikey who smiled back knowingly.

"Celebrate your life," the song continued.

By the summer, Mikey was officially introduced as the newest member of The House of X at The Confirmation Ball held at The Sanctuary to a club packed with every ego in New York City that paid the $20 or more admission at the door and waited during the two-hour delay.

After the other children had been individually called out to the catwalk during the Grand March to contribute their share of shade and attitude to the event, Mikey emerged.

He served the runway with enviable ease and confidence in a black sable Armani suit, which his House sistas had stolen for him.

It was the happiest time of his life to be finally accepted into a family that would accept his locuras and not consider him 'una desgracia de la familia'. He was admired not condemned for his deviance here.

Damian and Jorge walked behind him, wearing the same stolen outfits, dark designer sunglasses enhancing their notoriety. When reaching the edge of the runway, they took the sunglasses off to reveal eyelids, which motioned that they were better than the colorful sea of spectators. It was a moment of almost laughable absorption as Dominick spun "Plastic Dreams" from the deejay booth.

After they had walked off to undying applause, Hector emerged tapping violently on the microphone.

"Excuse me! Excuse me!" he yelled, creating a sudden armor of silence. "Thank you!" he smiled in a tone of mingled wrath and self-amusement. Then with almost mocking conviction, "Now I'd like to introduce you to the new mother of all these lovely children!"

The entire club was victim to a sudden dramatic blackout before the stage lights slowly faded in with clouds of smoke. The children of the House of X re-emerged carrying a large black lesbian resting on a bed-like throne.

"Get into her! She's a hundred percent tuna!" Hector continued.

The stage ignited at once as the crowd hollered their approval. Dominick mixed in the fiercest house groove as the children slowly lowered the throne to the ground and started voguing in unison to a choreographed number.

Sista Mama X, the new mother of the House of X, featured a brown patterned tribal gown, a matching turban wrapped around her head, as she threw roses into the drowning flood of roars from the audience. She was replacing Mother Alexis X, a pre-op tranny hooker arrested for stabbing one of her clients. She casually chewed on an incredible piece of gum while examining her nails, unbothered by all the screaming. When she had had enough, Sista Mama raised her hand, demanding silence.

Nevertheless, the crowd continued to cheer with the electric current that ran beneath the rest of the night.

A few nights later, at The Sanctuary with a group of X-Men, "Jorge, I need to speak to you!" Mikey said with child-like eyes.

"What papi? What's da mattah?"

"Privately!" Mikey insisted with deadening urgency.

Jorge excused himself and followed Mikey toward the dark lounge area, which graffiti artist Keith Haring had decorated shortly before his death. Neon lights brought out the fluorescent caricatures painted against the black walls. Except for a few comatose K-queens staring intensely at the paintings for hours, the lounge was virtually empty.

"Sit!" Mikey said, his youthful features suddenly becoming old.

"What's wrong?" Jorge asked, dreading the answer.

"Jorge ..." Mikey began, "... I ... I ..." he hesitated, stumbled, turning to hide his quickly reddening eyes. He had given this a lot of thought and rehearsed this revelation for hours in front of Alberto's bathroom mirror. Aware that he had only used Jorge to be in the House of X, Mikey had developed something of a conscious.

"I don't love you!" Mikey said, gathering all his strength and conviction.

There was stillness. There was silence. The silence seemed like forever. Jorge held himself together and pretended not to seem upset.

"I can't say I do either!" he lied while searching Mikey's eyes for any signs of pain and hurt.

"Jorge, I do care for you a lot!"

Jorge raised hopeful eyes up to him before Mikey added, "Just not that way!" Jorge looked away as Mikey continued, "Enough, however, to tell you this! I couldn't go on with this any longer!"

"How long have you felt this way?" Jorge asked the one question Mikey was trying to avoid.

"Jorge, you don't understand!"

"OF COURSE I DON'T UNDERSTAND!" Jorge yelled.

Mikey fell silent in light of Jorge's anger, the words slapping him across the face the way he knew Jorge really wanted to so badly.

"Jorge, I've been through so much in my life. I couldn't even begin to explain!" Mikey begged callously.

Jorge stared at him with tears in his eyes, forcing a smile just a minute too late, not caring about Mikey's sob story.

"I've lived as much hell as you have Mikey but that doesn't absolve me from using other people! I fuckin' loved you, kid! I should've known better than to fall in love with a hustler! Always hustling to get to the next place! I knew you were a self-absorbed little fuck but I never thought you'd turn on me after all I've done for you!"

"Jorge! You don't understand! You don't understand!"

was all Mikey was able to let out before falling apart in public. Whatever words he needed to say were lost forever, drowned out by his tears.

Jorge continued examining him, studying Mikey for some revelation. "You don't even love yourself! Do you? You don't even love yourself enough to consider falling in love with another person! You're so sad!" Jorge's words flowed out like a sudden torrent.

Something in the arrangement of the words grasped Mikey before he stood up and ran out of the club, pushing past all the club kids he had tried so hard to impress.

Mikey continued running until he had reached the piers like a repentant lover. He was back invading the empty docks where it had all started. He felt cold but not by the weather, by his heart. He could not understand why he was so fucked up. It seemed impossible for him to settle down and love someone in return. Maybe he was a glutton for punishment like Alberto said. It seemed he was always caught somewhere between the tears and the laughter, in and out of love, always glimpsed briefly but intensely felt.

He knew he had fed from Jorge ruthlessly—becoming Mikey X, enjoying all the attention, the fierce jealousy of others, the unfounded rumors. Mikey had loved it all but never loved Jorge in the way he deserved to be loved. Now he was all alone again at the piers, staring out into the Hudson, waiting for another ship to dock the harbor.

SERMON ON THE MOUNT

Johnny sat on the large couch, which Mikey called his bed, staring out the vast window while puffing from a cigarette. He was really sick and now staying with them so that Alberto could take care of him. Mikey really did not know much about Johnny except that he was Alberto's lover and that he was white. He was much too self-absorbed to deal with the fact that Johnny was dying and someday Alberto would die too. He knew people who were living with HIV but had yet to know someone who had actually died from AIDS.

Johnny wore the white robe that Magdalena once gave Mikey as a birthday gift. Johnny smiled a ghost of a smile as he listened to the sounds of nature from the CD player Alberto had bought him. Alberto was out shopping for groceries, mostly vegetables and fruits to regain Johnny's strength. Mikey was in the kitchen talking to Sheba as if she were human while heating up some leftover chicken soup. It was early in the morning and Mikey had just arrived from The Sanctuary.

"Get out of my face, girl! Why don't you go find yourself a mouse to play with? Fuera! Pa'fuera de aqui!" Mikey echoed the words Magdalena used when he was a little boy to get him out of the kitchen. He wondered if she now used those words on that bastard Emilio. Sheba ran out of the kitchen leaving behind a trail of attitude.

'Sheba X', Mikey had nicknamed her, sometimes putting on a house record, grabbing her, and making her vogue like a puppet. Sheba would stare off to the side allowing him to move her paws around and shake her like a toy. Mikey loved cats and swore one day to have at least one of his own.

"You remind me so much of myself when I was your age," Johnny said, meeting Mikey's eyes over the glass living room table which separated them. Mikey, uncomfortable to be left alone with an ill man, now rested on a cushioned chair to his right while giving the soup time to cool off.

"I do? But you're a gringo!" Mikey smiled.

"How old are you?"

"Me? Twenty two!"

"Wow! Twelve years younger than me!" Johnny said, trying to remember what he looked like at twenty-two. Johnny remembered the days when new wave began replacing disco over the airwaves and roller-skating was as popular as rollerblading. Johnny had been wild and carefree when hanging out at Fire Island every summer, sleeping with the most beautiful boys without any protection, without fear of death and without fear of AIDS. He had been the most handsome bartender in New York City with a provocative smile that sealed the many fates of those who fell helplessly in love with him.

Mikey curiously watched Johnny as he drifted off to another place and time. Shadows revealed bright patches of yellowing skin. Johnny looked as thin as a twig wrapped inside the white robe Mikey was afraid to wear. It reminded him of those recurring nightmares, of howling wolves, of lonely deserts, of chanting music and of death. Death now surrounded Johnny who sat there with a faint smile and closed sunken eyes as if welcoming it. The crashing waves from the CD became chant-like, entering his soul and putting him in a trance.

"Are you ah-ight?" Mikey awakened Johnny from his

element, knowing this man was quickly fading.

"Huh? Oh, yeah! I was just remembering how beautiful it is to be young. So full of life and so innocent!"

"Johnny, being in your thirties does not exactly make you old!" Mikey insisted, with words he had used on many a trick for better tips.

"I'm forty!"

There was silence and then. "So! It only makes you wiser! Not to mention better in bed!" Mikey continued, trying to give him something to look forward to.

Johnny laughed at his kindness.

"Oh, my dear child, wisdom has no age and neither does death!" he laughed, focusing his gaze with eyes which were once as blue as the ocean but now a bone-chilling grayish-white on Mikey's pearl-black eyes.

Sheba jumped onto the couch, purring as she made herself comfortable next to him. Johnny brushed bone-like fingers against her soft shedding fur.

"It comes when it wants to!" Johnny continued, "That is why you live your life to the fullest. Enjoying every moment. Every sound. Every breath!"

Mikey blushed, aware Johnny was trying to tell him something, as Sheba purred ecstatically.

"Mikey!" Johnny leaned over to whisper, "Don't ever let anybody tell you how you should live your life! Just live!" He held out the last word by stressing it out, "Just love your family, your friends, yourself, your life!"

That was it. That was his goodbye. That was his swan song for Mikey.

That night, Alberto rushed his lover to St. Vincent's Hospital. Early the next morning, he called Mikey in tears.

Johnny was dead. His last words to Mikey filled every space in the apartment where Mikey sat alone. He contemplated them. He stared at himself in the bathroom mirror several times repeating them. He sat exactly where he had been the day before listening to the advice of a man already dead; a man who had died long before reaching the emergency room doors; a man caught somewhere between life and death who had left him with a profound message.

Hearing Alberto's pain over the telephone had left him unnerved. They had been together for many years and he knew Alberto had really loved Johnny. Though he had come close, Mikey had never experienced the death of a lover, except maybe Supreme who was gunned down by the police. Johnny's death made Mikey face the reality that his cousin Alberto was also waiting in the wings for the epidemic to take him too.

It was not enough that Mikey had been in love with Ricky and Juan Carlos, who were dying of AIDS. He feared that after everything he had experienced, he too might be carrying the disease. He had always used condoms and played safe but he was always afraid. Mikey was left to live the life Johnny had told him to live.

Mikey lifted himself up off the chair and stumbled over to the CD player where he pressed the play button and turned up the volume. Expecting the room to fill with the sound of crashing waves from the CD, which he thought Johnny had listened to last, instead he was overwhelmed by a lonely drum. Soft music instantly haunted the empty apartment and Mikey immediately recognized the record from his junior high school days. Cyndi Lauper's "True Colors" broke through the silence like a ghost with distant memories and not so distant tears.

"... but I see your true colors shining through/ I see your

true colors/ and that's why I love you ..."

Sheba emerged yawning from the closet-turned-bedroom as Mikey sang along to her.

"... so don't be afraid to let 'em show/ your true colors/ True colors are beautiful/ Like a rainbow ..."

It was not too much longer before Damian and Dominick were calling Mikey to find out how he was doing. Months had passed and even his cousin Alberto had moved on to start dating again. Jorge was now dating someone they all despised, someone Mikey had once been friends with, one of Jerry's many religious godchildren.

"That fat nasty obnoxious queen!" was how Damian described Raul Rodriguez over the phone to Mikey.

Mikey had known Raul Rodriguez since high school and, because of similar features, they had often been compared to one another. Raul, however, was never a match to Mikey's arrogance and bad boy image, and had gone on to gain a few extra pounds almost to throw off any comparisons. Despite this, they were always at each other's throats fighting over the same guys. Mikey had to be pulled off Raul one night at Hatfield's to the horrified eyes of Jessica Foxx, the Jewish drag queen who hosted the club, in the middle of her lip-synch rendition of Taylor Dayne's "Can't Get Enough of Your Love." Raul had always carried a vendetta against Mikey and was carrying it out by dating Jorge simply because he knew Mikey had dated him. Raul was the only person Mikey had ever lit black candles for and killed some chickens.

"I thought he said he was straight?" Dominick asked himself over the three-way-calling phone conversation.

"Straight? Straight to Jenny Craig!" Damian barked as all

three of them coagulated the phone lines with laughter.

"Well, how does Jorge feel about him?" Mikey asked casually, trying to conceal any hints of jealousy.

"Well, I guess, he's hooked!" Damian admitted as Mikey fell silent.

"Hooked? That bitch betta get hooked-on-phonics[61] if she wants to stay with Jorge!" Dominick cackled as a wave of laughter once again flooded the phone.

"That queen!" Damian continued, "When I saw him with Jorge at Great Adventure I said, 'what chu doin' here?' and he said 'I fell from the sky!' I said 'Bitch, it looks more like you crashed!'"

Mikey threw the phone on the couch and fell apart. Once again, he was one of the boys, one of the girls, one of the members of The House of X.

Despite the fact that Raul was his religious godson, Jerry's loyalty primarily belonged to his former partner-in-crime, Mikey. Aware that Raul was only using Jorge as a vehicle to become a member of The House of X himself and antagonize Mikey, Jerry proved his allegiance by shedding light on Raul's biggest secret.

Mikey, of course, just had to pick up the phone one evening and invite Jorge out for a chat.

"About what?" Jorge demanded.

"Oh, about things!" Mikey said sadistically at what promised to be an eve of destruction.

They were to meet at a hustler bar in Jackson Heights, Queens called The Magic Touch, which the queens had dubbed

---

61 A commercial brand of educational materials popular in the '90's. It was originally designed to teach through phonetics.

'The Tragic Touch'.

"What are you guys doing here?" Jorge hollered that fateful evening when he showed up and spotted Damian and Dominick smiling like two Cheshire cats from a table deep in the corner sitting with Mikey.

Jorge immediately caught on to a conspiracy as a flickering candle produced dancing shadows on their already purring faces. Before Jorge could repeat his question, the lights suddenly blacked out and the stage lit up to reveal a Raul they had never seen before.

Emerging from a thick cloud of smoke, his narrowed eyes absorbed the sounds of clapping hands behind a black leather mask and bright red lipstick. Raul touched himself all over a black patent leather bustier and matching bikini-shorts with his black elbow-length gloves completing his tribute to Madonna with black fishnet stockings and knee-length patent leather high heel stilettos.

Raul expressed only two emotions—hot and bothered. While lip-synching to the words of the ruling diva's "Erotica," he pulled his short black hair in total ecstasy.

Allowing himself to fall on his knees, he rubbed his erecting cock in front of the audience simulating masturbation. Squeezing his rubber breasts, Raul bent over and fondled his fat Puerto Rican ass. Crawling all over the floor, he was engrossed in his performance. The audience cheered excitedly as Jorge screamed, Mikey smirked, Dominick laughed and Damian chanted "Work Shashonna! Work Shashonna! Work!"

Raul searched the crowd through the slits in his mask for the unannounced guests. With eyes bulging, his gaze stopped at Mikey who sat there with his characteristic raised eyebrow, nonchalantly sucking his teeth.

Mikey joyfully lit himself a joint and literally glowed, in his moment of divine glory.

Jorge sat next to him with both hands holding up his crumbling face. He was confused, shocked, ready to vomit as the crowd continued chanting, "Work Shashonna! Work Shashonna! Work!"

Shashonna pulled her mask off to reveal Raul, the music still playing, as he stood there horrified.

"Ahhhhhhhhh!" he screamed before stumbling off the stage in four-inch heels, disappearing into the darkness.

Damian and Dominick hollered maliciously at the look on Jorge's face. He stared at Mikey, hunting for an answer, a comment, anything. Mikey coolly smoked his joint seemingly unbothered and unnerved. He puffed smoke out his nostrils before finally cracking a vicious smile to reveal a gold cap with the letter "X" sparkling from one of his two front teeth.

Jorge sat quietly at the piers as his friends maliciously dished out his latest flame along with Mikey.

"Did you see the size of that belly hanging out from underneath that bustier? I thought he said he was straight. What closet could he ever fit into?"

There was laughter before a stoned Dominick jumped in while sipping alcohol from a brown paper bag.

"I just feel sorry for poor Madonna! I almost wanna write huh a letter!" Dominick fixed his puffy eyes on Jorge, "To tell huh all about Shashonna—the fat Puerto Rican straight drag queen who disgraces huh every week at some seedy bar in Jackson Heights!"

Jorge alone made no sound while fixing Dominick with a look of silent reproach.

"I just wanna know one thing!" Mikey pulled at his fingers until they cracked and took a drag from his cigarette in sheer ecstasy before asking, "Did he evah wear that outfit when you fucked him?"

Everyone except Jorge let out a brief, sputtering laugh. His eyes were a perfect orgy of hate and embarrassment. Several emotions curiously mingled in the way he stared at Mikey who sat there with a mute smile planted on his face.

With Raul now exposed as Shashonna, Jorge and Mikey reluctantly rediscovered a new friendship. Mikey had after all saved him from somebody else using him to become a member of The House of X. He apologized profusely for his selfish insensitivity and revealed hints of his past to try to make Jorge understand why he was so fucked up. Gossip within the club scene had them "secretly involved," "having an open relationship," even "hustling together."

They celebrated these unfound rumors about their camaraderie by holding hands and kissing in public with vague sarcasm. They quickly became the gay darlings of the club scene and together with Damian and Dominick formed an impenetrable clique of ex-boyfriends. Together they would terrorize the nightlife night after night, wherever bouncers would ceremoniously usher them past velvet ropes. They read and battled the other queens, tearing apart anyone that crossed any which one of them. It was not long before they were dubbed "The Shady Bunch" and feared by the most vicious of queens for their unethical means of vengeance.

Their reign of terror began on Sundays starting at the piers. There, they would agree on who's face to slash, what records were hot enough to be ovah and with whom not to be seen. Sunday nights belonged to the infamous Cafe Con Leche where their growing mood swings would escalate on the dance floor amidst straight banjee boys and wannabe straight banjee boys.

Always on top of the competition, Dominick would find whatever means, however ruthless, to complain about the deejay. Nicknamed 'DJ Dominatrix' and quite often 'DJ Doom' or 'Gloominick' by one too many of his bitter peers, Dominick always managed to send them running for their money. Because of his influence, many of them either found themselves playing at some dive hellhole or altogether out of work.

On Monday nights, they frequented Sugar Babies at CBGB's[62] on the Lower East Side. With only hard-core party people haunting New York City's nightlife on a Monday night, there they sealed their invitations into private parties and permanent guest lists.

Tuesday nights found them laying low at Dominick's West Village crib where he would sample new records for them while they tested coke, K, crystal, ecstasy, and acid.

Drugs were often given to them compliments of the most notorious dealers in club land with the knowledge that their approval would provide for numerous sales and free advertising.

People always approached them at the clubs for drugs and the proper referral is all it took for any dealer to stay in business. Ernesto, the most popular of them all, was the main sponsor of their Tuesday night drug-fests. Marie Antoinette, always dressed in a baby doll with a Mickey Mouse backpack used to stash her drug supply, was another proud sponsor.

62 Country, Blue Grass, and Blues was a famous music space located on the Bowery area of Manhattan that became a forum for punk music during the '80's. During the '90's it also briefly sponsored a popular weekly dance party. CBGB's closed in 2006.

They always ran into her with three other women all of which were rumored to be working for the Latin Kings.

By Wednesday night, they were all strung out and crashing whatever party comforted their Godless yearnings. Sometimes they would venture to a sex club with flashlights to feast their eyes on the grand orgies of men sucking one another off. They would often run into ex-boyfriends, enemies, and would-be lovers there to humiliate and crush with their exposing spotlights.

Friday nights, they stalked Christopher Street bringing fear to the eyes of many as they paraded down toward the piers only to walk back down toward Seventh Avenue. They would dub this event 'walking the runway' and they would get stoned and pick fights with anyone who just looked at them the wrong way.

They became absurdly unapproachable and devious by nature, kicking off their Saturday afternoons by mopping throughout the city. They shoplifted only the finest baggy oversized clothing just for the very thrill of it. They would walk out mostly with expensive baseball caps to add to their already sizable collections. Sometimes a brand new pair of costly sneakers would leave the store unpaid.

Saturday nights they modeled the latest in stolen merchandise at The Sanctuary featuring the likes of Hilfiger, Lauren, Diesel, and Nautica. The latter designer was victim to Damian's vicious "Nautica? It looks cute but not-on-huh!" This was directed at Flaca Pendavis, Damian's fiercest competitor on the dance floor, who appeared at The Sanctuary one Saturday night wearing Fila from head to toe. "Feed huh! Feed huh!" became the label's new nickname.

Dominick would be spinning from the deejay booth kicking

everybody's ass with only the very best and latest in house music. He played nothing commercial, nothing popular, only his mood swings generating through the state-of-the-art sound system. His style was usually dark but always intense—perfect for the tweaking drug addicts. Dominick would start the night off smoothly, testing new records on his audience until building up to his insufferable peak.

It was during this time that the club was the most crowded with queens at the door fighting to get in. Straight girls from Jersey were usually fighting, "Why do the fags get chosen first over us?" Police cars filled with Maggie would prowl back and forth while homeless East Village punks begged for money to buy more drugs outside The Sanctuary. Children smoked crack, hidden behind cars and alleyways. Their laughter drowned out the sounds of groaning men getting their dicks sucked off inside the cars by prostitutes, transsexuals, and young boys.

Inside the club, the smell of cigarettes, marijuana and crack blended to create a thick air of nostalgia. Muscle boys escorted beautiful drag queens. Mean-looking hard-core hoodies[63] hung out with voguing queens. Expensive models wrapped themselves around aging sugar daddies and houses battled on the dance floor.

Confrontations between the House of Aviance and the House of Infiniti served as a backdrop to the waging wars between the House of Pendavis and the House of X. It was old school versus new schools of facetious faggot gangs staring each other down behind designer shades. Each house gathered within their own boundaries throughout the club making sure not to step on enemy ground. The club divided into territories

---

63 A slang term for someone from the neighborhood. Also refers to sweaters with a hood that usually feature one big pocket in the front where one can put both hands in.

and turf wars were common. It may have seemed comical to the regular partygoer but to the Houses, it was serious.

Mikey, Jorge and Damian hung out unapproachably by the deejay booth surrounded by the House of X. While snorting coke and K, they gathered there to read the opposition, to laugh at them and to score the pieces as they walked by. They were always too high to tell the difference between the 'fierce pieces' and the 'nasty seeds[64].'

"Ovah!" Damian would yell rather suddenly.

"Ovah? Ovah-weight!" Mikey would correct him.

Damian would look twice to realize the shirtless man he was cruising had a belly bulging over his too-tight denims.

"Excuse me? Are those Bugle Boy jeans[65] you're wearing?" Mikey would add insensitively to stimulate his jaded nerves.

Jorge would mentally collapse from too many bumps of cocaine while Steve the bouncer glared his harsh repellent flashlights to make sure all the dealers were in their designated spots.

Beefy male strippers tried desperately to keep up with Dominick's musical trickery. One night, Damian spotted one stripper in particular whom he absolutely detested for once trying to pick up Hector dancing up on a speaker in a somnambulistic trance, stoned out of his mind.

Damian quickly grabbed Mikey by the arm, motioning him to follow as Jorge instinctively tagged along. The dancer was excessively absorbed in his high to notice Damian tying his shoelaces together. In a moment of complete euphoria, unable to balance, he fell over off the speaker and onto a crowd of

---

64 Gay slang for undesirable men. It originally came from another slang term referring to the undesirable seeds found in marijuana.

65 A brand of jeans popular in the '80's which featured elastic cuffs at the bottom and cross-stitching patterns.

horrified spectators.

Damian just watched with vindictive eyes as Janet X yelled, "You better work, Ms. Damian!" She laughed so infectiously that even the collapsed stud was careless enough to crack a smile making Janet a concubine to Damian's crime.

WOES OF THE PHARISEES

Eventually, they all decided to get the same tattoos to signify their commitment to one another. A two-inch letter X was inked in gothic letters, confined by two tribal lines running parallel around their left arms. Dominick, venturing into the art of body piercing, now exhibited a silver hoop impaled into his left eyebrow. Never a step behind, Damian showed up to The Sanctuary one night with a silver stud through his tongue.

Then there came the day when the whole New York City nightlife no longer intrigued them. Their predictable evenings would leave them becoming more irritable and vindictive than ever after the drugs-and-boredom induced haze of the night. They would scan the clubs for new faces, not the familiar ones, who would walk around wondering whether they had slept with one another. The only battle left in their quickly fading lives was adjusting some stray wisps of hair in the bathroom mirrors.

They traveled together into the outer boroughs on the prowl with the questing look of those desperate to find adventure. Mikey, the outer borough gay club connoisseur, introduced them to Hatfield's in Queens. There, they terrorized everyone with bitchy comments, even resident drag diva Jessica Foxx. They assaulted the guidos[66] at Spectrum out in Bensonhurst

---

66 An entirely American phenomenon found in the New York and New Jersey metropolitan area. Mostly of Italian-American descent, interpretation of their European heritage usually falls short with focus on status symbols, regional dialect, and mall culture.

and started riots in Long Island.

Soon enough, their reign of terror stretched out as far as South Beach down in Florida where underneath the curious moon and stars, Damian finally questioned his belief in love.

After a two-year relationship, Damian and Hector were no longer a couple. Damian had been caught sleeping with one of their friends. Hector, devastated and wounded, retired from the nightlife altogether, though he remained Father of the House of X. Damian was still allowed to stay in the House of X but Hector scarcely tolerated him as a friend.

"I know I fucked up!" Damian told Dominick and Mikey.

The three of them were sitting somewhere on an empty beach while Jorge was out getting laid. The darkness, the solitude, the sand reminded Mikey of his nightmares and made him feel slightly uncomfortable. The light from cigarettes and joints cast ominous shadows on their tanned bitter faces. Damian's sudden flash of vulnerability made him look even more strikingly handsome to Mikey. Damian appeared almost human. This moment bound for one of those memories Mikey would remember in future years.

"I never meant to hurt him!" Damian continued, lost in his own thoughts while Mikey silently listened to the crashing waves.

"Two men should be able to have sex with other people without loving each other any less," Dominick suggested while staring morosely out into the ocean. "Why are gay couples trying so hard to be like breeders? Even they can't stick to monogamy with the right to marry and kids."

The silence that followed seemed long enough to shatter. Mikey looked up at him with uncertainty—baffled, irritated, depressed.

"You know it's really hard to have a one-on-one relationship with someone when you can't sleep with other people!" Damian thought aloud.

"That's not a relationship!" Mikey flared up like an ignited match.

At that moment, Mikey hated the selfishness of his friends. Unwillingly, he forced out a chuckle to evade the stunned pause that followed his sudden outburst.

"Love is something special shared between two people, not a party of five!" Mikey found himself saying, wondering if his vulnerability was not his own worst enemy. He was surprised at his own statement.

Their silence was profound.

"I hear ya mama! I once believed in love too!" Dominick jumped in. "But when you've been hurt over and over again you just can't help but become bitter and jaded."

Mikey brightened, discovering an unintended hint of Dominick's lingering love for Frankie and possibly even Damian.

"Now here!" Dominick handed Mikey a joint, "Smoke this and you'll feel much betta!"

Mikey reluctantly took his advice, allowing himself to relax so that the conversation would continue.

"At first, I was just using Hector to get into the House of X," Damian admitted. "I learned to love him but I guess I was never really 'in love' with him. I kept telling him that I wanted an open relationship because I wasn't sure I was ready to settle down with him but every time I brought up the subject, he would shut me up and buy some expensive gift. Hector always treated me like I was some stupid kid and never really wanted to listen to anything I had to say. I might've used him at first but he used me too. I was like his trophy wife. I was supposed to look great by his side all the time but never think for myself."

"Why'd you stay with him?" Mikey asked.

"I don't know. Why'd you stay with Jorge?"

"I was only with Jorge for several months not several years and I never cheated on him!" Mikey said defensively. "I never moved in with him either! But I guess I know where you're coming from. I thought I would eventually fall in love with him too. It just never happened."

They sat in silence, listening to the crashing waves while smoking more weed before Damian continued.

"I never meant to hurt him!" Damian started to cry much to the shock of his friends. "I kind of liked the fact that he tried to daddy me. I never met my real father, you know? But it's really hard for me to get that close to anyone. I always end up finding some way to fuck it all up!"

With these tears, Mikey realized how much he had in common with them. The conversations continued to unfold throughout the course of the night with more curious reactions and revelations as the marijuana thinned their minds. The waves created a soft breeze adding to this rare bonding moment.

When they returned to New York, Mikey's cousin Alberto had a surprise in store for him. His name was Joey and he was now living with them. Alberto had met Joey through some friends shortly after Johnny's death. They had dated extensively during their brief two-week courtship, both of them longing for a relationship. After only two weeks, Joey was now part of the household.

Concerned about his cousins lesbian tendencies, Mikey

cornered Joey at The Monster one night. Joey was an Italian guido from New Jersey complete with thick gold chains, massive amounts of hairspray and the most up-to-date collection of dance music. Joey was the typical queen Mikey was susceptible to antagonize immediately.

"I've heard so much about you. I've been dying to meet ya!" Joey admitted, cursing himself after having said that.

However, with nowhere else to go, Mikey had no choice but to welcome Joey into the family. Though Mikey felt Alberto had replaced Johnny too quickly, he was genuinely happy that his cousin had found happiness with Joey. Apprehensively and instinctually, he came to love Joey like a surrogate mother.

Mikey, looking more like an eighteen-year-old but acting more like a twelve-year-old, quickly became Alberto and Joey's pseudo-adoptive son. They fed him, cleaned up after him, and helped him look for work.

"You can't make a career out of being a house queen!" Alberto would lecture, irritated with Mikey's lack of responsibility and free-spirited 'Life is just one big party' attitude.

"Oh, leave him alone! The kid's just having fun!" Joey would defend Mikey.

"Well, the kid either better get himself a job or get his ass back out on the pier!" Alberto threatened.

BEATITUDES

A few days later, Mikey had his very first encounter with the Mother of the House of X, Sista Mama.

"Mama, I needs a job!" he demanded while examining his nails and chewing an amazing piece of gum.

Sista Mama was fascinated by Mikey's tempestuous audacity. Most people were intensely frightened by her fabled violent temper and yet, there was Mikey trying her patience. He stared back at her behind a lost child's eyes while a Beastie Boys record blared from her CD player. Sista Mama got him a job at the gay and lesbian bookstore where she herself worked.

"If you fuck this up, I'm gonna shove my beeper up your ass and page you repeatedly on vibrator!" she threatened.

As usual, Mikey became immediately intense with Sista Mama and they became soul mates as if truly only separated by Mikey's birth. Mikey brought his party atmosphere into the lifeless West Village bookstore with a crank of the volume. He would pump the sound system, insisting that the gay clientele preferred listening to house music rather than "That tired old elevator crap!" He was always on the phone with one of his sistas when he was not flirting brazenly with one of his preferred customers. Instead of asking customers if he could check their bags, he would yell, "Can we snatch your products, please?"

He would drag his ass into work with only a few hours of sleep or straight from whatever club he had just left, still stoned. At the bookstore, he would crash, abuse the customers, sleep in the stockroom and do more bumps of cocaine in the bathroom to stay awake. His only enterprising contribution was to flip through the porn magazines sold in the back and write obscene messages on the sample copies which humored the clientele. In short, Mikey was always out to lunch.

However, it was there that he was first introduced to gay culture. Dan, the assistant manager, was the queen of camp and cult and taught Mikey about the importance of John Waters, Bette Davis, Joan Crawford, Judy Garland, and "No wire hangers, ever!"

"I know you're just a jaded, little queen but I'm beyond jaded, sweetie. I'm bitter!" Dan would tell him, widening his huge baby blue eyes. "I've been through it all! Little pier queens like you only amuse me! Pretending to be so fierce and immortal! Dahling, one day you too will suffer the agonies of menopause, hot flashes, and changes of life! One day, you too will find yourself balding, wearing tight jeans and pierced nipples, drinking too much beer at Rawhide's, the Spike and the Eagle, and begging for a decent fuck!"

With that, Mikey had newfound respect for his elders and eyed Dan with great curiosity as he paraded throughout the bookstore with his Charlie's Angels, Police Woman, Brady Bunch, and Wonder Woman tee shirts. Rumors had him willing to do anything for a Roseanne tee shirt.

"I'll even sit through an episode of Baywatch if I have too!" Dan would insist devilishly, walking away with cheeks sucked in.

Behind the counter, Mikey was a cunning parody of himself always fluttering his eyelashes and posing vampishly.

"Oh, Ms. Thing don't you get too fierce on my time!" Mikey had become comfortable enough with Sista Mama to threaten her when she ordered him around.

Mama would stare bug-eyed, as Mikey would prepare to fight her like a true banjee girl. With one hand, he would pretend to open hairclips using his teeth while, with the other, pretend to hold back his long imaginary luscious black hair. Clipping it back, he would then proceed to raise his calves to pull off fictional high heel pumps and toss them to the side. After pushing up his invisible breasts, he would stand there with his hands on his hips ready for action.

"Oh! Wait!" Mikey pretended to pull out a jar and open it.

"What in the world are you doin'?" Sista Mama asked, completely puzzled by his performance.

Mikey rubbed some fantastical cream on his face, "Vaseline! In case you scratch my face!"

Sista Mama would laugh, "You're so adorable! And so young. I get chicken pox just looking at you!"

This was probably the happiest time of his life. He was working legally, found himself a new surrogate mother, and was learning there was more to gay culture than the club scene.

Sista Mama would invite her children to some of the most lavish parties in the city. The most memorable, however, were always the ones thrown by DJ Kenzo and his drag queen lover Flora, who had gotten her name from a Midwest waitress they once encountered on the road. These were major drug parties where the minute they got to the door, someone would shove a half gram of K into each of their hands. Mikey always knew before walking into the large, crowded Gramercy Park apartment that they would all stumble out totally fucked-up, if at all. Here, familiar faces from the underground club circuit would emerge from the darkness with powdered noses.

"Hey, Mikey! Wassup?"

"Wassup?"

"Who that?" Jorge would ask.

"I have no idea!" Mikey would respond, "Some queen!"

Once inside, they were cast immediately into a dangerously smoke-infested room filled with sweaty people who stared at them as they pushed their way through. The music would blast from every angle, the crisp rhythms ostentatiously running through them. Semi-nude girls and bare-chested men tried desperately to keep up with Kenzo's frenetic madness. Moist, oiled muscle queens rubbed themselves excitedly against each other with hands openly exploring, and drenched in salty manhood.

For Kenzo's thirtieth birthday, the entire apartment was decorated with pink pastel streamers and ribbons underneath a radiant disco-ball. Outside, in the patio, a "Happy Sweet Sixteen" banner hung over a tall pink and white Valencia birthday cake decorated to look like a dress around a Barbie doll.

Kenzo grinned from the deejay booth as his lover paraded throughout the madness in a pink Sweet 16 prom dress. That night, Sista Mama wore her favorite oversized dress shirt, the one Mikey always joked "Ya look like you're ready to jump off a plane!"

Mikey remembered falling into a K-hole after too many bumps of K, unable to move, with Flora that night while watching some little black girl with pig tails and a Nancy Drew lunchbox snort cocaine like there was no tomorrow. Flora sat next to him with her frazzled blonde wig and ripped prom dress. By the end of the night, she looked like she had been repeatedly run over by a bus with her badly smudged lipstick and splattered blush.

"I'm beautiful damn it! I know I am!" was all she kept saying to Mikey throughout the night. Mikey stared down at the aging drag queen beside him and wondered where the insanity of his life was taking him. He knew he was running away from something by losing himself in the drugs but from what, he did not know.

One night at the bookstore, Sista Mama was having a loud and elaborate conversation over the phone while Mikey flipped through the latest copy of Machismo magazine to see which one of his friends had finally made it in the porn industry. He would always come across someone he had slept with and seriously considered becoming the next Latino Fan Club boy toy.

"You so crazy! I can't believe you went out with him!" Sista Mama's phone conversation reverberated throughout the bookstore followed by, "A good date is when you can't walk the next day and you're two hundred dollars richer!"

Mikey dropped the magazine on the floor and curiously asked, "Who the fuck are you talking to?"

"A friend of Ellen's!"

"Boy or girl?"

"Boy!"

"Is he cute?"

"Very!"

"Describe him!" Mikey demanded.

"Short, stocky Puerto Rican, very handsome!"

"Give me that phone!" Mikey snatched it out of her hands, "Hello?"

"Hello?" the voice on the other side asked, sounding vaguely familiar, "What's your name?"

"Mikey!"

"Mikey? That's funny! I used to go out with a Mikey!"

Monumental silence was followed by Mikey's sudden shriek, "Juan Carlos?"

"Mikey?"

"Ahhhhhhhhh!" Mikey tossed the phone, "I'm gonna kill you, Sista Mama!"

"Hello? Hello? Mikey are you still there?" Juan Carlos's voice begged from the receiver.

"What? What did I do?" Sista Mama fidgeted nervously.

"My God! That's ... that's Juan Carlos! My ex-lover Juan Carlos!"

Sista Mama stood in complete shock, staring at him as if watching a slowly developing Polaroid. Mikey continued screaming as Juan Carlos's voice called out his name.

"Well, nobody told you to snatch the phone away from me! That's what you get for trying to hook yourself up on my time!" she half-joked.

Later that night, after work, Sista Mama approached Mikey about his estranged ex-lover as they were cashing out the register.

"I don't wanna talk about it!" Mikey's eyes had lost a shred of liveliness.

"Mikey!" Sista Mama's maternal instincts flowed, "Whatever it was, I'm sure it wasn't that bad!"

Mikey stopped dead in his tracks before she finished that last sentence, his face flushed with fury, "The man is HIV positive!"

Sista Mama looked at him like a whipped schoolgirl, sorry for her unpremeditated yet significant discovery. Mikey shut his eyes tightly with the hopes that when he opened them he would be somewhere else. Instead, he found Mama standing before him looking Christ like with her arms stretched out.

"I loved him Mama!" Mikey cried, "I thought he would save me from myself with just one perfect smile but instead he made it all worse! I was so much younger! So stupid!"

"Younger and stupider than you are now? That's impossible! Oh, baby!" She wrapped her thick arms around him as Mikey rested his head on her bosom. There, he cried uncontrollably and allowed himself to fall apart.

"What was I thinkin'? I didn't know Mama! I swear!"

Sista Mama's warmth and the words he chose made him feel like he was buried deep in Magdalena's arms.

MIRACLES

Mikey tested himself once again for HIV and with the days that followed his wait for the results, he visited Magdalena in Bushwick to celebrate the Thanksgiving holiday. They did not speak much as Mikey thought that Magdalena wanted to hear nothing about his life. Not wanting to upset her, he pretended to be enjoying the approaching Christmas season.

However, through the small talk he sensed that Magdalena was showing signs of sympathy. Emilio was out getting the car fixed and so Mikey and Magdalena both had the opportunity to say all that needed to be said. Nonetheless, except for a tender moment when she reached over to fix his hair, nothing much happened.

He spent most of his time back visiting the neighborhood with Jerry in between his killing chickens or casting spells. Ever since becoming a full-fledged santero, every outburst out of Jerry was a premonition. Any event out of the ordinary attributed to one of the orisha's whims—the squeaking from an old wooden door, the falling rain, the growth of fungus on outdated bread. They all represented evil and restless auras from the dead.

"Wassup sista?" Jerry welcomed Mikey as he followed him up the stairs with the smell of urine rising from the wooden hallway floors and the olive green walls peeling away.

"Ay mi'jo!" Esperansa greeted him. "Yo pense que te habias muerto!" she said while cooking something full of too much garlic, "Que milagro que vienes a visitarnos a los pobres!"

Mikey smiled at her bitter sweetly wondering what Jerry had told his mother about Mikey's latest adventures. Jerry's room was now more of a botanica[67] with statues crowding every inch and dolls staring back at him uninvitingly. Pictures of beefy men still posed underneath jars of honey but Jerry's followers now stretched out overseas.

"Mira, he's from Spain. Muerete loca, I'm international!" he glowed as an old freestyle[68] record played in the background.

"Did ya hear the latest about Angela?"

Mikey shook his head a quick, curious 'no.'

"Well, let me tell you! She's dating some fat old man in Queens with lots of money!"

Mikey remained indifferent. He was still anxious to know the results of his HIV test.

"You know what they say, 'Why buy the cow when you can get the milk for free!'" Jerry was still trying to get some reaction out of Mikey. "I must admit I miss her. It was fun being some irresponsible menace to society."

Mikey was still silent.

"Have you spoken to Victor?" Jerry tried to strike a nerve.

"Huh? Yeah, he finally sold his little red Festiva."

"Ay, Lucky's head would've split wide open and huh brain would've popped out if she knew ya two were gonna end up becoming friends! She must be rolling in huh grave!" Jerry unaware Mikey only spoke to Victor on rare occasion.

Jerry looked chubbier and hairier than Mikey had

---

67 A retail store which sells religious statues, candles, folk medicine and other products regarded as alternative medicine or magical which caters to the Latino community.

68 Electronic dance music that originated in New York City in the '80's and was popular amongst urban Latino and Italian-American communities.

remembered him. Mikey suddenly thought of Teddy Ruxpin[69] possessed by the spirit of Rosie Perez.

One of Jerry's little brothers, about five-years-old, ran into the room giggling fiendishly.

"Wok, Ms. Thing! Chu sooo fiace!" he laughed before dashing out and leaving Mikey confused and Jerry tittering.

"I see he's quickly picking up on the Queen's English!" Mikey looked at Jerry almost scornfully.

"It's that Jose & Luis record! They love it! My little brothers, the future of the Houses!" Jerry gloated. "How's your mother?"

"Ah-ight! But she still doesn't like you!" Mikey snickered.

"That's ah-ight! She still doesn't like you either!" Jerry laughed, "Besides, Magdalena's just jealous cause I look better in her dresses than she does!"

He reminisced on the times he would try on her clothes with Mikey while she was working. They would sneak in and get whatever Mikey needed. Mikey was always afraid Jerry would stretch out her dresses or leave traces of his hair stuck in one of the zippers.

"What's the mattah, sugah?" Jerry finally asked, sensing Mikey's depression.

"Nothin'!" Mikey pouted. Jerry caught the lie.

"Come on, Cuca! I know you like a book!" Jerry reached over, sitting next to him.

Mikey lay back, defeated, on Jerry's bed, "I spoke to Juan Carlos!"

Jerry crunched his eyes like a child just finding out where babies come from, "How is he?"

69 An animatronic talking bear from the '80's who would move his mouth and eyes as he read stories from an audio tape deck located on his back.

"Still alive!" Mikey sounded unintentionally hateful.

"How did ya get in touch wit' him?"

Mikey answered from a semi-catatonic state where flashes of his life with Juan Carlos still lingered, "You know the mother of the House of X? Sista Mama? She tried hooking us up ovah the phone."

Jerry unsuccessfully tried holding back his erupting laughter.

"It's not funny!" Mikey yelled sharply.

"I'm sorry!" Jerry briefly regained control before Mikey's reproachful eye made him fall apart once again.

"I was ready to kill huh! That bitch!"

"What did he say?" Jerry calmed down with curiosity while Mikey searched the room for a phantom to change the subject.

"Oh, he's doing fine! Probably living off of some stupid queen that'll put up with his bullshit until he dies!" Mikey almost whispered the last few words leaving silence to linger like some sort of terror.

"Well? Are you gonna see him?"

"No!" Mikey flared, "You know I only want ta forget everything about those days!" He jumped up violently, "About Juan Carlos, about Ricky, about hustling, about Lucky. About everything!"

"'Everything?" Jerry was stunned by Mikey's sudden disposition, "Pero mijo, no te me pongas histerico!"

Mikey simultaneously laughed and cried, "I'm just scared!"

Those three words called back the silence that had fled the room during his brief outburst. The statues from Jerry's altar stared back at him with consolation.

"Do you want me ta read your cards?" Jerry suggested.

He had learned to read everything from playing cards to coffee spills on the carpet.

"Jerry, you know I could do that myself if I really wanted!" Mikey said rather unconvincingly.

Both of them questioned his abilities and without another word, Jerry opened a drawer and pulled out a deck of cards. Sitting on the floor, Mikey sat across from him while Jerry shuffled the cards expertly the way Mikey never could. Jerry looked much older and wiser than his twenty-three years of age. He chanted something in the Yoruba[70] language, which Mikey tried desperately to translate.

"Pick a card, any card!" Jerry gave his best imitation of an Atlantic City card dealer.

Mikey stalled for a moment before pointing to a card buried beneath three others. Jerry picked it up, his face becoming a perverse white.

"What? What is it?"

His mystified eyes revealed the answer before he exposed the ace of spades. Mikey's heart sunk to his feet as the big black goblet stared grotesquely back at him.

"Oyá is coming! Death surrounds and walks with you!" Jerry said, both of them turning their heads to look up at the altar where St. Therese smiled down on them with a glow behind her painted eyes.

The day finally came when Mikey had to pick up his HIV test results. He was prepared for anything, planning how, and if to tell his mother. He even decided which medicines he would take, debating whether to come across as a fighting hero

---

70 A dialect continuum of West Africa spoken by the Yoruba people from which the Santeria religion eventually evolved.

or a morose victim.

"Your results are negative!" the counselor told him.

Mikey was stunned, the word 'negative' buzzing around the room like a bee. A mingling of joy and confusion caused his heart to pause briefly while relief massaged his tense muscles.

"Are you sure?" he asked in disbelief, as if expecting the counselor to yell out "Surprise! It's all a joke! You've got AIDS!"

Instead, "That's what the tests show!"

Mikey was ecstatic as Jerry's premonition still lingered in the air.

That night, at The Sanctuary, in celebration, Dominick dedicated to Mikey the song by which he would always remember him. The club overcrowded as usual with familiar faces everywhere; people Mikey had seen a million times before but never bothered to say 'hello.'

"Music is the basis of all life ..."

Dominick blinded him with his flashlight from the deejay booth.

"... Without music we have no meaning, no joy, no soul ..."

Jorge's baseball cap bounced up and down from the deejay booth next to Dominick as he danced along to the song.

"... It comes from the innermost thoughts and emotions ..."

Damian cleared the dance floor area by the deejay booth and vogued, battling his own shadow.

"... Music is a celebration of life ..."

Mikey lost himself in the music, for the first time not high, perverse with the delight of being alive to see yet another Christmas as all the lights in The Sanctuary ignited at once.

"... Celebrate your life ..."

TRANSFIGURATION

Juan Carlos was almost twenty-nine and knew he would not make it into his thirties. The day was quickly dawning with a t-cell level under a hundred. He felt weak and tired and nothing really mattered anymore. He was living alone in some welfare apartment in the South Bronx with only some stupid cat and a ferret for the mice. Listening to some cheesy freestyle record, he remembered the days he used to dance back up for freestyle singers. Juan Carlos had always wanted to be a singer himself, forever trying to put together some group or another. He had even performed at a few clubs and the girls loved him. They went crazy over his once handsome Latin features and sexy smile. If he had really wanted to, he could have been a singer, an actor, a model even.

Juan Carlos had been beautiful in every way except for his personality. Having people constantly telling him how sexy and gorgeous he was had made him pretentious and superficial. He always thought he could have anyone he wanted. In his mind, they all lived for him and loved him. Now they were all gone. Hearing Mikey's voice over the phone had made him realize what a prick he had been taking advantage of someone so naive and vulnerable. Mikey used to buy him stuffed animals and try to cook him dinner. Even the look in his cat's eye reminded him of Mikey's need to be loved.

The cat and the ferret were blatant reminders of things that would last longer than he would. Juan Carlos still looked beautiful, in the way dying young men looked beautiful. He had lost a lot of weight but he still had his sexy smile.

When he walked down the streets all the girls still looked at him. He was still quite a sight to see but every time he met one of them, he had to push them away, not because he was gay but because he was sick; because he had AIDS; because he was dying. Sometimes they did not even care. Some of them still wanted to 'get down' with him but he never would because he was too scared.

He was afraid the condom might break or he would hurt them the same way he hurt Mikey. He was afraid he might do to them what someone else had done to him. Juan Carlos was afraid to wake up the next morning and see the same death in their eyes that reflected from his own. His eyes were still so young, so full of life, so full of fear and so full of death.

"Merry fuckin' Christmas!" he told himself aloud while staring out the window knowing that the dying live somewhere between life and death.

Outside, the fallen snow glistened under the feet of children playing with snow piled on the sidewalks. He watched with detachment the blinking lights, which sparkled from every bodega. Banjee boys and girls modeled the latest in winter gear—turtleneck shirts that snuck out from underneath baggy sweaters that, in turn, were covered by thick long-sleeved shirts. Monstrous Triple Fat Goose coats boasting Fila, Nautica, and Polo topped these off. Balloon-like baggy jeans tucked inside Timberland boots and their fades and shaved heads hidden beneath baseball caps and puffy cotton hats. Sometimes they wore court-jester-like hats with bells ringing while beepers sounded off every five minutes drowned out by speeding cars, which blasted loud obnoxious rap songs.

Mothers carried large shopping bags full of gifts and toys avoiding the snowballs, which hurled playfully from one gang to another. The smell of marijuana crept up from the front porch steps while old women begged for money. It was Christmas in the South Bronx; Christmas 1992; Juan Carlos's last Christmas. He wondered if people lived every day knowing that they were going to die, would they still do all the stupid shit they did.

ENTERING JERUSALEM

The holiday season brought uncharacteristic warmth to the House of X. Damian, fresh off the heels of his 'divorce' from Hector, was now seriously chasing after a beefy Puerto Rican bartender named Cesar. Jorge was exclusively dating some nineteen-year-old member of the House of Latex and even Dominick, aware that Frankie only wanted to be left alone, was giving a famous male model the time of day. Everyone seemed to be paired off but Mikey.

Mikey had become too capricious and demanding about his men. He dated them all—black bodybuilders from the Bronx, roughneck Puerto Rican banjee boys from the projects, steroid-enhanced muscle queens from Chelsea, eccentric East Village white boy hipsters and artists.

Soon to be twenty-three-years-old, Mikey was beginning to panic. In almost five months, he would be twenty-three.

"Twenty-three!" he screamed.

He had never had a relationship that lasted more than a few months.

"I'm just too much of a fuckin' bitch!" Mikey told Alberto. "I need someone who's gonna slap me around and not take my shit! Otherwise, I'll just walk all over them!"

All the men Mikey met were either "not dominating enough" or "much too aggressive." Mean-looking daddies with a reputation for being sadistic would turn out inconceivably dedicated and lovable toward Mikey. They would become 'pussified' and expect him to take control while boys that promised to be loyal and wholesome turned out to be anything but. The madness that surrounded Mikey's life left him twisted and jaded. There was no satisfying him. He could have the most gorgeous, finely structured man sweating[71] him and be bored stupid.

They tried unsuccessfully to fix his attention upon them, wining and dining him incessantly in the most peculiar restaurants or fast food joints. Mikey felt like an oddball while they talked to him about modern art or the latest muscle gain. Mikey tried to keep up with them through his self-absorbed eyes while they tried desperately to break down the walls he built around himself. They all seemed eager to know the mysteries of his darker side but Mikey kept mum about his past. Some of them managed to stir something in Mikey but he never allowed them to get too close.

By mid-January, Mikey had saved up enough money to look for an apartment with a roommate. He was beginning to feel he had overstayed his welcome. Alberto and Joey were having problems of their own. They argued every day reinforcing Mikey's skepticism about relationships.

At work, Dan was also looking for a change of pace and someone to pay the other half of the rent in his large West Village railroad studio-loft. Half-desperate and half-blinded by Mikey's innocent smile, Dan asked Mikey if he would be interested in moving in with him.

The illegal commercial space was conveniently located above a 24-hour Korean deli featuring old wooden floors, brick walls, and two fireplaces. Redesigned in the early Sixties, the

71 Slang for being very attracted to someone or liking very much.

doors oddly shaped in upside-down V curves, were curiously reminiscent of the Star Trek emblem. The only bathroom, located in Dan's room all the way in the back after the kitchen, featured an antique toilet complete with pull-string to flush. The kitchen was large and spacious and included a washer and dryer. Almost a New York city street block down in length through a dark corridor was what Mikey would call his bedroom. Large windows on Mikey's side of the apartment opened up to a balcony-like fire escape, which overlooked the streets of Sixth Avenue between West Fourth and Washington Place. His own fireplace topped it all off and pin lights glowed a gloomy whisper of light onto the brick walls. Dominick lived only a few blocks away and Mikey could almost wave to him from his fire escape.

"Oh, I guess I should tell you! The reason the rent is dirt cheap aside from it being an illegal sublet and a commercial space is that it's supposedly haunted!" Dan smiled lavishly.

"Huh?"

"The woman who used to live here back in the Sixties died of a heroin overdose in this room while staring out this window!" he smiled, pointing at what would become Mikey's view of the world.

Mikey brilliantly glowed with excitement, "Ovah!"

The following week, Mikey was sitting on an old beat up couch from the Salvation Army staring out that same window with his characteristic smile. Magdalena had bought him a twin-size captain's bed, big enough for only him and maybe a teddy bear, indicating her unspoken distress over Mikey's sexual activities. Still he was grateful and knew she was slowly but surely coming to terms with his sexuality. The unfinished walls were covered with homoerotic black and white images of beefy naked men (gifts from some of the Chelsea Queens he had dated) while his own statue of St. Therese stood regally above the fireplace. She glowed happily over bright candles, fresh eggplants and an offering of bones.

To the side, Mikey built a small altar with tall plaster Catholic representations of Chango, Yemaya, Oshun, and Obbatala reigning ominously over offerings of apples, seashells, honey, and white eggshells respectively. Elegua, located by the entrance to Mikey's room, smiled up at him from the floor, flooded with toys, candies, cigars, and bottles of rum.

"I didn't realize I was renting the space out to a botanica" Dan half-joked.

Hanging from the ceiling of Mikey's room was a teddy bear that Juan Carlos had given him and Mikey had named UmFumFum, which supposedly meant pussy in some African language, according to an Eddie Murphy movie he had watched as a teen. UmFumFum was now bound in leather with a joint sticking out of his mouth.

Mikey had moved from Bushwick to the South Bronx to Riverdale to the West Village. He thought himself worldly simply because he had lived in different parts of New York City. He walked down the streets as if he owned them the way many before him had—blacks, whites, Latinos, Asians, Indians, Jews, Catholics, Muslims, Buddhists, Pagans, straights, gays.

Every race, religion, sex and culture was represented at least once somewhere on the streets of the Village unlike anywhere else Mikey had lived.

Mikey would cruise the streets, a sudden prisoner to a pair of eyes or a smooth face or an inviting smile. Warm waves of heat rose from the subway stations and the smell of marijuana and garbage lingered in the air. Taxicabs sped down the avenue past the basketball tournaments held in the small park near West Fourth Street. The piers, which Mikey now avoided like the plague, were only a few blocks away. There were restaurants, stores, dogs, cats, pigeons, and rats everywhere. Mikey was finally home.

It was five o'clock in the morning and Mikey was still lingering at The Sanctuary. Dominick was up in the deejay booth collaborating his musical madness with the new lighting boy who Mikey was flirtatiously trading glances with. The white banjee boy tried hard to focus on the beats to avoid Mikey's penetrating stare.

The lights bounced on and off, pin-lights reflecting off the disco-ball with spots of yellow, red, blue and green revolving around drunken faces, stoned faces, tired faces, hungry faces— all starving for that last-minute love. Mikey won the trophy in all categories—drunk, stoned, tired and above all, hungry. Fed up with his loneliness, Mikey was dying to meet someone to love again. He was not really expecting to pick anyone up this late. Loneliness clung to him, refused to let go, leaving Mikey afraid of going home alone.

It was not long before the sexy, green-eyed white boy who was working the lights came down to dance next to him. This time, Mikey was the shy one avoiding his stare. He was practically sitting on his tongue, dancing in front of Mikey who turned to look the other way. The boy casually danced over within Mikey's range. Mikey was unable to conceal a growing smile. Dancing his way over to him, Mikey had felt his warm breath brush against the back of his neck.

"You're one of Dominick's friends!" The white boy spoke with a jagged yet squeaky voice. Mikey was nonetheless charmed.

"Yeah, what of it?"

He was trying to come across as defensive. He realized that he had seen this boy many times before, especially the tattooed vines running down those milky white arms. Mikey remembered cruising that perfectly tweezed light brown mustache (a look he had once mocked Jorge for) and goatee surrounding his seductive smile before.

"What's your name?" he butched up his squeaky voice, making it tenser.

"Mikey! Mikey X from the House of X!" Mikey laughed at his own pretentious conceit.

"Oh? Really?" he responded before taking a bow and introducing himself, "Chris! Chris Infiniti from the House of Infiniti! Pleasure to meet ya!"

The dance floor had moved.

Mikey and Chris's first encounter was something of a scandal in New York City club land, not to mention an irony of senses. Members of two opposing Houses, much like the Capulets and the Montagues, together they quickly became one of the most notorious couples in club history (or at least in their own minds). It was West Side Story with Mikey cast as Maria.

"Mikey, what are you doing with that white boy?" Jerry asked, jolting Mikey's cool demeanor.

"Ay, hangeando con mi pato!" Mikey would respond facetiously.

"Hangeando? That's not even a word!"

"Yes it is! It's Spanglish[72] for 'hanging out'!"

---

72 Used extensively throughout this book, the code switching of English and Spanish words by people who speak both languages.

"You just made that up!"

"Yeah, I did! Whatever!"

At first, like budding rock stars, they presented each other with their best songs and dance—the most beautiful infectious rhythms recorded to perfection with lies and laughter to evade their fear of one another. Yet, slowly but surely, they revealed their selfish and vindictive ways. Chris constantly cursing himself for falling in love with Mikey, confused as to whether he wanted to grab and kiss or just slap the living shit out of him. Chris was terrified of Mikey's intentions and Mikey quickly became apprehensive to Chris's jealousy. The both of them, however, were madly in love—at last, truly, profoundly.

"I believe that for each soul, there is a mate. When these two souls find each other, they create love. A love that lasts through many lives" Chris would tell Mikey, who tried not to laugh at the corniness of his ethereal quote.

Chris was serious, insinuating that they had loved each other in a previous life and will love each other repeatedly through time. Chris would teach Mikey the beauty that belonged to gay lovers alone—how to properly shave. Soon enough, to the delight of Jorge, Mikey was sporting his own perfectly tweezed mustache and goatee. Between the hugs and kisses, however, they argued incessantly.

"What the fuck do you think you're doing? I saw you cruising that other guy!" Chris yelled at Mikey outside The Sanctuary one night after pulling him out of the club.

"Who? Eric Santiago? He's just a kid!" Mikey laughed.

"Yeah, whatever! You were all up in his face ready to tongue him down!"

"Bullshit! So, I think he's cute. Would you rather me lie?

Just because I already placed my order don't mean I can't look at the menu!"

"You know, you're such an asshole!"

"Yeah, and you're such a prick!" Mikey screamed back.

That night, Mikey and Chris had the best sex they ever had. Fights were essential to their being. Growing up and watching Emilio beat his mother brutally and Magdalena, in turn, beating Mikey had left his definition of love associated with some sort of violence. Chris had also come from an abusive family and harsh words had become habit. Making up became the sole purpose of their relationship. They were on-again, off-again so many times that Mikey had lost count.

During the on-again periods, they would form the words 'I Love You' with their lips in crowded subway cars and steal kisses from each other on the streets when no one was looking. Holding each other lovingly while looking out onto the Hudson River piers, they followed in the footsteps of many gay lovers before them now long dead.

Stimulating each other's arrogance, Mikey and Chris would have long conversations in bed, laughing at their ignorance, at their differences, both wanting only to conquer the world (or at least just the club scene).

"I want to be on every guest list and throw the fiercest parties!" Chris revealed one night.

"Is that all you want from life?" Mikey crunched his face.

"What more is there?"

"I dunno, but we can't be club kids forever."

"Why not?"

"'Cause we're not even kids anymore! We're like grown-ups, you know. There's more to life than just partying all the time." Mikey's eyes widened, "Did I just say that? Oh my God!

I sounded just like my cousin! Quick, get me some drugs!"

When they first met, Chris had insisted he was half Puerto Rican and half Irish but Mikey soon discovered that Chris was actually a hundred percent Jewish. Chris had also told Mikey he was twenty-three-years-old when he was actually twenty-eight.

"You're so full of shit!" Mikey teased him one evening, "But I love you anyway!"

"What are you talkin' about?"

"I went through your wallet while you were taking a shit and I found your driver's license. You're not twenty-three. You're twenty-eight and I thought you said your last name was Rodriguez. What the hell is Rubenstein?"

Mikey broke up with Chris that night but after only a week, took him back. This time around, however, Mikey had become increasingly defensive, giving off subconscious outbursts of insecurity. Mikey would brush off his incipient jealousy and suspicions, determined to have faith in the power of love. Mikey lingered on, reducing the relationship to mere divergence while catching on to more of Chris's petty lies and unintelligible carelessness. Chris eventually began projecting his guilt onto him and Mikey finally became restless with the relationship. By now, both of them were hurling words at each other older than the Bible. It was the perfect fight, the perfect match.

"You're just another white boy trying to pass as a Latino! You THINK you're fooling everybody with your fake tan! But you know, just because you adopt our characteristics and talk the talk doesn't mean that everybody can't see you're totally lost in the translation!"

"Yeah? Well, you're just another filthy pier queen who'll never make it past the West Side Highway! Without me, you're nothing! Do you hear me? You're NOTHING!" Chris yelled.

"Fuck you!"

"I'd say fuck you too but you've already fucked half of New York City!" Chris silenced Mikey down with this harsh reality.

"You asshole! I hate you!" The words 'I hate you!' venomously expelled through Mikey's clenched teeth while, for some strange reason, the words 'I love you!' still glistened in his eyes.

It was always like this until an occasional dry and lonely sob made them realize how much they hurt each other and reminded them of their love. Mikey often wondered if this is why Magdalena had stayed with Emilio for all these years.

Magdalena lay on her couch listening to the latest Luis Miguel CD. It seemed he put one out every other week. Her bleached blonde hair crumpled against a pillow and her face was still beautiful but now showing signs of aging. The years of stress and pain had wrinkled her soft light skin and she had gained some weight through the years. However, like most Latin men, Emilio found her sexier than ever. Her parakeets chirped loudly and viciously from their cage reminding her that she was all alone. Emilio was out visiting his kids.

She started to cry. It was sudden and uncontrollable. Magdalena had just gotten off the phone with Titi Yoli and found out that Chino was returning to New York. Her hand had trembled as she hung the phone up on the receiver and before collapsing to the floor, she managed enough strength to lay herself on the couch.

Chino had been deported years ago on multiple drug

charges. He had become the most ruthless drug dealer in Coney Island. It seemed like only yesterday that Titi Yoli had called Magdalena in tears to tell her Chino was being deported back to Ecuador. Magdalena had held back her tears of joy and vengeance.

All she could remember was the day Mikey had finally told her about the sexual abuse. They had not discussed the molestations or referred to them since. It was an unspoken understanding in their odd relationship. He would come over and visit her while Emilio was out and, despite so much to say, neither one of them ever made an effort to talk about any of it. It was almost as if it had never even occurred.

Had she even known that Chino was on trial several years ago, Magdalena would have been more than happy to testify against him. Titi was still in the dark about her son molesting Mikey. Magdalena wanted so much to tell her and have somebody to talk to but knew it would break her aunt's heart.

Titi Yoli was already dealing with Alberto's HIV status and Beto, who was now a grown man but still a child in need of being taken care of. Titi Yoli would already cry over the phone about all of her motherly hardships, not to mention Chino's drug bust and deportation. Mikey's molestation was their own suffering and she longed for the day they could both somehow come to terms with what had happened.

It was a Saturday and Magdalena remembered all those Saturday mornings when Miguelito would wake her up early to watch his cartoons. She would watch him as he gleamed innocently in front of The Super Friends and Bugs Bunny. Later, when he was older, he would wake up early to shower and run out of the apartment before she could even offer him a decent breakfast or some "corn flaks" like he would say. She would lie on the couch waiting for him angrily before he would be dropped off late from vehicles, which carried several people in two-passenger cars.

She lay on the couch where he used to sleep, where late at night or early in the morning, he would hear them arguing in the bedroom, where he would probably dream of other men. The day Miguelito had told her Chino had molested him was still fresh in her mind as if it was only yesterday that a part of her almost died with her son on that hospital bed.

Since he had left, Magdalena and Mikey hardly ever spoke about his experiences in the outside world. All that was left was the guilt and the memories of spanking Miguelito with her chancletas while he lay crying on the linoleum floor. She would yell at him at the top of her lungs, even if just to summon him for dinner in the one bedroom apartment. Miguelito would run to the kitchen only to be yelled at for walking barefoot. Her frustration with men had definitely been taken out on Mikey.

Even though he was now in her life again, she regretted the harsh reality that her son suffered through all of this while keeping the secret of his molestation to himself. Mikey was still angry with her for his turbulent childhood.

It was in the way he looked at her, in his tone of voice, in the silence, which prevailed every time he came over to visit. His personal life was a complete mystery to her and they were about as close as New York and Ecuador. His visits were always brief and distant. Their relationship appeared to have died that day on the hospital bed after he had tried to take his life. All that was left was a ghost that came over to haunt her with an innocent smile and a fusion of love and hatred in his eyes.

She had finally given up on the possibility of a girl in his life, which he would have many children with and marry. She only longed for a child to hold; to start all over again; to protect from the world, from the people, from Chino.

Her soft black eyes remained misty with tears and the shadows of a dream pervaded her loneliness. Miguelito smiled back at her from a high school picture. She was afraid to touch him, to hold him, to tell him she was sorry. If only she had known about Chino, things might have been different.

Her caged parakeets sang happily, as Magdalena noticed the picture of Christ, which hung above their metal prison. For the first time in a very long while, Magdalena started to pray.

Through Chris, Mikey met a host of club personalities far more colorful than those he already knew.

Janet, a loud-mouthed Puerto Rican transsexual prostitute, lived down the hall from the Chelsea hostel where Chris was staying. Even though Janet was a member of the House of X, Mikey had only recently started hanging out with her. Barely nineteen, Janet featured naturally long luscious black hair to bring out her feminine curves. Janet's street-tough smile revealed a few missing teeth lost in trying to pass herself off as a real woman in the meat packing district of the West Village. She was always in a bustier and cut off shorts. Janet would yell at the drivers and grab her crotch while massaging her implants seductively.

On Saturday nights (or more like early Sunday mornings), Janet religiously attended The Sanctuary mass. She was often getting into trouble for beating up some banjee girl who dared look at her the wrong way. Janet only dated the fiercest roughneck banjee boys that liked to get their dicks sucked off by 'girls' like her. The bugarrones loved Janet and came out of the woodwork for her titties and mangina[73].

Chris also introduced Mikey to Marsha Milan who, years ago, had been Mother of the House of Milan. Marsha was now a homeless transvestite working the piers for her next meal. She was always running around with her, "Oooh honey, chile! I is stahvin'! I'd do anythin' fo' a dahlah!"

Mikey and Chris would usually invite her to eat with them or buy her food. Sometimes they would leave her with a joint.

"Gawd bless ya sowls!" she would say, her ashy dry skin crumbling like aluminum foil to form a fearless smile that had once snatched many trophies at the Harlem balls.

Then there was Ernesto—the most fascinating one of them all. Mikey already knew him from the House of X's Tuesday night drug parties at Dominick's apartment but what he did not know was that they would all eventually end up working for him.

Ernesto was the most notorious drug dealer in the New York City gay club circuit. A handsome, twenty-two-year-old Puerto Rican from the Bronx, Ernesto dealt drugs in only the most popular clubs. The Sanctuary was his home base. He sold 'designer drugs'—coke, K, ecstasy, crystal meth—no marijuana, or crack.

"That's so ghetto! I don't take welfare checks!" he would say.

Liquid K and steroids were also available upon request.

Ernesto knew where the money was. The white muscle boys who always talked so much shit about the little Puerto Rican drug dealers were always the first ones to buy drugs from him. Ernesto knew they looked down on him for being a dealer

---

73 The vagina of a male to female transsexual. However, this term is also used as a slang term among gay men referring to their assholes.

but, "If it weren't for them tired white faggots, I would be out of business!" They would flirt with him, buy him drinks, and sometimes even let Ernesto fuck them if he wanted to. They would do anything for his drugs.

In fact, Ernesto had slept with nearly half The Sanctuary. He knew exactly what size their dicks were and what they liked to do in bed before anyone would even work up enough nerve to ask for details about a guy. Ernesto was no stranger to the sex scene and bragged glowingly about sleeping with every hustler and porn star in the city.

Cruising the local party magazines to see which ones were in from out of town, Ernesto always had some beefy bare-chested escort fetching him water and cigarettes. He was the archetypal drug dealer, only gay. Faces were always being confused with others so Mikey did not even bother getting to know any of Ernesto's pieces.

Ironically, Ernesto never touched alcohol in spite of all the free drink tickets he was showered with at the door. He preferred hiding out in the bathroom stools to do bumps of coke and K.

"People try to take advantage of ya when they think ya drunk! Sometimes I pretend ta be just ta see who tries to fuck wit' me!" he would say while sober from alcohol but shit-faced from drugs.

"Then what?" Mikey would ask.

"Then I smoke 'em!" he would smile devilishly, proud of his notoriety. Ernesto's tendency for petty revenge and exhibitionism made him irresistible to Mikey.

With that same tough banjee exterior, he would turn around and yell, "Ay que lindo! Don't you just wanna put him in your pocket?" running to chase after some scared little Puerto Rican boy. Ernesto's femininity inevitably reeked through his thick layers of ghetto gear canceling out his masculine image with coy gestures and suggestive passes.

Ernesto also had a strong undying passion for Broadway theatre. His favorite musical was "Les Miserables," which he went to see every other week, usually a Sunday matinee straight from The Sanctuary. He would sit there, one of the most wanted criminals in New York City, singing whole-heartedly to every song with a handkerchief in hand from his private balcony seat.

His penthouse apartment in Chelsea was always filled with steroid-injecting prostitutes and boys from out of town.

"Who's that?" Mikey asked one day, accidentally stepping on some muscular white boy sprawled out unconsciously on Ernesto's floor.

"Oh! That's Little Rock! Don't mind him! He's been there for like two days!"

One day, Mikey and Chris together with Ernesto and Janet rented a car and the four of them traveled to Washington, D.C. for the weekend. Chris, the designated driver, was the only one not doing bumps of K in the backseat during the whole trip. A recovering coke addict, Chris watched as they enjoyed the powdery poison, which would lapse them into the excitement of childhood with occasional laughter punctuating the air.

Staring intensely out the window, they seemed mesmerized by everything they passed, wowing astounded at buildings they had seen millions of times before. They had never before noticed the 'unique structures' and 'immense proportions.' Lost in their insanity while Chris dangerously sped through the highways, their heads snapped back like Pez dispensers every time he would step on the gas to go faster.

"Wait! Wait! Stop da cah! Pull ovah!" Janet screeched after joyfully discovering a Friendly's restaurant along the highway.

"I want a cheeseburgah with French fries and a Diet Coke!" Ernesto demanded as Chris nervously pulled up to the parking lot.

Janet raced out of the car in red patent leather, three-inch pumps, hopping excitedly toward the entrance, titties bouncing.

"Well done!" Ernesto added, Mikey chasing after Janet without asking Chris if he wanted anything.

Once inside, the world stopped spinning and all eyes rested on Janet. Janet slowed her pace down to a snake-like slither, caressing her voluptuous butt-cheeks, which popped out from tight denim short shorts. Tossing back her exquisite hair with long luscious nails painted Yummy Red. Janet strutted her way through the restaurant. Left. Right. Left. Right. Left. Right. Left.

"Eh-Q me! Do chu have a ladies room?"

Mouths dropped. Faces fell. Heads turned.

"Toward the back, to your left!" a young man's prepubescent voice nervously answered from behind the register.

"Wai tank'u!"

Left. Right. Left. Right. Left. Right. Left.

"Ooops! Dropped my gum!" Janet giggled impishly while purposely spitting her gum out on the floor, bending over ever so slowly to pick it up.

Her implants hung out of the tube top like a dozen roses making eyes gleam, lips curve, and dicks rise. Janet tossed her hair back once again, licking the gum back into her mouth.

Pulling it out through her teeth like a rubber band, she laughed excitedly at the success of her own deceit.

Left. Right. Left. Right. Left. Right. Left.

Janet stopped somewhere between the men's and the ladies room, looking back to give a look of confusion as if to arouse suspicion; giving them a full minute before opening one of the wooden doors.

"I like to pee standing up!" Janet smiled back to her audience before disappearing into the men's room.

The only sound heard was Mikey's delirious laughter behind thick black sunglasses.

"I'll have four cheeseburgers with French fries and four Diet Coke's to go please. Oh, and a caramel sundae with nuts for the lady!"

Another time, they were all hanging out on Mikey's fire escape—whistling, yelling, screaming, and harassing the boys walking down Sixth Avenue with their girlfriends. Mikey was arguing with Chris as usual when Janet started screaming out, "Over there! Catch it! Catch it!"

They all turned simultaneously to spot Steve, the bouncer from The Sanctuary, appearing from around the corner flaunting his muscular body with a tight, white tank top tucked inside a pair of loose baggy jeans.

"Ay papi! Estas tan chulo[74]!" Janet yelled brazenly. "Mira! Mira!" she waved, trying desperately to get his attention. "Yoo-hoo, papi!"

Steve smiled back politely to look up from down below as Ernesto began, "Girlfriend, he could turn me out any day! His

74 A Spanish word that loosely means pimp but is used mostly in reference to an attractive man. It is also used in reference to something that is cute. *Chula* is the feminine use of the word.

shit is mad fly, yo! Did you catch the size of his bulge?"

Janet was gone.

"Where the fuck did she go?" Ernesto asked as Mikey and Chris stared at each other, puzzled.

"I guess Janet bounced early kid!" Mikey playfully gave his best banjee effect.

"I'm gonna fuck that bitch up one of these days!" Ernesto continued with a childish whine, which undercut his threat.

From the corner of his eye, Chris spotted Janet running down the street, "Look! There she goes!"

Janet dashed after Steve in her patent leather open-toe pumps, turning back to make sure they noticed while she laughed insanely.

"Get him Janet! Spray him! Spray him!" Mikey giggled.

Between the drugs, partying and decadent friends, Mikey hardly ever took the time to visit his mother and think about his past. He was so distracted by the insanity of his life that nothing else in the world mattered more than getting stoned and hanging out with his friends. Mikey embraced the amnesia.

Mikey could not trust Chris as far as he could throw him. Nonetheless, he still loved him and was, by all means, unstable. He convinced himself that he did not care that Chris had lied to him about most everything—his age, his background, his last name.

"So! Is there anything else I should know about you?" Mikey taunted him.

"What are you talkin' about?"

"Well, maybe you were once a woman. Or maybe you're like some crazed serial killer and they're gonna find my head in the fridge one day with really bad frostbite!"

"That's not funny, Mikey!" Chris yelled.

"No, but do you wanna know what is funny? That you think I'm so stupid I'd believe anything you tell me!"

Chris was not a good liar. Every time Mikey would confront him about his deceit, Chris would swallow or choke on his own defense. He would fall to pieces.

What bothered Mikey was how incredibly facetious Chris was. Chris promised Mikey many things, none of which ever materialized.

"I'd love to take you to Europe! You would love England!"

"When should I pack my bags?"

"It might be too much of a culture shock for you though, considering all you've ever known is Bushwick and the West Side Highway!"

"Ugh! You're so fuckin' tacky!"

"I'm not the one who used to sell myself at the piers!"

He always made Mikey out to be inferior to him the way Emilio used to make Magdalena feel. Chris always told Mikey that he was "NOBODY" and was used to dating little Spanish boys who allowed themselves to be controlled. Chris never once raised a hand to hit Mikey but his words and air of superiority were enough to make Mikey feel abused. In spite of the continued dysfunction, Mikey remained with Chris.

They argued incessantly. With each quarrel, they killed everything they had together. Chris was naturally insecure about Mikey's history as a hustler and eventually began to distance himself. Chris began to find his solace in street trade and sex clubs only to feel worse when it was over.

With the intent of going into a sex theater, Chris would walk up and down the block, making sure nobody he knew was in the neighborhood. Baseball caps bent over strange faces, downcast to suggest their shame. They would pass each other invitingly. Chris prowled near the entrance to see if any cute boys would walk in so that he could follow and suck them off in a booth.

Inside, the smell of urine and disinfectant engulfed the theater while eyes adjusted to the sudden darkness. Men desperately tossed each other needful glances while waiting for an inviting smile, an attractive body, or an exposed penis to call them down to their knees. Strangers feasted on one another or walked with studied casualness. Shadows floated around hungrily, sometimes recognizing one another as someone in the club scene, someone's lover, or someone's husband. However, they never acknowledged each other as individuals and only spoke in groans while on Ecstasy, cocaine, acid or AZT. The only voices were those of porn stars who filled the movie screen.

Mikey ran into Chris at one of these notorious sex theaters.

"What the fuck are you doin' here?" Mikey demanded.

"Mikey!"

"You filthy son-of-a-bitch!"

"What are you doing here?"

"You left me at The Sanctuary and told me you were going home. I went to look for you. Of course, you weren't there!"

"Well, how'd you know I was here?"

"Are you really that stupid, Chris? Do you know how many people we know between the two of us? The New York City gay club scene is not as big as you think it is! It wasn't so hard to track you down after making a few phone calls! What the fuck are you gonna tell me now? Are you gonna tell me you got lost?"

"I was just tagging along with some friends from out of town. I wasn't gonna do anythin', I swear!"

"Yeah? Then why is your shirt all open? How come you're walking around exposing your fuckin' scrawny chest?"

Mikey grabbed him by the ear and dragged him out of the club as the other queens quickly dodged into the darkness in fear they too might be caught by their boyfriends.

It was there and then Mikey realized that what he found in Chris was his own reflection. Mikey had whored around all his life searching for some meaning to his life through sex. He remembered Alex telling him about homosexuals being like vampires as men emerged from the shadows.

CURSING OF THE FIG TREE

The early morning of Easter Sunday, the subway station was filled with hung-over, partied-out teenagers coming from parties lasting until morning or still going on. Smelly strung out bums also hid underground from the crashing rays of the bright early sun. These were the only creatures alive besides the man behind the token booth and those cleaning the platforms.

Headlights gleaming on the rusty metal tracks and a sudden roar signaled the arrival of the train. Mindlessly, the awaiting flock of slaughtered lambs stumbled onto the subway cars clashing drastically against the array of little girls in Easter bonnets and churchgoers who stared in horror and disbelief.

Dark sunglasses and bright sunny smiles came face to face as homeless bums scattered around for a place to sleep. Their treacherous odors enough to peel ads off the wall and destroy the holiday spirit.

Chris sat hidden behind a pair of shades unbothered next to one of them. He yawned, stretching his mouth to reveal the damage years of cocaine can cause to teeth while Mikey stared lifelessly from across. Chris was drunk and Mikey was stoned yet again.

Through his high, Mikey envisioned St. Therese getting on the train and accommodating herself next to Chris opposite from where he sat. The silver steel of the subway was not flattering to her brown and beige robe and she smiled with her cross and pink roses. She seemed intent on saying something

193

to Mikey but he could not understand what she was trying to say.

She faded slowly as the train struggled to the next stop. A few stops later and Mikey forgot all about her, vaguely remembering catching Chris making out with some guy in a dark corner of The Sanctuary. Chris stared back at him silently with ears still ringing and lights still flashing on his face. Mikey felt the Ecstasy slightly wearing off as the train pulled into the next station.

Even more strung-out, drugged up, party leftovers stumbled in, along with a fat woman wearing a purple jumper, which made her look like Barney[75]. She sat removed, wearing a ferocious look on her face wide-awake with anger.

While Barney pretended to read the Bible, those who had not found a piece for the night continued to hunt and cruise each other with drained faces. Attitudes collided and children with puffy eyes glared wickedly at younger children in pastel Easter colors. Barney began to read from the Bible aloud urging a group of pier queens on the train to begin yelling at her.

A young police officer stepped in from the other car, handsome and radiant in his uniform, smiling at the women and waking up the bums. Barney and the pier queens quieted down. For a brief moment, Mikey wondered about Officer Williams as the young cop casually strutted to the next car.

This is when Mikey caught Chris drooling unabashedly as the cop disappeared, probably imagining the young police officer naked with his chiseled chest and big nipples. He seemed not to care that Mikey was staring at him. Chris no longer even hid the fact that he longed for the taste of somebody else's dick.

---

75 A purple anthropomorphic Tyrannosaurus Rex popular with children in the '90's who conveyed learning through song and dance.

"You fuckin' prick!" Mikey seethed before lunging over to slap Chris dead in the face. "To think I actually loved you!"

Chris stared back in disbelief behind his sunglasses, grinning nervously. He had hoped that Mikey would at least wait until they got home to have this argument.

"Tu eres una sucia!" Mikey continued, turning all heads including Barney. "In front of my own face! How could you? How could you do this to me?"

Chris held himself back. Barney was mortified. The queens became rowdy. The churchgoers gagged.

"Tell me! Tell me! How could you?" Mikey grabbed Chris by the jacket and shook him violently as if to wake him from his sudden stupor. This time there was something else to the tone of his voice.

Barney got up to get the police officer in the next car while one of the pier queens yelled out, "Work! Let him have it!"

"Tu no eres nada!" Mikey continued in his best dramatic telenovela moment, "You hear me? NADA! You are nothing!"

Once the train pulled into the next station, in his drug-induced frenzy, Mikey ran out leaving behind another shattered soul on the subway. The love affair between Mikey and Chris was over.

THE TEMPLE INCIDENT

That night, the House of Infiniti held a ball at the Marc Ballroom in celebration of the Easter holiday. Every House in New York City, old and new, showed up to compete in the brutal display of arrogance and shade. As traditional, "The Ha Dance" by Masters at Work boomed from the sound systems. During the Grand March, the children from the House of Infiniti hid their vicious eyes behind thick shades and featured painted whiskers and Easter bunny ears, crudely flinging jellybeans out into the audience.

It all almost ended in a riot when someone threw a rotten egg on stage at Chris toward the end of the House of Infiniti Grand March. Though rumors made Mikey X out to be the culprit, none of the members of the House of X was thrown out and they were still allowed to walk the categories.

Queens screamed out "Get huh!", "Chop huh!" and "Slaughter huh!" as each House fought against each other for the tall beautiful trophies laid out inside Easter baskets filled with chocolate bunnies, jellybeans and colored eggs.

Mikey X won a trophy as usual for Schoolboy Realness, where he emerged freshly-shaven and featured a new Caesar-like fade adding youth to his already tender years. He walked down the runway in his baggy oversized gear carrying a book-bag on his back while sucking a lollipop and bouncing a handball.

"Ay nene, te botastes!" Janet X told him later that night

after winning trophies for Banjee Girl Realness and Femme Face herself.

Princess, the newest transsexual member of the House of X, snatched the trophy for Schoolgirl Realness in her Catholic school uniform complete with knee-high socks, knickers, pigtails and a Dukes of Hazard lunch-box. Princess later walked away with another trophy for Best Runway with Crucifix.

Damian bitterly won only two trophies himself, both in the voguing categories. He beat out Flaca from the House of Pendavis in Best Vogue the New Way but lost big to him for Best Floor Work Vogue. Damian gleamed when Flaca was disqualified in the Butch Queen Arm Control category. He vogued joyfully and easily won his second trophy for the evening.

"The category is butch queen! Butch queen! Not just queen. BUTCH queen" the emcee yelled before Flaca walked away spewing obscenities.

The war between the House of X and the House of Pendavis was officially on.

A few days later, Padrino called Mikey to tell him Juan Carlos was back in the hospital with full-blown AIDS and this time he was laying in his deathbed for sure. In between the partying and K holes, Mikey only brought himself to visit him once. Only a week later, Mikey found himself at Juan Carlos's funeral. It was a warm May afternoon when they buried him. The sun gleamed down harshly on the multitude of black surrounding his burial place. The fiery rays penetrated through Mikey's suit as the priest rambled like a character in a Charlie Brown cartoon.

Dominick, Jorge, and Damian joined Mikey at the vast

cemetery, none of them listening to the priest's sermon behind their stolen collection of designer sunglasses.

Padrino stood next to Mikey, unrecognizable as the man he had once admired. It turned out that he too was HIV-positive. He stared at the coffin as if imagining himself there soon.

Behind the drooping black shades he wore loosely around his face, Mikey fought unsuccessfully to hold back the tears that streamed down his tanned skin. He had never prepared himself for this day and in spite of all the misery and pain Juan Carlos had brought him, Mikey never wanted to see him dead. Truth told, he still loved him and no drugs in the world could numb him from this fact.

He almost felt his presence there haunting him as if they had never left the streets of the South Bronx. Mikey remembered Juan Carlos telling him, "I motherfuckin' love you, ah-ight, kid!" with that gorgeous smile Mikey had always been a sucker for.

"When people die, they become one with nature," Padrino would tell them every time somebody on one of the telenovelas was killed off while having his Cafe Bustelo, which he had after every meal.

"Well, when I die, you will always find me in the wind," Juan Carlos would turn to Mikey, making that funny pointing thing with his nose toward Padrino meaning he thought Padrino was insane. When Mikey would look at him confused, Juan Carlos would use his lips for emphasis.

Mikey searched through the crowd in hopes of finding Juan Carlos smiling back at him from behind a tree like the night he found him lurking underneath the bleachers. Instead, he rested on Juan Carlos's stunning black eyes, wet with tears, staring back at him from behind a black veil—Juan Carlos's mother, crying over the death of her only son. Behind her lay clusters of crucifixes and tombstones with the city emerging far in the distance.

A light breeze wrapped itself gently around Mikey's feet, rustling up dried leaves.

THE PASSION

Mikey looked down on the city streets from his rooftop and noticed the night featured cloudy skies and a mysterious fog surrounding the top of the Empire State Building. The cold breeze crept up his flannel boxer shorts. The irritating crash of rusted metal from the subway trains echoed from way down below the concrete pavements cutting into his heart.

He looked out onto the heavy traffic. For every two cars, he counted a taxicab. They were bright yellow colors parading down the avenue. People were still out, shopping and walking around the restless city. It was a beautiful night but it was getting windy. Mikey realized he was not wearing any socks and wondered if anyone could see him from the lit windows on the murky West Village buildings. He felt a chill race down his pelvic area as he looked up toward the sky while standing on the edge.

Mikey was scared of heights and wondered why he was standing on the edge. The thought of peeing became so overwhelming that he had to walk over to the rooftop door and unleashed a steady stream of urine instead of simply going back down to the apartment.

Mikey lit a joint and stared out at the New York skies with no stars for him to see. Everything was cloudy and gray. Reaching over, he lit the citronella candle he had used to climb the lightless stairs. It came in a metal bucket and Mikey watched as it created a light around the darkness. Like the breeze that made the candle flicker and the flame grow tall, Mikey felt a sudden rush of loneliness.

The wind played on his bare feet as the first teardrop fell from his eyes. Mikey was consumed with how fucked up his life had been. Maybe he was just suffering withdrawals from the drugs but Juan Carlos's death had brought him back full circle to that pain he longed to forget. Mikey wanted the memories to fade into the darkness but Juan Carlos's smile kept haunting him to an unusual extent.

The candle blew out and the wind soothed him, temporarily lifting him from his emptiness. Beginning to cough, he thought maybe he should not be out in the bitter cold in his boxer shorts. However, Mikey felt dead inside and did not care about the fact he was freezing his balls.

"That bastard!" Mikey heard himself say.

The sound of his own voice startled him. Mikey bowed his head to weep, feeling lost and insecure. He wanted to die, maybe come back to a new life, a completely new existence.

He remembered his only visit to Juan Carlos in the hospital and the crazed look of fear in Juan's eyes. Juan Carlos had broken many hearts with his sensual smile and rough, masculine features but he had been left to nothing but bright yellow skin on bones. All Mikey could remember from that day were his eyes filled with fear. Juan cried for help, for some salvation while his mouth, covered by respirators, filled with fungus. There were tubes in his chest and his penis because he had no control over his bodily functions. Piss and diarrhea had covered the bed sheets and Juan Carlos trembled violently with a fever of almost 120 degrees.

The door squealed and Mikey looked up in horror. His bare feet were now icy and yet Mikey felt detached from them.

"Why? Why?" he cried aloud, destroying the notion that this was just a bad dream.

Mikey wanted to run down the pitch-black corridors in search of something, anything to take away the pain but all he could do was cry. "Pull ya'self together!" he told himself.

Lifting himself, he searched his flannel pockets for his only escape, which he had been trying to avoid. Twisting the cap off, Mikey poured himself a large bump of K. He snorted it quickly before the wind would blow it away. Walking back to the ledge, he lit himself another joint and smoked it lavishly.

He no longer felt scared as he looked down to the city streets. He no longer felt cold. The Ketamine began to take over and the yellow taxicabs became giant bumblebees flaring down the avenue.

Swerving through traffic, a bike sped by causing Mikey to burst into laughter. He remembered the time he was with Juan Carlos when his bike was nearly stolen. They had been arguing outside their South Bronx building, probably about some guy—the bike parked by a fire hydrant. Not knowing that Mikey was watching, some crack head started walking away with it.

Mikey chased him down the street screaming curses. The thief, scared, tossed the bike aside and ran for his life but not before Mikey had taken a big gulp of saliva and spat in his face. Mikey drove away only to be hit on the back of his head with a can of Vienna sausages.

Mikey had fallen to the ground only to have the thief, spit dripping down his face, grab the bike and smash it down on him.

He listened to himself laugh in his loneliness as the rest of the K kicked in. Flying cans of Vienna sausages and bikes hurdled at him as he pulled out the vial to snort two more bumps. His nose felt tender and soft. The powder ran down his throat like aspirin and his eyes began to melt.

Yawning, he walked away from the ledge unaware he had stumbled and almost fallen onto the streets of the West Village. Once again feeling anxious, memories of Juan Carlos raced through his mind as he walked down the stairs back to his botanica-like apartment. Dan had recently taken in a stray cat, which waited patiently behind the door. The cat meowed as Mikey kicked him gently back into the kitchen. Mikey grabbed a bag of chips as he paved his way toward his room where one of Dominick's house tapes still pounded away. Now irritating him, Mikey hit the stop button and plunged himself onto the worn couch.

Drug-induced images raced through his mind—flashes of his sexual abuse; bikes hurdling at him; Magdalena beating him; Juan Carlos dead; getting fucked by Juan Carlos. When Juan Carlos would fuck Mikey, he would stare into his eyes as if pounding that memory deep into Mikey's soul with every thrust. He would fuck Mikey so hard that the condom would often break. Mikey tried to remember if Juan Carlos ever came inside of him with a broken condom.

The next night, the taxis drove by pretending not to notice Mikey, Janet, and Damian. The cabs scurried on as if they did not exist. The trio flagged them down, whistling, ready to show a little leg if they had to. The taxicabs ignored them completely. Some slowed down, took a quick look, and then dashed off. They had been waiting for at least a half hour as millions of yellow cabbies paraded down Sixth Avenue never stopping for them.

A straight white couple stepped up to the corner next to

them. Instantaneously, a taxi pulled up in front of them. The couple ran in and the cab raced off.

"You fuckin' prick!" Damian chased after it.

Another couple, this time two white men, stepped up to the corner. A black taxi driver pulled up at their feet.

"Back up, queens!" Damian yelled, jumping into the back seat.

Janet pushed the two guys aside and sat next to Damian followed by Mikey. The driver asked them to get out in his harsh Jamaican accent.

"Whaddaya mean get out?" Mikey slammed the door.

"I'm no going your way!" he insisted.

"All you have to do is drive forward!" Damian demanded, snapping his fingers simultaneously with the word 'forward'.

The irate cabbie stepped on the gas and cursed them underneath his breath.

"We're going to The Sanctuary! Do you know where that is?" Damian pressed, noticing a photograph of a much younger, thinner face than the driver in front of them above the glove compartment.

The driver nodded as Mikey quietly looked out the window.

"Can I ask you a simple question?" Damian pushed himself all the way forward. "You're black just like me aren't ya?" Damian insisted.

Before the cabbie could even respond to the first question, Damian asked, "Why, if you're black and I'm black, didn't you wanna pick me up?"

The question bounced around inside the car and their ears perked up anxiously awaiting to hear his explanation. The driver mumbled unintelligibly as their faces crumbled with confusion. All they heard was something like "Da luke! Da luke!"

"What?" Damian screeched.

"It's da luke! Da luke!"

"Oh, you mean 'the look'?"

The driver nodded again while going on incomprehensibly about "Peep-ole like shoo!"

"People like who?" Janet blew up.

"Bitch, you don't know us from a can of paint!" Damian added while Mikey leaned back in his corner aware that the driver was in for trouble.

"Peep-ole like shoo ..." Damian repeated mockingly, "... are the reason people like us are so fucked up!"

Damian's nose flared and the gold stud pierced into his left nostril looked like it was ready to pop. The cabbie tried desperately and unsuccessfully to explain himself.

"No! No! Shoo luke like bad peep-ole! No luke right. No luke good!"

Damian turned to Mikey and Janet, "I don't need this shit! Let's get out of here!"

When the driver pulled up to a red light, they opened the door and got out. Janet hopped away teasingly singing "You're gonna get it! You're gonna get it!" Damian slammed the door ferociously and walked around to the driver's seat. He opened up his pocketknife and pulled it out while reaching in to grab the cabbie by the neck with his other hand. Yanking him through the window, Damian placed the side of his switchblade on his cheek.

"You are ..." Damian slashed the driver's cheek with his switchblade, "... a prejudiced asshole!"

The cabbie screamed in horror as Damian smiled savagely, "That's from one brother to another!"

FLAGELLATION

Chris was still harassing Mikey. He was now showing up unexpectedly at the bookstore while Mikey was working and demanding a conversation about the egg incident. Mikey simply ignored him until Dan or Sista Mama would ask Chris to leave by threatening to call the police.

One day, Chris stopped by to annoy Mikey at the bookstore once again while Mikey was working a Saturday shift. Mikey had just gotten off the phone with Dominick who had seen Chris at the piers making out with some hustler only a few hours ago.

The minute Chris stepped into the bookstore; he was greeted instead by Mikey yelling. Something in Mikey had snapped and Chris, scared, tried to leave but Mikey followed him outside.

"That's bullshit! I wasn't making out with no hustler!" Chris insisted.

Mikey had had enough. The more Mikey looked into Chris's face, the more he realized how much Chris reminded him of Emilio.

"How could you? You filthy bastard! You come to my job and annoy the shit of me while I'm trying to work and the whole time you're picking up hustlers at the pier? You're more fucked up than I thought and, yeah, I threw that egg at you at the ball! You're lucky it was only an egg, you motherfucker!" Mikey screamed loud enough for everybody to hear from inside the bookstore.

"Oh, no he didn't show up again to the bookstore!" Sista Mama said, calling the others to watch while drinking her cup of coffee.

Mikey was waving his hands in Chris's face while everyone inside the bookstore joined to watch the commotion outside.

"That boy needs to get his ass kicked!" Sista Mama added.

"Oh, come on! Dominick just saw you at the piers! Not that I really care who you are fucking these days but you need to leave me alone! I'm going through enough shit right now and I've had it with you! I've had it with you, you hear me?"

Before he knew it, Mikey had punched him in the face. It was unexpected and seemed quite natural.

Chris turned back, only to be punched again and feel his wisdom tooth crack. Mikey went on to kick him in the groin.

"You go, girl!" Sista Mama screamed as the others joined in.

Mikey pushed Chris to the ground and kicked him in the face as he crawled on the street with blood spurting from his mouth. He went to kick him once more before realizing what he was doing.

Sista Mama stopped cheering as Chris stared up at Mikey. Disgusted with himself and disgusted by him, Mikey sucked up one huge gulp of saliva, which seemed to rise all the way from his feet and *FUA!* The fluid landed all over his horrified face as Mikey turned to run away as fast as he could. Mikey looked back. Chris just lay there. A massive gob of spit dripped down his bloodied face. It was Magdalena on the floor and he had become Emilio.

That night, Julee Cruise echoed from Mikey's radio. He

was once again alone up on his rooftop. The music made Mikey feel spiritual and at peace with himself. From his rooftop, he could smell something sweet flowing from someone's kitchen. He was able to make out pancakes.

Mikey glanced down at the people and traffic running along Sixth Avenue. He then focused on the empty roof, the cloudy skies, and the buildings glowing in the distance like huge candles. Mikey watched the clouds move majestically, hiding heaven from his eyes. Sometimes, if he stared up long enough, he thought he could catch glimpses of God smiling down at him.

The sweet smell of pancakes haunted him. Juan Carlos would sneak out of bed sometimes and cook pancakes while he slept. Mikey would wake up to the sweet smell, pouring syrup all over them before kissing Juan Carlos sweetly on the lips. Sometimes he would glaze syrup all over his lips before kissing him.

He took out his vial of K and snorted a few bumps. Soon, the night became darker and the music became haunting. Mikey's heart pounded along with the escalating music as the night became morbid and grey. God laughed at him from up above.

Mikey decided to go out that night and returned at 11:45 on Sunday morning tremendously trashed from The Sanctuary. His ears were still ringing as he sat by his window. Staring out the window, Mikey heard a faint music in the background. Maybe he heard the sounds from the passing cars or maybe he still heard the occasional laughter and unintelligible screams from the club ringing in his ears.

People were either out shopping early or on their way to church. Because it was a bright and sunny morning, he thought about going to the roof and falling asleep there to wake up crisp like bacon.

Mikey had taken a Red Devil, a red dyed hit of acid, and smoked about three joints. He had taken about twice that amount in bumps of K and felt like a disastrous mess on the verge of a massive crash. An eerie depression dawned over him. It held him down onto the chair by the window as he stared helplessly outside. Mikey caught a glimpse of his reflection on the window. He looked crazed as he admired the numbness in his mouth.

His knee leaned too hard against the windowsill, yet he pushed harder. Mikey did not feel anything. He thought about Ricky high on crack. Is this what he felt like when he got high? Mikey was sweating and yet shivering at the same time. He shook uncontrollably.

Raising his hand up to his face, Mikey watched it quiver. He did not recognize his own hand and was unable to make the quivering stop.

He remembered Jerry was hosting a tambor that day in honor of Oyá but Mikey could not find his way to the phone. He wanted to call Jerry to apologize for not making it. He knew he would sleep all day without even calling Magdalena to tell her he was not coming over to visit as he had promised.

It would just be another wasted Sunday. Mikey would be a useless wreck for the rest of the week. He allowed his mind to travel aimlessly as he closed his eyes and fell asleep on the couch.

He only prayed not to be haunted by the memories of his past; his childhood; Chino; Emilio; Ricky; Juan Carlos; Chris.

The church was quiet and solemn. The statues, handcrafted

beautifully in Italy, glowed radiantly above the small candles, which lit the church. Shadows created sinister smiles on their finely featured faces. Their eyes followed him as he walked to the altar and a faint chant echoed from the walls. A light breeze crept in from underneath the wooden doors as he watched Christ crucified at the altar. Christ watched him, as he got closer with terror in his porcelain eyes. Mikey held a shining gun in his hands that sparkled from the glow of the candles. The eyes of Christ widened with every step Mikey took. Each step reverberated in the emptiness as he reached the altar and stared scornfully up at Him.

In the morning, his body would be discovered lying at the altar, dead at His feet. Christ looked down helplessly at Mikey as he did all the times Chino would fuck him up the ass. Mikey had prayed all those times for Him to lunge off that cross and save him from the beast that pierced his soul. Mikey laughed insanely in midst of his confusion and through his tears searched deeply into Christ's eyes. He longed for some explanation; some last minute salvation.

"Whhhyyyyyy?" Mikey fell to his knees as tears leaked down his face.

He raised the gun up to his mouth realizing it was heavier than he had expected. Shadows lurked restlessly through the pews as Mikey wrapped his lips around the cold metal. His body would now be free to fall off the cross he had carried all his life. He imagined lying limp on the ground with red streaks of blood which would race out to their freedom.

Suddenly, one incredible gush of wind kicked the church doors wide open and raced through him.

Mikey shrieked before running out of the church as fast as he could.

Dominick and Mikey sat at the piers with glazed eyes and a morbid look of death on their faces. Looking out into the Hudson River, they seemed dumbfound by Mikey's revelation of the night before. Mikey's impending death and suicide attempt seemed unimaginable. They both looked a mess, strung-out and puffy eyed.

Mikey giggled as if with forced delight. Dominick stared at him curiously wondering how many bumps of K he had taken.

"I just can't believe you never told any of us what you were going through, bitch!" Dominick angrily broke his silence. "You would've walked away from us with your totally self-absorbed insensitive ass without even saying good-bye!"

A single lonely tear raced down Mikey's face. Mikey lowered himself to the ground and crunched himself with his head between his legs to hide the onslaught of emerging tears. This had been his second attempt at his own life and he did not even have Magdalena to blame or for an apology. His mother was estranged because he had pushed her away and now he only wanted to be held by her.

"You're wrong Mikey! You are so wrong!" Dominick choked on his own tears. "I thought we was your family, stupid! We're sistas! Remember?"

Dominick grabbed Mikey by his jacket and pulled him up into his arms. "I know we're not the best fuckin' influences but we love you, asshole!" Dominick cried as Mikey fell apart on his shoulder.

"I'm just scared! I don't know how to love! I don't know how to be loved! Every time I do I get used or left behind!"

Together, they cried pathetically and had a real moment before eccentric laughter reminded them of their thick skins.

"Next time ya even think about overdosing ya'self, let me know and I'll push you into the goddamned Hudson you dumb cunt!"

Mikey just held on tight to him and pretended Dominick was Magdalena. He realized Dominick knew nothing of his sexual abuse and wondered what had brought them together as friends and just how much they really had in common.

MOCKING OF CHRIST

Marsha was starving. The rumble in her stomach made her feel light-headed and dizzy.

"Not even a fuckin' joint!" she told herself while picking up a cigarette butt, hoping to find some way of lighting it. People passed her by looking disgusted and horrified.

"Get away from me ya fuckin' freak!" someone usually told her, pushing her aside.

Sometimes, if she got lucky, they would even toss a bottle at her so she would not have to dig into the garbage. Marsha was always on the hunt, currently hoping to find herself a new dress besides the usual leftovers. The pink one she wore already ripped and torn, was beginning to smell of excretions and urine. Finding herself a new pair of shoes was also on the top of her list. The pumps she wore cut into her ankles and her feet were full of calluses and blisters. The shoes were too small and one of them was missing a heel.

Marsha's prized possession was the purple Easter bonnet, which Sista Mama had given her recently. It was decorated with little plastic grapes, which Marsha only wished she could eat. Sista Mama always gave her a dollar or bought her food.

They had known each other for many years. Sista Mama was just a young lesbian and Marsha was still mother of the House of Milan and not yet physically homeless. As soon as she became mother of the House of X, Sista Mama had taught her children to respect Marsha and help her out whenever they could.

Marsha had been part of the West Side Highway scene from the time she decided no longer to put up with her father fucking and beating her at fourteen when she was still a little boy confused about gender.

That old bastard was eventually shot three times in the chest for breaking and entering and that bitch of her mother got pushed into a speeding car.

Marsha had found a new family in the House of Milan and ruled the pier scene back in the days, more than a decade ago. Those days were before the arrests for prostitution and before her hotel room went up in smoke. The children loved to hear her stories about sleeping all night in only the choicest clubs (or so she thought). They enjoyed her tales about battling the legendary Anji X and stabbing Cuca Pendavis in the leg at the Marc Ballroom.

Those were the days when the piers belonged to the children of the Houses. Those were days before the West Side Highway piers became a roller rink for steroid-enhanced, tanned muscle boys. "Balloons on wheels!" Marsha would call the muscle boys that never gave her a dime or the time of day. They only laughed at her or called her names.

Marsha's stomach was roaring as she dug through a recently deposited garbage bag. She found a half full can of Coke and a McDonald's bag filled with five cold French fries and some lettuce with mayonnaise. She was delighted to find a blue lighter with just enough fluid to light her cigarette butt. Inside a shiny silver can, Marsha nearly cried when she found her favorite dish still wet with oil and enough chunks to fill her tummy.

"Tuna fish! Work me, god damn it!"

"Yo, wassup Mikey?"

Mikey turned around from throwing out his garbage to find Eric Santiago standing outside his Sixth Avenue apartment.

"Hey!" Mikey unsuccessfully tried to hide his look of surprise.

"Sup? Don't I get a hug?" Eric invitingly stretched out his long Puerto Rican arms.

Mikey reached over to wrap his arms around him. Holding each other just a second long enough to feel Eric's warm breath caress his neck, Mikey pulled away feeling aroused. He had always had a crush on Eric, even when he was with Chris, and Eric seemed to be fully aware of this.

"What are ya doin' 'round hea?"

"I'm on my way to a friend's house!" Eric blushed.

"Oh!" Mikey said as he noticed Janet across the street gawking at Eric behind his back.

Janet had taken to prostituting Sixth Avenue right across the street from Mikey's apartment. She knew he would keep an eye out for her and let her drop in to use the bathroom and take a break from the streets. If it was late and she had still not scored a trick, Mikey would call her up from his fire escape to sleep on his couch. It would save her from having to pay for another night at the hostel.

Janet pointed to Eric from the other side of the street and mouthed the word "Ovah!" while snapping her fingers.

"What are you laughing at?" Eric looked behind his back but Janet had quickly dodged behind a car.

"Nothing!"

Eric continued staring at Mikey and asked the likely question, "So, I heard you broke up with Chris!"

"Yeah!" Mikey looked over Eric's shoulder to find Janet lighting a cigarette and waving to him, pushing up her implants to make them more noticeable for potential clients.

"Whatevah! You know what they say, 'When the ship leaves, another one docks the harbor!'"

Eric's face expanded into a big smile, "That's too bad! Ya need someone to beat him up?"

Mikey laughed as Janet made funny faces while walking away aware that they were having an intimate moment. "Nah thanks! I've done that myself! As a matter of fact, he's probably pressing charges against me for assault and battery!"

"What? Get outta here! For what?"

"I kicked his ass outside the bookstore for lying to me! But I don't give a fuck!" Mikey's laughter died out thinly. "Anyways!" Mikey fidgeted, "I betta be goin' back in!"

"Ah-ight! Catch ya later, kid!" Eric casually pulled Mikey into his chest and hugged him tightly.

Off guard, Mikey tried not to get excited as his erection rose to the smell of Eric's sweet cologne. Mikey pulled away abruptly.

"I'll see ya around!" Mikey said, turning to go back in.

"Yeah! You betta!" Eric demanded, tossing Mikey a smile so intense that Mikey had to turn from it.

Mikey walked back into his apartment confused about his bitterness.

CROWN OF THORNS

A rap song by the group Cypress Hills blared in the background from a boom box as Damian, Dominick, and Mikey sat at Washington Square Park. The night fell quickly upon them as they shared a blunt. Mikey sat above them resting his feet on the bench where the others sat. With eyes squinting from the smoke, Damian inhaled and choked.

"This shit is good!" Damian said as he passed it over to Mikey. Dominick kept a look out for the cops as Mikey nodded to the homeboys walking by and took a long puff before passing it over to him. Dominick's eyes were already bloodshot red to match his baseball cap and pullover windbreaker. Dominick's pale face almost seemed to gain some color as he sucked on the lighted herb. Everything seemed ethereal and in slow motion.

"I know you've been going through a lot lately and this may not be the best way to help but has Ernesto spoken to you?" Dominick asked Mikey.

"Huh?" Mikey asked back, too stoned to move.

"Has Ernesto spoken to you?" Dominick yelled and they all began to laugh.

"About what?" Mikey cackled.

"About working for him!" Damian answered as Mikey's laughter lost its force.

"No!" Mikey said dumbfounded.

"He wants you to work for him. He'll probably call you soon!" Dominick passed the blunt back to Damian.

"Doin' what?"

"Sellin' yaself at The Rounds!" Damian joked.

Mikey silenced Damian down with a threatening stare so that he would not slip in front of Dominick about their adventurous night at the infamous hustler bar. Damian was still bitter because he had only gotten two hundred dollars from an older Italian advertising executive while Mikey had made three hundred and fifty dollars from a gorgeous Jewish doctor that he would have laid for free.

"Did I miss sumethin'?" Dominick asked as Damian laughed knowingly.

"He wants you ta sell drugs for him!" Damian quickly returned to the matter.

"Chacho! What's the cut?" Mikey asked, deviously twitching his face like some satanic rabbit.

"Well, you know he only sells the hard stuff! Coke and K for forty or fifty depending on whether he likes you or not! From that, he's offering twenty dollars a bottle!" Damian laid it out.

Mikey's eyes widened with curiosity as he tried to multiply figures in his head. Five bottles a night added to $100 in maybe less than an hour. That was easily doubled by the amount of cokeheads and K-queens they knew at the clubs. He would be making more money than ever working for Lucky in Bushwick.

"Then there's also whole grams which go for eighty bucks!" Dominick added.

"Don't forget his Ecstasy which you can sell like candy!" Damian jumped in.

"And you know the queens need their vitamins!" Dominick insisted.

Mikey was dimly aware that they had already come to some

sort of an agreement with Ernesto about Mikey's fate. In an effort to help Mikey get his life together and feel better, they tried to help him the only way they knew how. Suicidal or not, these pendejos thought offering Mikey the opportunity to sell drugs again would help him feel better.

Damian continued, "In one night, you can make anywhere from three hundred to a thousand dollars depending on the night and the event!"

"What if I get caught?" Mikey asked.

"Well, you end up in prison with a boyfriend named Bubba! Ernesto only works inside The Sanctuary and you'll have bouncers and security guards looking out for you! How do you think the club makes its money?" Dominick's eyes gleamed devilishly. "If it weren't for the drugs, there would be no party!"

"Besides, when was the last time you saw anyone get arrested at The Sanctuary?" Damian snickered. "You would only be working inside the club and you could make yourself some really cute money doin' what you like best which is partying!"

"If I even suspect that it's getting too dangerous for you, I'll make you bounce early, kid! Have you ever noticed how I lower the music just before the cops come in for whatever reason? That's to cue the dealers that Maggie's about to come in so they have a chance to get lost!" Dominick revealed.

"Mama, I need to speak with you!" Mikey said as he walked past Sista Mama into her East Village apartment, which featured the bound and gagged mannequin of a naked woman hanging from thick metal chains against a brick wall.

"Excuse me, but you can't just barge in here!" she flared.

"Oh, Miss Thing! Don't pop an attitude just because you think you're fierce!" Mikey tossed back his imaginary long hair preparing for a catfight.

"You miserable bitch!" Sista Mama quoted Krystle Carrington from Dynasty[76], "What do you want?"

"Not you!" Mikey huffed. "Have any of your other children spoken to you yet?"

"About what?" Sista Mama asked as Mikey debated whether to tell her or not. His entire shtick was a facade to seem heartless and tough much like Dynasty's Alexis Colby.

"About me working for Ernesto?"

Sista Mama no longer smiled.

"I'm seriously considering working for Ernesto!" Mikey stared deeply into her big black eyes.

"Ernesto? The drug dealer?" she asked to make sure.

Mikey nodded a yes as Sista Mama yelled, "You want to sell drugs again?"

"Mama, what do I got to lose? Besides, we all know I'm gonna get fired from the bookstore! I haven't been there for like a week!" Mikey said as Sista Mama collapsed onto her purple couch with a portrait of herself dressed in African garb hanging behind her.

Mikey stared at her, determined.

"It'll only be for a little while, maybe a few months! Just until I get myself together! I could really use the money!" Mikey said, trying to convince himself more than Sista Mama. "It won't be dangerous! I'll only be working at The Sanctuary and Dominick will be looking out for me along with the rest of the House of X. I'll have security guards and bouncers keeping

---

76 A popular prime time television soap from the '80's about a wealthy oil family living in Denver, Colorado.

an eye out on me and it's not like I haven't put myself in worse situations. It's a wonderful opportunity for a kid like me, you know, really!"

Mikey was begging Sista Mama like some little boy asking his mother permission to play with the neighborhood pit bull. Mikey was surprised to be considering selling drugs but after everything he had been through it was conceivable. He really had nothing to lose at this point in his life. His innocence (if he had any before the age of three) was gone. His dignity was gone. His self-respect was gone. Hope was overrated.

Sista Mama felt her heart sink to her toes realizing that no matter what she would say Mikey had already made up his mind. Her face seemed haunted as she reconsidered her position as mother of the House of X. This was not what she had agreed to. She took her role as mother seriously but realized these were not really her children, these were not even children, and they only turned to her for some sort of false motherly support. It was wearing her down. For all the positive things that the House of X represented, crime and violence were always a lingering aspect of their existence. It was their defense against the world.

"I'll have nothing to do with this!" she yelled, her voice suddenly harsh and with the brittle inflections of irony. Taken over by fury, Sista Mama lunged off the couch and marched up to Mikey's face as he stared at her daringly.

"You want to sell drugs for Ernesto? You go get your sorry faggot ass arrested but don't expect me to bail you out! How dare you? Barging in here telling me you're gonna be selling drugs!"

"Mama, it's not like we haven't done worse things in life!" Mikey yelled then laughed in disbelief.

Silence took over, golden and painful as the crazed sparkle in Mama's eyes began to swell. She stood there as if her blood pressure was about to explode.

"What do they care about us anyways, Mama? Sooner or later we're all just gonna burn in hell just for being gay! Selling drugs, selling myself, being gay—What's the difference?"

"The difference is . . ."

Mikey furiously cut her off, "Do you really think they give a fuck about whether or not I become an outstanding citizen or not?" Mikey's anger emerged like venom through his clenched teeth and his flaring black eyes were once again red with tears, "They don't give a flying fuck! No matter what I do, I'll always be a drug addict, a prostitute, a child molester, and criminal to them!"

Choking on his own rage, Mikey trembled uncontrollably as he stared into Sista Mama's frightened eyes and realized he had shouted her down to a mere whimper. His words had leaned down over her and all she could say was, "It's not like that anymore, Mikey!"

She did not know how to break through his anger.

"Yeah! Well, then tell me why I need some stupid House of X to make me feel like I've got a home!" Mikey gave Sista Mama one last daring look before running out of the apartment and racing down the stairs, leaving her without a chance to answer.

Mikey pretended to be absorbed by a syndicated television repeat of "Roseanne" while Magdalena sized him up from the corner of her eyes. It was like this every time he visited. They had everything and absolutely nothing to discuss. She would sit there pretending to be knitting even though they both knew she could not even sew. Except for the laugh track from the television, there was nothing but silence.

He should have been telling Magdalena about how he had just survived another failed suicide attempt.

He still had not made up his mind whether or not to tell her he was going to be selling drugs for a living and had survived the streets as a hustler. However, the way she looked at him, she already seemed to know.

Emilio was out as usual and Magdalena seemed worn and disheveled. Her beauty had faded down to leave her with just a shell of who she had once been. Mikey did not look any older—not fatter or thinner. Except for a foul attitude and the dark circles underneath his eyes that revealed many sleepless nights, he was practically unchanged.

After some time, hoping to begin a conversation, Magdalena asked, "How is your cousin Alberto doing?"

The silence doubled, culminating with an eerie and untimely laughter from the set. Something pressed against Mikey's chest.

"He's doing fine, I guess!" Mikey presumed with a flat tone

to his voice and eyes glued to the screen. He had not spoken to Alberto much since moving into the West Village, avoiding his familial lectures to indulge freely in his decadent choices in life.

Though he was dying spiritually, Mikey remained self-absorbed in order to survive.

"Did you know Chino is back?" Magdalena asked.

Instantly, she got his attention. The television faded into the distance as Mikey's head spun around and stretched over his shoulder. Magdalena glared tragically into his eyes and Mikey finally recognized her depression and shame.

"What?" Mikey's heart palpitated and the expression on his face revealed panic. "I thought he was deported?" Mikey nearly cried.

"He's coming back to stay with Titi Yoli." Then, as if in a genuine attempt to bridge the distance between her and her son, "God help him if I ever come face to face with him again. I swear Mikey! I'll kill him for what he did to you!"

Mikey just sat in silence. Whatever revelations he may have had for Magdalena about his current life situation were no longer up for discussion.

He realized only the two of them along with his cousin Alberto, and perhaps Beto, knew about that terrible period in his life. He had hidden all of that away in the unknown gutters of his soul. Throughout the years, Mikey had never shared anything about his sexual abuse to any of his tricks, boyfriends, not even his friends.

That night, Mikey had violent nightmares. In his dream, Mikey followed a trail of bloodied diapers to the room where Chino would molest him as a child. Walking in on them, Mikey watched Chino cover Miguelito's mouth before penetrating him. Mikey would later find Miguelito crying underneath a table with blood on his face and a pool of blood emerging from his ass.

Mikey saw himself hustling at the piers as a twelve-year-old boy sucked Chino off in front of him. Chino's dick was still wet with Miguelito's fresh blood. Mikey ran to the nearest church only to discover his own dead body lying in a pool of blood at the altar with blood splattered onto the image of Christ. Mikey only awakened after attending his own funeral where he was buried in a coffin while wrapped in bloodied bed sheets.

CRUCIFIXION

"There's only one lesson to be learned from dealing," Ernesto told Mikey with contempt in his eyes, "Never trust anyone!" An unmistakable aura of evil surrounded him like a gathering of unclean spirits.

Mikey smiled, "That won't be so hard to do!"

Everybody at The Sanctuary paid unfailing homage and due respects to the dealer whose drugs would turn the night into a four-dimensional spectrum of lights. Ernesto was sure to point out exactly who was full of shit and whom Mikey should keep an eye on. It was agreed that Dominick would lower the music to warn Mikey in the event of police raids, which were becoming more and more frequent under the new mayor's reign. Mikey pretended he was just finding out about this subtle cue for the drug dealers at The Sanctuary.

Security guards and doormen would pace back and forth with their walkie-talkies while keeping an eye on Mikey to make sure he was all right. Mikey greeted everybody Ernesto introduced him to with an inviting smile to hide his disinterest and disdain. Steve, the main bouncer, would clear Mikey's space from K-holed queens that would tag along trying to talk Mikey up for more drugs. He would be responsible for Mikey's safety and make sure Ernesto's pawn was well taken care of.

Mikey was only allowed to leave his spot (located underneath a statue of St. Therese) for drinks, the bathroom, or severe emergencies. As each weekend passed, going to The Sanctuary became a burden for Mikey. When he was not working for him, Mikey would have to entertain Ernesto's demand for attention. Mikey liked Ernesto but he was beginning to find him too needy.

Being a drug dealer, Ernesto had nothing close to a meaningful relationship. He bought Mikey's friendship with weekly haircuts, expensive shopping sprees, and fancy dinners at the finest restaurants. Mikey was now bombarding the stores he once used to shoplift. They ransacked the record stores for the latest house tracks and imports for Dominick before picking up drugs and rushing to Dominick's apartment to double-check the merchandise and plan out the evening.

Mikey arrived home with shopping bags and briefcases to take his disco nap and prepare for the long nights ahead. Ernesto either called or paged Mikey incessantly to wake him unless Mikey was already shacked up in one of Ernesto's guest-rooms with one of the many hustlers Ernesto hired to entertain Mikey.

Mikey arrived at The Sanctuary in limos where he emerged to hand the doorman a guest list and a list of who not to allow into the club each night. Once inside, Mikey remained sober until the last few hours before the club closed and watched his clients indulge in vial after vial of cocaine or K while enjoying the orgy of flesh and gossip. By the end of the night, Mikey would be stumped on some couch with pockets filled with twenties and fifties yet so exhausted one could mistake him for a Save the Children poster boy.

Dominick joined him each night after the closing of The Sanctuary, doing so many bumps of coke that his already soft and tender nose would bleed. Ernesto would meet Mikey to pick up his money. On Sundays, they would catch a Broadway matinee. Straight from The Sanctuary, they would distract the Broadway actors from high above in their private balcony seats.

Mikey slept all day and woke up only after the vicious sun had fallen from the sky. The moon was the only occasional light in Mikey's darkness, as he assisted some drugged up one-night-stand out of his bedroom and onto the streets.

On non-Sanctuary nights, Mikey haunted the competition at other popular gay dance clubs and risked his life by selling drugs on the down low without Steve watching over him or Dominick's cue to exit the club.

The demand for Ernesto's drugs made Mikey's popularity skyrocket and left the other dealers in the cold. It was not long before Mikey would be stopped at the door of some infamous club and kept behind the velvet ropes.

The Sanctuary, however, belonged exclusively to Mikey.

The House of X brought him potential clients, entertaining the regulars and casting shade at anyone buying drugs from other dealers. Most of the members had fun so long as there were enough drugs to keep the nights from becoming utterly intolerable. Mikey felt trapped, however, no longer able to dance underneath the disco ball with the rest of his sistas. He wanted so bad to run out and join them on the dance floor like he used to.

Mikey found himself getting more and more bored with the whole scene. Though he had a glamorous life, Mikey would give it all up in a heartbeat for a new life.

Mikey still found himself traveling from one meaningless one-night-stand to another but his dreams (whatever good ones he had) belonged to Eric Santiago. He could not wait to run into him again and jump his bones.

Mikey had been currently dating one particular muscle boy that he later found making out with someone else by the bar.

On that one occasion, Mikey used his drink tickets to get actual cocktails and offered them innocently to the Chelsea queen and his new beau.

"This drink's on me!" Mikey offered with the sweetest of smiles to them. "Now it's on you!" Mikey threw the drinks in their faces and walked away psychotically. Mikey had Steve throw them out and added their names to his growing 'do not let them in' list.

It was not long before Mikey brought his nocturnal crimes to his West Village share and argued ceaselessly with Dan about the loud music Mikey would blast. Mikey had quit working at the bookstore and told Dan he was now working as an assistant to Dominick at The Sanctuary. Mikey tried desperately to drown out the sounds of money being counted and cocaine being snorted. Dan noticed all the strangers that constantly visited Mikey to "borrow something to wear" while walking out with the same clothes and hundreds of dollars of drugs stashed away in their pockets. Different wide-eyed muscle boys emerged from Mikey's space and paraded in their underwear through Dan's bedroom every night to use the only bathroom in the apartment. Dan pretended to watch television while they showered. He knew something was up with Mikey and was growing annoyed by the constant invasion of privacy.

The phone rang off the hook at all hours of the morning for Mikey with strange voices asking for Ricky, Juan Carlos, Chris, or whatever other names Mikey would give. Mikey got a certain thrill using his ex-lovers' names to protect himself.

Though Mikey was not working at the bookstore anymore, Dan took particular notice when Mikey finally had his own private line installed and bought himself a state-of-the-art beeper and cellular phone. Mikey used various codes and alternate names in case the lines were tapped and talked about what 'vitamins' they were looking for and how many. Mikey seemed to be quite the expert on vitamins C, K and E.

Mikey stumbled home early in the morning wearing heavy sunglasses to hide the black circles underneath his eyes which bulged as if a roller coaster ride were about to derail. He stared at fantastical gargoyles, which hid behind his Santeria statues and watched everyone outside his window stagger in slow motion. Mikey seemed fascinated by the sound of traffic and fell into K-holes while taking bubble baths.

At The Sanctuary, there seemed to be a fight every night that always ended with someone else being thrown out. Mikey had become paranoid by rumors that the cops were on to him and he was beginning to lose his edge. Mikey became meaner and heartless and this negativity had rubbed off on his friends as well.

"Back up, bitch!" Damian sneered one night at Flaca from the House of Pendavis, who was taking up Mikey's spot as Damian watched it for Mikey. It was rumored throughout The Sanctuary that Flaca was now selling drugs too.

"Eh-q me?" Flaca demanded, "Now I know chu weren' talkin' to me!"

"I said move bitch before I beat you down with this pole here!" Damian said, referring to the column that separated them from the dance floor.

Flaca, quite daring, would not budge from his location as people shoved past him toward the bathroom for more bumps.

"Vamos pa'encima, puta!" Flaca taunted Damian; fully aware Damian did not speak Spanish.

"Miss Thing! If you don't move off this spot," Damian threatened viciously, "I'll get security to haul your tired Flaca ass out onto the pavement!"

Flaca stared Damian down defiantly; unaware that Damian was keeping guard for Mikey until Mikey returned from the bathroom.

"Get the fuck out of my spot!" Mikey yelled loud enough for Steve to hear and run over to remove Flaca from the club.

Damian smiled salaciously, "Can't she see my sista is trying to do business here!"

From the deejay booth, Dominick searched the dance floor for faces he could fall in love with while waking up to some drugged up queen asking him for a tape of his music. Dominick had lost sight of himself and his life. Sometimes he stayed home all day doing bump after bump after bump of cocaine. Nosebleeds were now all too common and sometimes dribbled on to the record Dominick was spinning causing it to skip. The bags under Dominick's eyes looked like someone had stuck empty vials beneath his lower lids.

Dominick had even lost one of his front teeth one night and could not remember how or when. He now featured a porcelain tooth that flew out of his mouth every time one of his friends made him burst out laughing while they were out scouting other clubs. All of them would drop to their knees at once with their lighters in search of Dominick's missing tooth.

Dominick, himself, once hunted for his pearly white underneath some woman's skirt. The woman screamed as Dominick crawled out from beneath her yelling, "I found it! I found it!" He held the tooth up to his missing gap and added, "By the way girlfriend, your panties smell nasty! I almost got another nosebleed down there!"

Mikey became a childish menace always looking for new ways to antagonize someone. He dubbed people 'Sleestak'[77], 'The Fly', and 'The Chicken' depending on what they reminded him of. Mikey mocked how they danced and imitated them in front of their angry faces. He was always yelling at people to "Move the fuck" out of his way and pushed K-holed queens down the stairs on purpose. Mikey chased shady drag queens that stepped on him without apologizing and set their wigs on fire with his lighter. He immaturely used straws to spit gumballs at people and stuck his leg out to trip enemy forces.

In short, if Mikey or anyone else from the House of X did not like someone, that person might as well find another club to party. Chris became Mikey's biggest target. Chris no longer stirred Mikey up by flaunting his new boyfriends in his face or staring at him from the other side of the bar. Chris was unaware that his very presence had become a sort of suffocation to Mikey. Mikey's despise of Chris combined with the loving memories he had with him caused Mikey to build a wall around himself.

Rumors circulating around The Sanctuary made Chris out to be a broken man wretchedly and emotionally absorbed in Mikey's memory for the rest of his life. The look in Chris's eyes suggested his longing for the day when whatever love he may have had for Mikey would die. Despite the fact Mikey had beaten him down and knocked out one of his teeth, Chris was

---

77 Large green humanoids from the children's television series "The Land of the Lost" with insectoid and reptilian features.

still in love with Mikey.

"Would ya like to dance with me?" Chris finally asked one fateful night, interrupting Mikey's conversation with Jorge.

With newfound spitefulness toward Chris, Mikey returned with "Only if you know how to do the dis dance!"

"What? The this dance? Nah, I never heard of it!" Chris looked puzzled, "But I can try!"

An immediately suspicious glow leaped into Mikey's eyes. "Oh, it's easy! You just go over to that side of the club," Mikey said with Jorge listening next to him, looking almost sorry for Chris. "And I stay here, okay?"

Chris looked dejected, "Oh, I get it. I just got dissed and you prefer me at a distance."

Furiously aware that he had just been snubbed, Chris's once seductively green eyes were now hollow and strained. Chris never bothered Mikey again (until surprisingly hooking up later with Jorge).

It was not long before the House of X began fighting with Mikey about who should be paid and how much for looking out after him and bringing him clients. Greed quickly became the proverbial reason for the growing arguments, especially between Mikey and Jorge. Periods of sporadic hates, disguised envies, and ruthless jealousies began to last longer than just a few days. Ernesto tried to convince Mikey that friends were like cocaine.

"Ya take a few bumps and enjoy the high!" Ernesto said, "Afta a while ya nose begins to develop calluses and starts ta bleed but ya continue taking the bumps to feel that high once again!"

Those senseless words of wisdom and the realization that

his world was falling apart helped Mikey develop the skeleton, fragile, yet definite, of a conscience. Mikey would force himself to sleep by avoiding the angry glares from his statues only to wake up from nightmares even more frightening than the ones that already recurred. Overwrought by guilt, he had trouble sleeping.

"Mikey, I don't mean to interrupt your life but I heard a rumor recently that you've been dealing drugs and not just at the clubs. You know kiddo, I really don't care what you do with your personal life, but when you start selling drugs from this apartment it becomes my problem!" Dan confronted Mikey one day.

"I'm not a drug dealer, okay!" Mikey lied to Dan but the fact that he was paying his share of the rent with drug money became increasingly obvious.

"I'm not stupid. I really do like you, kid. You may hate me now but one day, hopefully, you'll realize I did what needed to be done."

Dan asked Mikey to move out and gave him only two weeks before Christmas to pack his bags and leave. With nowhere else to go, Ernesto hired Mikey an all lesbian moving company, appropriately called The Amazons, and had Mikey's statues and furniture put away in a storage facility. Mikey would sleep on Dominick's cat-infested couch until he saved up enough drug money for an apartment of his own.

Mikey's spirit was dying. He had lost his apartment in the West Village because of selling drugs. Mikey was now forced to reflect on his entire history and the insanity of his life. The House of X had nurtured his strange behavior but he still had no place to call home. Using more and more drugs and sleeping with more and more strangers to take away his pain had ultimately left Mikey numb.

Mikey celebrated Christmas in a deep K-hole in which he swore he experienced death and reached the gates of heaven.

"They told me I wasn't even on the guest-list!" Mikey told Dominick after he had been resurrected, "I said 'Excuse me? There must be some mistake!' and St. Peter said 'God doesn't make mistakes!' Can you believe I wasn't even on the guest-list? So, I snapped my fingers in his face and said 'Well then, you betta send me back to The Sanctuary!' and here I am!"

Besides the sound of his own voice and the hollow laughter, Mikey only heard the continuous buzzing in his ears. He was flushed with his own impassioned gibberish.

New Year's Eve found Mikey having the busiest night of his life. Dominick, in an effort to retain his title as New York City's best deejay, was kicking everybody's ass with his music. The Sanctuary was jam packed with what seemed like all of New York City nightlife. Damian assisted Mikey as people formed lines just to buy drugs from him. Selling out rapidly, at increased holiday prices, Mikey sold them as if he were selling them for half price.

In less than two hours, Mikey was out of business for the remainder of the night. He had made enough money to retire for the next few months and with the last few minutes to midnight remaining, Mikey and Damian ran up to the deejay booth to join Dominick in the celebration.

Dominick, shirtless, slowly faded the music out and illuminated the old church to reveal the stained glass windows and crumbling saints.

"Ten-nine-eight-seven-six-five-four-three-two-one. HAPPY FUCKIN' NEW YEAR'S!" they chanted. The sounds of roaring from the crowd below were reminiscent of the sounds of the Romans feeding the Catholics to the lions at the Coliseum.

Outside, a crowd thronged to be admitted.

ASCENSION

Emilio died shortly after Mikey and the others had fled from the cab driver they left for dead. Mikey watched his mother, dressed beautifully in black, cry over his casket. Magdalena stared down at the man that for whatever reason she had always loved. This man had abused her both physically and emotionally for over twenty years. Magdalena's heart seemed to ache with misery and loneliness.

Mikey, the prodigal son, was stumped in the suit he had purchased with drug money on the wooden pews. His mouth trembled in an ecstasy of remorse and relief. Mikey only remembered Emilio's intense power over him and Magdalena.

However, there was now also an onslaught of repressed memories. He remembered his hatred toward the man that would leave his mother bruised. He remembered himself as a little boy screaming as Emilio punched Magdalena over and over again leaving her unconscious across the floor with blood and bruises. He remembered running into his mother's arms and huddling into her bosom, wet with tears and blood.

He had prayed many nights for the day that Emilio would die and leave them alone. He never really expected that somber day to come. Mikey always assumed that he would die first.

In his coffin, Emilio represented most of what Mikey was trying to run away from. Emilio's ignorance, prejudice, and hatred toward homosexuals had made it easier for Mikey to believe that he was evil and condemned to sin forever. It had added to Mikey's history of tears and bitterness and given him license to embrace his dark side. Mikey wondered what in life had made Emilio so cruel and searched for a reason to cry; a reason to miss him; a reason to love Emilio. Instead, an overwhelming sensation of relief lingered over him.

"Tu eres maricón?"

The words were still fresh in his mind as if it were only yesterday that Emilio taunted him from the driver's seat of his car. Mikey only remembered all the torture he had to endure from the man he was forced to call 'papi.' The word itself left dryness in his throat.

Mikey rose and walked down the aisle toward his mother and his dead stepfather. Mikey glared at his ghastly pale skin and noticed the hands resting over a golden crucifix that, more than once, had sent his mother to the hospital. Emilio rested peacefully, absolved from all hatred and sin.

Mikey was unable to shed a single tear. He was only sorry that the last hope he ever had for a father was lying there, in a casket, with eyes that would never rest on him again.

Magdalena cried next to him as Mikey jumped out of his thick skin to reach out and hold her. Her worn face formed the shadow of a smile as Mikey wiped away her tears and a brand new sensation of life rushed through him. It was over. At least one of his many demons was laid to rest. He felt sad, not because Emilio was dead, but because Magdalena still suffered because of him.

As he held his grieving mother, unsure of whether she actually heard him or not, he whispered into her ear, "Mami, I love you and it was not your fault!"

The Sanctuary never reopened. The mayor of New York had

decided that the church where it had been located for almost ten years belonged to the State of New York. In a desperate effort to clean up the city, the church that had once been home to hundreds of New York's "Godless degenerates" was going to be destroyed. The Sanctuary would crumble to the ground to create a new K-Mart for the people of New York. Apparently, this had been planned for many years. Because they had lived in their own deluded little worlds, the queens were just beginning to take notice of an existence outside The Sanctuary. The West Side Highway piers, also city property, was also rumored to eventually become a park with waterfront stores and malls to replace the gay and lesbian youth which had once haunted the only place they ever fit in—the edge of the city.

At last, everyone had something to talk about as if cast for parts in some dark comedy. The closing of The Sanctuary and the closing of the piers were ultimately conceived as the destruction of Satan's temple.

When the press found out, rumors began to leak from all angles sensationalized with preposterous and sinister lies. The newspapers spread ruthless truths and lies about The Sanctuary. The faithful children waited patiently for the day when, like the phoenix rising from its ashes, The Sanctuary would be born again in all its unholy and eternal haunts.

New York City would be doomed to hungry children lurking the city streets with the ancient restlessness of their souls creeping over them every Saturday night.

"Hello? Dominick? Are you home?" Mikey yelled as he entered the apartment.

He looked around for him until he realized Dominick was not home. Mikey headed toward the door on his way to

Dominick's rooftop. One of Dominick's cats quickly scurried into the kitchen, expecting Mikey to launch his foot and send her flying across the room.

Instead, Mikey reached out to pick her up and caressed her lovingly.

Once he reached Dominick's rooftop, Mikey brazenly drifted toward the very edge. Because of everything else he had confronted in his brief life, it was inevitable that Mikey should dare himself high above the hostile city. Stretching out his arms in a Christ like gesture, Mikey searched the cold gray skies for any signs of God with his bright eyes. He imagined God smiling at him from behind the dark cheerless clouds. Mikey no longer questioned the meaning of his painful existence and ceased to be an individual full of hatred and anger. Mikey no longer wanted to be some miserable little fuck intolerable unless he was under the influence of drugs.

Juan Carlos was gone. Emilio was gone. The Sanctuary was gone and in spite of all the death that surrounded him, Mikey had discovered life. His will to survive breezed through him like the wind and Mikey began to laugh in his solitude. He wondered what it would be like to fly through the air audaciously as he looked down at the streets below. Mikey was mystified by the swarm of yellow bee-like cabs buzzing down Sixth Avenue.

The wind pushed against him ever so mildly as Mikey felt the sudden urgency to piss. He looked up to explore the heavens one last time as the strained and hollow voice of Oyá rose from below the concrete streets and called him by name. A realization suddenly crept into his eyes.

After calling Ernesto to tell him that he no longer wanted to work for him, Mikey stepped into a yellow cab and asked the driver to drive him around the city as he cast himself in the back seat. The Indian cabbie stared back at him through his rear view mirror as Mikey simply handed him fifty dollars in advance.

"Keep da change if there is any! Just drive, I've got money!" Mikey slouched himself on the corner behind the driver and rested his face against the window. The driver asked no questions and stepped on the gas to drive aimlessly until Mikey's voice gave him directions.

Mikey wanted to travel through New York City and pretend he was still Miguelito sitting in the back seat mesmerized by the sights and sounds of Manhattan while Emilio and Magdalena laughed and kissed in the front seat.

The taxi passed the apartment where Mikey once lived and he noticed fresh new curtains up on the windows where he had blocked out the harsh sunlight with black paint-splattered bed sheets. The cabbie drove him in silence through the noisy streets of the West Village as Mikey stared out at the many wild and eccentric faces. He recognized a few people he knew and at least two or three he had slept with.

The driver hurriedly raced straight toward Times Square where he was met with heavy traffic. Mikey was happily absorbed by the fantastic jeweled magnificence of lights before heading up to Central Park and cruising back down Fifth Avenue. He smiled as they passed FAO Schwartz remembering the day Juan Carlos brought him there to buy the teddy bear he would call UmFumFum.

Before ending up bitterly hung from his West Village apartment, Mikey used to sleep with UmFumFum every night, holding him tightly as if by some sheer force of nature he would metamorphosis into Juan Carlos by the morning light.

Mikey finally asked the driver to drop him off by Rockefeller Center to see what was left of the Christmas spirit. The cab driver pulled up to the curb and cursed Mikey under his breath as Mikey got out. A few ice skaters surfed on what was slowly melting into a huge swimming pool. Sparks of laughter emanated from Mikey as he recalled the days when Emilio and Magdalena foolishly tried to teach Miguelito how to ice skate. Most of the time, they had all tumbled down on to the cold ice.

Mikey focused only on the few happier times of his life letting go of all the evil demons that he called his memory. He had long yearned for the day when all the madness and the insanity of his miserable life would end. Mikey had spent an entire quarter century lost in total darkness. He never knew what life had in store for him next, if there was to be life at all.

Mikey had doomed himself into loneliness and wretchedness. He had condemned and kept himself from discovering his soul and essence. Mikey had coexisted in a realm of false contentment and despair.

By selling himself and selling drugs, Mikey had become everything he thought society had expected him to be as a victim of sexual and physical abuse. It had been easier to believe all the negative things that people would say about someone like him. He had lived up to their expectations without regret. He still felt no regret because he had heard somewhere that everything in life happens for a reason. His experiences had manifested themselves into hateful bitterness but Mikey wanted the nostalgic days when he found love with Mario back in high school.

Mikey had been left but with the carcass of a soul never settling down long enough to allow anyone near him. He had laughed at anyone who imagined being loved by him when he did not even love himself. He had become so numb from all the pain that he had stopped caring and instead found his solace in sex, drugs, and anything else that could distract him from reality. Mikey now realized that he had created his own hell.

He used to keep his head held high through the prejudice he felt in elementary school for not having a father by imagining himself the son of someone very special. A rich powerful father was supposed to rescue him someday from all the bigotry and poverty. He would only be a bastard child until the day his charming father was supposed to return for him and his abused mother to take them back to a beautiful palace. That dream had evolved into another more religious fantasy where Mikey had two fathers to choose from—God or Satan.

It had been easier to believe that in the end his soul had been damned by a God who had betrayed him. A God who had allowed him to be sexually abused by Chino and watched as Emilio destroyed whatever chances Magdalena had for true love. God had never answered any of Miguelito's prayers when he begged for Magdalena's anger to end.

Indeed, the dark prince inside of him had comforted his pain by unleashing powers within Mikey that would defend him against all of God's wickedness. No amount of fire was able to challenge what Mikey had stored up in his ghostly heart. Mikey had built a fortress around his heart to keep him from the cruel yearnings for love and forgiveness.

Mikey only regretted that his notoriety had precluded whatever chances he may have had at settling down as the image of Eric popped into his head. The desire for love still blazed in his heart, beginning to glow around him like a bursting flame. The night no longer seemed empty and dark.

The day had finally come when a gathering of dedicated children displayed their authentic devotion to the place they once called their church. They had agonized unendurably over the destruction of what the newspapers were calling "The Synagogue of Satan." The sidewalks were peopled with vicious queens frowning heavily and casting shade behind their sunglasses at the pompous construction workers. The workers smiled triumphantly over what was about to take place with their caravans of tractors and tractor-trailers.

The sun they had only known on Sunday mornings when they were leaving The Sanctuary crushed down on them devastatingly. The noise of heavy monstrous machines and the smell of dust was everywhere. The tattooed rough-voiced construction workers shuffled about lackadaisically and their curses and mockeries were deafened by the raucous sounds of machines.

The children were outraged as their own complaints were drowned out by the grinding, churring, and screeching.

They were infuriated that the destruction of The Sanctuary could happen in so little time, as if ordered immediately by some cruel sardonic God. They had enjoyed living in their own oblivious world. They existed without the faintest care for continuity of others in their lives, only vaguely remembering having slept with each other.

Other clubs would open and the legacy of the Houses would always dwell within them but nothing could ever be like The Sanctuary. They all watched in utter desperation. Faces that had seen each other hundreds of times before, never bothering to smile the faintest hello, suddenly approached one another to comment on their grief. Eyes that once flashed restlessly through the smoky air in search of instant pleasure finally rested on each other.

Queens that once vowed to battle each other until the end stood together to share in the moment of their apocalypse. Rival Houses that once cast ruthless shade onto each other huddled in unity. Instead of verbally attacking each other, they cursed the army of soft-bellied men that tore apart what once belonged to them.

The vast orgy of somber faces included Sista Mama, surrounded by most of her children from the House of X, which held up lit candles they had mopped from The Sanctuary prior to its closing. Damian featured an arm-cast graffitied by all his sistas as Jorge wrapped his jacket around Damian's shivering body. Meanwhile, Janet hid behind dark sunglasses while battling a monstrous wad of bubblegum inside her mouth while Chris eyed her from behind with great curiosity.

Every other New York City drag queen that had ever graced their high heels on The Sanctuary stage gathered to sing a campy off-key rendition of "We Shall Overcome." The words 'black and white together' rhymed with 'gay and straight together.'

Princess, surrounded by her own entourage, hid dramatically behind a sheer black veil while her running mascara blended in with her glittering black funeral dress.

Condemned to a wheelchair after the fight with Damian, Flaca yelled for his painkillers from behind as transsexual prostitutes in sequined mini-skirts and fur coats sang along.

Sista Mama anxiously combed the crowds in hopes of finding Mikey. The Sanctuary God himself, Dominick X, was also notably absent. After the violent episode at the piers, neither one of them had been seen or heard of again. The peanut gallery spread the probable rumor that Mikey had finally been captured by the police. Other speculations of his sudden disappearance had him killed by enemy drug dealers and living in a luxury villa somewhere on the mountains of South America.

The men continued to bring down the unholy church with prejudiced curses and ignorant insults beneath their breath. They used grotesque machinery to crumble the walls that for many years kept the brutal sun from shedding light on their cathartic darkness. The walls that once muffled in the musical wizardry of Dominick's devious mastermind tumbled to the ground.

It was Monday morning and like every Monday morning, Jerry was feeding his Elegua and cleaning out his altar. Cleansing the ceramic plate on which the stone face of the child prince martyr rested, Jerry washed the blood and feathers from his sacrifices off with luke-warm water. Jerry changed Elegua's decaying week-old candy offerings with fresh new lollipops, bubblegum, jellyfish, chocolates and mints. He filled his own mouth with rum and then sprayed it all over Elegua through clenched teeth. Then, lighting one of his imported Cuban cigars, Jerry took three long puffs. Placing the lit end inside his mouth, Jerry exhaled thick clouds of smoke over the small smiling orisha.

During this weekly ritual, he would recite a Yoruba chant to Elegua while shaking two beaded maracas. Jerry ended his ceremony by gently kissing Elegua and lighting the three candles that surrounded the orisha. Jerry deeply petitioned for the end of all suffering, the omega of all darkness, the end of prejudice and hatred against all religions, races, and sexes. He prayed for the living and the dead while listening to the sound of his own coarse voice as a light wind drafted in from the open crack of his window.

Feeling it beginning to gust through him, Jerry prayed louder as the wind perpetually gathered great strength and built itself up into an ominous mini hurricane.

Jerry's heart beat faster and his voice escalated into a scream. The wind raced through a copy of the Bible and sucked up loose items and papers violently tossed against a shrieking Jerry.

He struggled against the wind on his passage toward the window as the vicious gush battled him back. Jerry was forced to turn away as his glasses flew off his ardent face to join in the spectacle of traveling papers and offerings. Achingly reaching the window, Jerry slammed it shut with tears in his eyes as everything suspended in thin air suddenly crashed ragingly against the cold floor.

Jerry's heart palpitated dangerously against his heaving chest as he sucked in deep breaths to recuperate. He slowly recovered from the wrath of the wind while searching through his raped apartment. Scattered victims of the sudden torrent were ruthlessly tossed around everywhere.

Jerry gradually raised his blurred confused eyes to rest upon his altar. His eyes widened with terror as they dismally focused in on the miracle, coincidentally heavenly and abominable. The statues that reigned over his tabernacle as the orishas of Santeria stood curiously untouched. They glared back at him indifferently. The candles, fruits, flowers and other offerings, which once rested at their feet, were cast throughout the room. One single candle, before Jerry's awestruck eyes, made the room gradually lighter as it regained its full flame to pay homage to the Catholic simulation of Oyá—St. Therese.

HOMELESS TRANSVESTITE FOUND
FLOATING DEAD ON THE HUDSON RIVER

The body of Carlton
Jones, a 27-year-old
Black man, also known
as "Marsha Milan",
was found floating on
the Hudson River.
Police reports
indicate that the
homeless transvestite
was severely beaten
and strangled before
being dumped from the
piers of the West
Side Highway off
Christopher Street.
Police have made no
connection between
Jones's death and the
brutal beating of a
30-year-old African
American cab driver
by a gang earlier this
year.

Dominick sat across the street from what was left of the
once legendary Sanctuary reflecting on days when he ruled the
dance floor. He would enter gloriously and all eyes would rest

upon him, in awe and fear. Dominick speculated what was left of his life now that his world had crumbled to the ground with nothing left but piles of cement and dust. His life, otherwise, continued on its normal route of anger and loneliness.

From the corner of his eye, he caught a glimpse of someone he had once despised and learned to love throughout the years.

"Hey, you!" Mikey said with a morbid hollow voice.

"Hey!" Dominick said indifferently, eyes still glued on the scene of the crime as Mikey sat down next to him on a small apartment porch entrance.

Dust from the destruction lay everywhere.

"Where ya been?" Dominick asked, rather collectively.

"To hell and back!" Mikey responded, cracking a faint smile.

"I haven't heard from you for days!" Dominick finally turned to look at him, frowning while holding back his tears. With the life sucked out of him, Dominick was beginning to look like a frail corpse dressed in banjee gear. "I guess you wanted to avoid the crowds too." He continued in reference to the scene before them, "Now this is all that's left!"

"I'm leaving!" Mikey said, ignoring Dominick's last comment.

Dominick caught the slightest glimpse of a twinkle in Mikey's dark eyes. He looked rested and almost heavenly.

"Because of the cab driver incident?" Dominick asked with the answer to his own question on the tip of his tongue.

A long shattering silence followed as Dominick traced Mikey's gaze back to where it all began and where it all seemingly ended.

"Because," Mikey quietly mumbled, "I have to!"

The words caused their eyes to meet for the first time in many days.

"I'm spiritually dying here!" Mikey said. Dominick detecting a hidden truth buried beneath this cryptic statement. "If I continue this path, I'm gonna die. And I don't want to die. I want to live! We've done some pretty fucked up things and I'm tired of being angry."

Mikey's feverish eyes were bright.

"I want ... to be ... happy!" Mikey continued, stretching each word as if by sheer force of nature he could make them real. "I want to believe in something other than pain and misery. I want to wake up in the morning and watch the sunrise. I want to enjoy the simple things in life that I've learned to ignore like birds singing and children laughing."

Mikey trailed off unconsciously into a utopian world where the trees were always green, the skies were always blue, and peace was always plentiful. Dominick's eyes narrowed at Mikey's delirium.

"I'm not high on ecstasy or anythin' so don't look at me like that!" Mikey said defensively. "I just have to get away from here, from all the madness, from all the anger and pain!"

Silence. Then, "I was sexually molested as a child and I've been blaming myself for it ever since!"

The release of those words lifted a tremendous weight off Mikey's shoulders as if Dominick listening to them broke some kind of spell. Tears of relief comforted Mikey's soft freckled cheeks.

"I was only a child. The worst part is ending up as a cliché. You know. The drug addicted self-destructive prostitute. I've been an insufferable punk ass! I need to get out of here and find myself. I know there's more to life than this. There has gotta be something good that comes out of this. I don't have any regrets but I need to get away and try to understand the insanity of my life."

Dominick stared at him with grave eyes, "I'm so sorry. I suppose we're all pretty fucked up. I guess it explains a lot! We'll miss you!" he confessed, ever so subdued. A rush of sadness and gloom overwhelmed the dusty air that confined them.

"I'll miss you guys too!" Mikey's eyes once again glowed to reveal the shadows of a peace he longed to obtain.

Without another word, Mikey rose majestically from off the porch on which they sat to leave behind the dust-filled doorstep with its ancient remains of something they once believed would last forever.

"Well!" Mikey said, smiling a handsome immortal smile that once before broke Dominick's heart, "I guess I'll see ya!"

The words lingered over them with an aura of unfinished business. Mikey turned to walk away as Dominick watched him vanish into the twilight. A light chill descended on him as he sat there helplessly.

"Mikey!" Dominick yelled.

Mikey turned to look at him one last time.

"Goodbye and good luck to you!" Dominick cried.

Mikey's radiant face extended into a warm loving smile before turning back to leave the cold lonely streets. Mikey disappeared into a darkness that seemed to have fallen early that February winter afternoon.

ACKNOWLEDGMENTS

I would like to thank:

Sven Davisson and Rebel Satori Press for making this happen.

Greg Wharton, Ian Phillips, and suspect thoughts press (for first looking to reprint this).

Mi querida madre Mercedes (te adoro, Mami).

My manager, best friend, BFF, and 'sista' Leo Toro (where would I be without you).

My dear friend Stephanie Holley who inspired the character of Sista Mama and watched me mature from a miserable little pier queen to a serious writer.

My beautiful boyfriend Chris James Cayler (I love you, mack daddy).

My cats who tried to keep me from finishing this book by falling asleep on my papers, Sable (rest in peace little buddy) & Alexis (get your fat ass off my pen).

Rodney Trice for all the laughter and good times.

Mi tia Cecilia, tio Alfredo and mis primas Monica, Veronica, Jessica y Fernanda.

My cousin Felipe and his lover Joe for giving me a place to stay when I needed to be off the streets.

Dominic Brando (rest in peace), David Mojica, Dana Williams, Jerry Estrella, Dan Sietler, Kurt and Mitch.

Michael TeVault for giving me the opportunity to work on this novel during its original publication.

Bill Sullivan for first giving this story the chance to be read.

Willi Ninja (rest in peace) for believing in me and

encouraging me to get off the piers and start writing.

Andres Duque for calling me out as an activist within the gay Latino community and forcing me to live up to that title.

The West Side Highway piers of New York City and Bushwick.

Ms. Regina Vogel and all the teachers who really care about what they do for a living.

Jaime Manrique, Michael Nava, Felice Picano, Richard Labonte, Sarah Schulman, Sharon Bridgforth, Leslie Feinberg, and every published writer who has been kind to me.

Shelly Weiss, OUTmedia, and every college and university organization that ever brought me out to their campus to share my work with them.

Kevin Joseph a.k.a. Flotilla DeBarge for keeping me real.

Michael Musto for being a friend throughout the years.

Fred Phelps and the Westboro Baptist Church—we'll see who burns in hell, bitches!

Andres Rodriguez a.k.a Mother Diva Xavier for standing by me and making the annual Glam Slam competition so much fun for so many years.

The Latino/a community who supported me even though I am gay.

The gay community who supported me even though I am Latino.

The Houses of New York City for continuing to bring it and inspire.

The fans for keeping the faith and the story of Mikey X. alive.

And Jesus Christ—whether you were the Son of God or not, you were a great man and your message of peace and love are worth aspiring to.

257

Printed in the United States
217776BV00001B/1/P

9 780979 083853